BORN AND BRED TO FIGHT

CLETE SLATER—A forgotten Confederate hero, he's changed his name to Slate Creed, but nothing could disguise his fiery passion for justice.

COLONEL BENJAMIN HILL—For this old soldier, the Civil War would never end—not until the South was victorious and the black man was in chains.

THE GOLIHAR BROTHERS—Once Creed's bitterest enemies, they were his staunch allies in a land where a man always needed someone to watch his back.

CATHERINE RAMSDALE—A wild Texan beauty, she was as explosive as Rebel gunpowder—and just as dangerous.

COLONEL ISAAC ROSE—He hid behind the authority of his uniform to work his own sadistic will—to capture and lynch Slate Creed.

SERGEANT MARCUS JONES—As a black man he hated the Rebs as much as anyone. But as a Union soldier he was sworn to uphold the law for blacks as well as whites.

CREED

POWDER KEG

BRYCE HARTE

BERKLEY BOOKS, NEW YORK

**To my good friends,
Jack Zabrowski and Brad McDowell,
who give bankers a good name**

CREED: POWDER KEG

A Berkley Book / published by arrangement with
the author

PRINTING HISTORY
Berkley edition / August 1991

ISBN: 0-425-12851-2

A BERKLEY BOOK ® TM 757,375
Berkley Books are published by The Berkley Publishing Group,
200 Madison Avenue, New York, New York 10016.
The name "BERKLEY" and the "B" logo
are trademarks belonging to Berkley Publishing Corporation.

PRINTED IN THE UNITED STATES OF AMERICA

10 9 8 7 6 5 4 3 2 1

REAL HISTORY

In 1985, the Victoria Advocate Publishing Company released a magnificent volume of history titled *300 Years in Victoria County*. This was a work done by several people, and it was edited by Roy Grimes. From the pages of this wonderful book came many of the events and characters portrayed in this episode of Slate Creed's life.

Of particular interest is the murder of the former soldier known as Black and the subsequent lynching of Colonel Hill by Federal soldiers. The author has attempted to present both sides of the explosive situation that exists in Victoria in late 1865. Nearly all of the details included in this story were taken from the point of view of Dr. Sherman Goodwin who was an avowed Unionist during the Civil War and who had no ax to grind with either side in that conflict.

All geographical details included in this story are precise to the time with the exception of the names of the streets in the city of Victoria. The streets of that community were not officially named until 1869. Until that time, streets were designated by the names of the people who resided along them, such as Dr. Goodwin's street. The author has employed the first names given to these thoroughfares in order to give the reader points of reference within the context of the story.

PROLOGUE

Although the battle for Matamoras was far from over, Creed had had enough of Mexico and its brand of civil war. He gave the Golihars one hard look, and they agreed to let bygones be bygones; after all, they were outnumbered now that Kindred had run off and the rest of his gang was dead, and besides, killing Creed wasn't going to bring their younger brother Champ back to life. Between themselves, Crit and Charlie figured Creed wasn't the kind to go shooting a fellow in the back—leastways, not without good cause, which made it all right then. They asked Creed if they could join up with him and his four friends for the long ride home, and he was agreeable to that notion.

Creed said his farewells to all his new friends except one, intentionally saving Silveria Abeytia, the beautiful and seductive daughter of the *hacendado* for last. He walked with her in the garden for one last time.

"When you left before," said Silveria, "I thought that I would never see you again."

"You wouldn't have either," said Creed, "if we hadn't run into that storm and been forced to meet up with Crit and Charlie like we did. We were on our way home, and we would have kept on going right past Olmito. We should be a hundred miles north of here right now."

"But you are here now."

"Not for long. We're riding out as soon as I finish saying what I've got to say to you."

1

"Please do not say it," she said, turning her face away from him.

"If I don't, you'll always wonder and so will I." He stopped, took her by the arms, and made her face him. "That night you first came into my room . . . I wanted you . . . to lie down beside me . . . so that I could make love to you." He swallowed hard, then went on. "I've wanted you more and more each time I've seen you. I've felt a great . . . need . . . in my heart for you."

"You are making this so very difficult for me," she said as she put her hands on his chest.

"It's hard for me, too. Especially because I've got a girl back in Texas waiting for me."

"And now I have no one."

"We didn't really have each other, Silveria. I know I wanted to have you, but it just wasn't meant to be, I guess."

"And now you will go home to your girl, and I will only have a memory of what might have been."

"Yes, I guess that's the way it'll be. But I'll often think about you. Every time I see a beautiful girl with raven hair and soft skin I'll think of you, and I'll remember your kiss and touching you and wanting you, and I'll be a little bit sad because I don't have you in my arms right then and there. I'll probably dream about you, too, Silveria. And when I do, I won't want to wake up and find you aren't lying beside me."

"But you will forget about me once you marry this girl back in Texas."

"No, I don't think I'll ever forget you. No, never. In fact, I'll probably wonder what it would be like to stay here with you and maybe ask your father for—"

She wrenched herself away and said, "No more! Please, say no more!" She turned away from him, tears streaming down her cheeks. "Please, Creed," she said hoarsely, "go now. Go and let me be. I have too much pain already."

Creed reached out and touched her shoulders, but Silveria squirmed away. "All right," he said, "I'll go, but I won't say good-bye. I won't say good-bye because we'll see each other again. In our dreams. I'll see you in our dreams, and there . . . there we'll make love . . . and we'll be in love . . . and there won't be anything to keep us apart ever again." He wanted to touch her one more time but didn't. He turned and walked away toward his waiting horse.

1

Old Mexico was behind Creed—for now. He might go back there again—some day. Who knew? Not he, although he suspected that he might be forced to return before he'd go voluntarily again.

For the moment, Creed was willing to risk his life by going home to the girl and the land he loved. Texada and Texas. To him, they were almost synonymous. Both represented the future. His future. Their future. Together. If it could ever be. It could, he told himself, as long as he could breathe and could determine his own destiny.

The road home lay through Victoria County. Riding with Creed were his friends, Jake Flewellyn, Bill Simons, the Reeves brothers, Kent and Clark, and the Golihar brothers, Crit and Charlie. Creed's friends had gone to Mexico to save his hide from the Golihars, who had gone there to kill Creed for shooting their younger brother, Champ, in the back. Creed hadn't been able to convince Crit and Charlie with words that he had shot Champ only after the kid had fired at him first and then tried to run away. But he had been able to prove the truth of his words by his noble actions in the battle for Matamoras. Not only did they believe him, they were now willing to accept him as their leader.

Of course, Creed was unaware that the Golihars' newfound friendliness toward him ran that deep. As far as he was concerned, they were merely along for the ride, seeking safety in numbers. They were wise to do this, of course, and Creed was actually glad to have them along. A fellow never knew

4

when a pair of extra guns might come in handy, especially when his trail took him through Victoria County, a place that many considered to be lawless and wild even before the War Between the States made so many good men into outlaws of one kind or another.

Creed could have chosen to swing west and go through Goliad, but his heart was in a hurry to get home to Lavaca County. And whenever a man let his heart lead him through dangerous country, he was inviting trouble to ride with him.

The town of Victoria was only an hour's ride in front of them when Creed and the others came to the crossing at Coleto Creek. Flooding from centuries of heavy rains had left the creek bottom strewn with brush-covered sandbars separating several branches of the rocky streambed, all of them dry now except the middle one. Cottonwoods and live oaks whose summer green was now yellow and orange grew everywhere in abundance. Among them were the evergreen anaquas, which were colloquially known as knockaway trees. Their dense foliage offered good cover for wildlife, whether it was feathered, four-legged, or two-legged. A man on horseback would have a tough time spotting any fowl or beast in this thick brush, especially on a dark gray day such as this one was.

If the war had still been on, Creed would have halted his men at the crest of the slope above the creek and sent a scout ahead to check out the other side of the stream before riding down to the water. But the war was over—officially, that is—and there wasn't supposed to be anything or anybody to worry about. Creed wasn't thinking in war terms; his mind was elsewhere, back in Hallettsville with Texada. Instead of scouting ahead, he and his friends rode casually down the decline and into the creek.

"Hold up there!" shouted someone hidden among the trees.

The sudden sound of a strange voice snapped Creed out of the reverie in which he had been indulging. In the very instant that Texada's image vanished from his mind, he drew his Colt's from the holster he wore on the left side of his belt buckle and simultaneously reined in Nimbus.

The others reacted in a similar fashion, each man pulling a six-gun and reining in his horse. Like Creed's, their eyes darted from tree to tree in search of the man who had challenged them.

"No need for that now!" shouted the hidden man. "We don't want no killing here."

"Then what do you want?" demanded Creed, still trying to locate the speaker.

"All we want is your horses and your weapons and any food y'all might have. We'll take your money, too, but I doubt that y'all got any."

Like the good soldiers that they had been in the recent war, Creed, Flewellyn, Simons, and the Reeves brothers sat tall, showing no fear by holding their ground and waiting for the right moment to act. The Golihars were a different story. Both of them were all afright for their insignificant lives and weren't sure of what to do or when to do it. Inexperienced in the ways of battle, they slumped down in their saddles, seeking protection from the would-be bushwhackers behind their horses' necks and heads.

"Over there," said Flewellyn without moving his lips and so softly that only Creed could hear him. "Amongst those scruffy little oaks. See the rifle barrel sticking out?"

Creed casually shifted his gaze to the left without turning his head and saw the black muzzle of a shotgun staring at him. "I see it," he said out of the side of his mouth to Flewellyn. "See any others?"

"Not yet."

"Keep looking," said Creed. Then louder, he said in his down-home twang, "I don't think we'd prefer to do that now, friend. You see, we're kind of partial to these critters, and of course, you know it ain't right to take a man's gun without at least giving him a chance to fight first."

"Know all about that, friend, but we ain't got time to argue with y'all. Y'all just climb down from those horses and tie them up to the first tree in front of you, then drop your weapons on the bank, and we'll let y'all walk out of here peaceful like."

"Got another one, Creed," said Flewellyn, again softly and without moving his lips. "Down low, behind the sandbar in front of the oaks."

"I see him," said Creed in not much more than a whisper. Then louder again, he replied to the bushwhacker, "I don't think there's but one or two of you, friend, and if you go to shooting, we'll spy you out and put you down for it. You getting my drift, friend? We're all veterans of Terry's Rangers, and we don't scare too easy now."

He was exaggerating a bit. The Golihars hadn't served in the Confederate army at all, and Creed had only been in Terry's regiment for a few months before being separated from Flewellyn and the others who had stayed in it throughout the war. He had ridden with Morgan and Mosby, and that was usually enough to command a decent amount of respect from other Confederate veterans.

"Y'all rode for Terry?"

"You heard right, friend."

"Got another one," said Flewellyn. "To the right. Up high on the ridge."

"Right," said Creed, spotting a tattered Confederate campaign hat and a pair of sullen, sunken eyes peeking over a fallen tree trunk.

"Y'all look too well fed to be Confederates like us," said the hidden man. "Y'all look like some of them Yankees with their carpetbags come down here to steal our land from us."

"Not true," said Creed. "We're from Lavaca County. Been down Mexico way recently, fighting the French, and now we're heading home. We ain't looking for no trouble. We're just passing through."

"Well, we're willing to let y'all pass through, but we'd appreciate it if y'all would leave your horses and weapons for us. We need them more than y'all look like y'all need them."

"'Tain't so," said Creed, finally getting his fill of this conversation. "These horses belong to us, and we're riding out of here on them, and if we have to, we'll shoot any man who tries to stop us."

"We'll give y'all one more chance to surrender them horses and guns or we'll go to shooting."

"I'd rather it didn't come to that," said Creed. Then aside, he said, "Better get ready to hunker down for a fight, boys. I think they're aiming to find themselves an early grave here."

"Then give us them horses and guns," said the bushwhacker.

"Already told you we can't do that."

"Suit yourself then."

And the shooting began. Little clouds of blue gunpowder smoke appeared in the brush and trees, and minié balls and buckshot sped through the air toward Creed and the others.

Creed charged the oaks where they had seen the first barrel. Flewellyn did the same. The Reeves brothers charged the ridge, and the Golihars rode after them. Simons took a blast from a shotgun and was toppled from his horse into the creek. He was badly hurt but not so much so that he couldn't keep his head above water.

Before the bushwhackers could fire another volley, Creed cocked the hammer of his Colt's, took aim at what he thought was the first bushwhacker, and cut loose a shot. A primordial scream followed instantly, and a gaunt man in a ragged Confederate uniform fell to the ground, clutching his lower jaw.

Flewellyn fired at the man behind the sandbar and put a bullet into his skull. The Reeves brothers wounded the man on the ridge, and the Golihars rode up and cheerfully finished him off.

A handful of other bushwhackers broke from cover and began running away. Creed and Flewellyn rode down on a pair of them, but instead of shooting them, they simply cracked them over the heads with the barrels of their revolvers. The Golihars rode down a third man and shot him— twice each—in the back, while the Reeves boys rounded up the other two as if they were steers and herded them back to where Creed had dismounted and was tending to the first bushwhacker. The Golihars followed them.

"You sure made a mess of his chin there, Creed," said Crit Golihar rather giddily from atop his horse. He cocked his piece and started to take aim at the wounded man. "Better let me put him out of his misery."

Creed turned his head slowly and glared at Crit. He said nothing out loud. He didn't have to. His eyes said everything that needed to be said.

Golihar sat back and lifted his gun away, easing off on the hammer as he did. He understood.

Creed turned back to the wounded man, who was already glassy-eyed with shock. "He's dying anyway," said Creed. "Forgive me, friend. This isn't what I wanted."

A bloody cough followed by a gurgling gasp was the only reply. The man died.

"Dammit all to hell!" swore Creed. "Why did this have to happen?" He looked around from face to face, at the Golihars, the Reeves brothers, then the two bushwhackers that they'd caught. "Why did you men do this?" he asked them. "Why?"

"'Cause we're hungry," said one.

"And so's our women and children," said the other.

"Hungry?" cried Creed, coming to his feet. "Hungry?" He grabbed the man by his ragged gray shirt and jerked him close to him so that their noses almost touched. "You dumb son of a bitch! We've got food. We would have shared with you. All you had to do was ask. Why couldn't you just ask us? Why'd you have to go to shooting and get yourselves all shot up like this? Why?"

The man gave no answer other than to stare wildly at Creed.

Creed released him and said, "I don't understand this. I don't understand why one man would want to steal from another when it's so much easier to earn whatever it is he wants with a little honest work."

"Work?" said the second captive. "There ain't no such thing, mister. Not around here there ain't. We come home same as y'all did, I'll bet, and what did we find? Yankees and more Yankees. And them what wasn't Yankees was Union sympathizers come back to take everything they couldn't have legal before the war. And there's the niggers, too. Yankees give them their freedom, and now they think they're all high and mighty. Calling us white trash and such. And them Yankees? Most of them is niggers, too, and their white officers ain't only backing them up when they do it, but they're encouraging them as well. And why? Because we fought for the South and lost."

"But we're Confederates, too," said Creed, "and we don't go around stealing from other men. We work for our food and clothes like honest men."

"How y'all doing that, mister? My empty belly would like to know. Tell me. How y'all got work up there in Lavaca County and we ain't got none down here? How is that now?"

Creed wasn't sure how to answer that question. He knew that he and his friends were the exception and not the rule

when it came to the postwar plight of Confederate veterans
in Texas. For certain, they had a ranch to work together, and
they had been able to earn some hard cash the summer before
when they drove a herd of mossy-horned longhorns to New
Orleans. But other ex-soldiers attempting the same thing had
failed, leaving them and the people who had backed them
worse off than before. Creed and the Double Star vaqueros
were much better off, but he couldn't explain why they had
been so fortunate.

Before he could even begin to offer a reply, Creed's attention
was drawn elsewhere.

"You better come over here," called Flewellyn. He was
kneeling beside Simons on the creek bank. "Bill's hurt pretty
bad. I think we'd best be getting him to a doctor as soon as
we can."

Creed hurried over to Simons and Flewellyn, knelt down,
and examined Simons's wounds.

Simons had caught several pellets in his left side from
mid-thigh to the middle of his rib cage and was bleeding
profusely. He was conscious and in a lot of pain.

"Let's get some bandages on those wounds," said Creed, "so
we can stop the bleeding. Then we'll get him on his horse and
ride into Victoria for a doctor." He looked at the two captives,
then at the Reeves boys. "Clark, you and Kent get these men
some food, and see about those fellows Jake and I cracked on
the head. Crit, you and Charlie get me the clothes off those
dead men. I need them for bandages. Jake, you give these boys
whatever food we got left."

Flewellyn, Kent, and Clark moved instantly, but the Golihars
hesitated, Charlie looking at Crit to see if he obeyed first and
Crit looking at Charlie for the same reason.

"Get moving!" snapped Creed.

"Sure, Creed," said Crit. He didn't like the job, but he did
. And so did Charlie. Because Creed had told them to do it,
'hich was good enough reason for now.

Creed took one more look at the bushwhackers and wondered
if he'd seen the last of them or their kind.

2

Creed barely noted the similarities between Victoria and Hallettsville as he and the others rode into the county town in the late afternoon.

Victoria was an old place as far as Texas was old. Older than Hallettsville, dating back to the days of the Mexican republic, it was situated on land originally granted to Martin de Leon, who named the town Nuestra Señora de Guadalupe de Jesus Victoria, then shortened the title in honor of his friend, Don Juan Felix Fernandez, who had taken the name of Guadalupe Victoria during the Mexican Revolution against Spain.

As a community, Victoria had changed as Texas had changed, from Mexican to Texican to Texian to very much Texan. Like most towns in Texas founded before the War Between the States, it was built on a rise of ground overlooking a river. In the tradition of his Spanish ancestors, Don Martin planned his settlement around a town square—the common of New England, the plaza of old Spain—with many of the major businesses facing it. When Texas gained its independence from Mexico and divided itself into counties, the county courthouse was erected on the block just west of the square as a sort of reminder that law and order and thus civilization were supposed to exist within the municipal limits. The usual stores, hotels, and saloons lined the streets, which were platted in the usual grid pattern, and surrounding the main business district were several hundred houses, ranging from the crude jacales of the few Mexicans who remained in the area to the fine mansions of the county's most successful planters and stockmen.

11

Creed and his friends crossed the Guadalupe River on the new bridge recently built by Captain Joe Wheeler. Victoria was a river port, and thus it had its waterfront district, much the same as Natchez, Mississippi, had its Natchez-under-the-Hill. The first block of Bridge Street coming from the river was lined with rough board saloons, gambling halls, and cathouses that catered to the rivermen in particular and, in general, anyone else who was ragged enough around the edges to take the risks of socializing in such places.

The men from Lavaca County followed Bridge Street up the hill to the finer part of town, where Creed was hoping to find a doctor for Bill Simons. He had managed to slow Simons's bleeding by stuffing bandages inside his shirt and trousers, then wrapping him in a blanket. For the ride to Victoria, Simons had ridden sideways on Creed's saddle with his right arm around Creed's waist and his head cradled on Creed's shoulder. The trip had been made as fast as Creed had thought prudent, considering his friend's condition.

Creed couldn't help noticing how quiet the town was. Very few people were out that day. Of course, the weather wasn't the most pleasant, but for early December it wasn't all that bad. The skies were gray but not threatening now, and there was only a hint of wind from the west. Then he realized that every street corner had a Yankee soldier stationed on it, and every soldier was a Negro. He couldn't say for certain, but he felt as if they were all watching him as circling buzzards would eyeball a dying horse. He decided to ignore them for now. He had more important business to attend to.

Noting that Main Street had more businesses along it, Creed led his friends over one block and continued looking for a doctor's office. Finally, he saw a sign, painted on the side of a drugstore, that advertised the name of Dr. J.P.T. January, Physician and Surgeon. An arrow beneath the name pointed east, and below that, it read, 1 Block. They went that way and found Dr. January's office in his house on Liberty Street. Another arrow, this one bent in the middle, indicated that the entrance to the medical man's office was at the top of the stairs on the side of the building.

Creed reined in Nimbus at the hitching rail in front of the two-story house, then waited for the Reeves brothers to help

Simons down before dismounting himself.

"Jake, run up and see if the doctor is there," said Creed.

Flewellyn gave a quick nod, then did as he was told. In a few seconds, he was back out on the landing at the top of the stairs. "He's here," he yelled down to Creed.

"Come on, boys," said Creed to the Reeves brothers, "let's get him upstairs. Crit, you and Charlie stay here and watch the horses."

Kent and Clark sort of nudged Creed aside, then one took Simons by the legs and the other by the shoulders, and they carried him up the stairs and into the doctor's office.

"Put him on the table there," said Dr. January, who held the door for them.

Kent and Clark followed the instruction and placed Simons on the table on his right side.

January appeared older than his fifty-three years, his pallid face lined with the signs of stress and fatigue, put there by four years in the service of the Confederacy, first as captain of Company A 13th Texas Cavalry Battalion, then as a field surgeon. Also adding to his elderly appearance were his long snow-white beard and hair and a small, pointed nose that was latticed with broken capillaries, indicating him to be a man who enjoyed his toddy. The only spark of youth that remained in his aspect was the bright blue-gray rings around the chestnut irises of his eyes. His attire of plain brown suit, scuffed brown leather shoes, and collarless, button-up gray flannel shirt gave him the appearance of a shyster lawyer instead of a man of medicine.

January's office wasn't much to look at either. Besides the portal through which Creed and the Reeves brothers had brought Simons, doors led to the front of the building and to the rear, and one window in the room was in the same wall as the entrance. The office had a high ceiling of two-inch tongue-and-groove boards painted white; a hardwood floor of four-inch tongue-and-groove boards painted colonial blue; and plain walls of lath and plaster painted sky blue and adorned only with January's license to practice medicine in Texas, his degree from Transylvania College in his native Kentucky, and a testimony to his competence as a surgeon signed by General Kirby Smith and accompanied by the medal of valor that Kirby had presented to him after the Battle of Sabine Cross Roads. A chart of the human form—male but without any indication of sex, of course—was hidden behind a dressing screen in one corner of the room. January's desk and chair were in another, and the examining table and an instrument cabinet were in the third. The fourth corner had a pair of straight-back chairs that were supposed to be used by people who accompanied patients to the office but never were employed for that purpose—as now, when Creed, Flewellyn, and the Reeves brothers crowded around the examining table to watch and possibly assist the doctor with Simons.

January removed the blanket from around Simons, noting that it was damp but not bloody. The same couldn't be said of Simons's shirt and trousers, which were soaked with water throughout and were stained with blood on the left side.

"Shotgun do this?" queried January.

"Yes, sir," said Creed respectfully. "Bushwhackers. South of here."

"I see," said the doctor, sounding somewhat disappointed. Then he went to the instrument cabinet and removed a probe, a forceps, and a scissors. Returning to Simons, who was still conscious but in control of his pain, January began cutting away the shirt.

Simons cocked his head and said, "Don't cut it up too bad, Doc. I ain't got but one other."

"If you don't shut up and lay still and let me do my job," said January, "we'll be burying you in the other one day after tomorrow."

"I heard that," said Simons, lying back and relaxing.

"Is it that bad?" asked Flewellyn.

"I've seen worse that lived," said January as he finished cutting away the shirt and started snipping down the trouser leg. "But those men didn't have their friends standing around asking fool questions while I was working on them." He removed the rags from the wounds, and then he looked up at Creed and said, "Who put these on him?"

"I did," said Creed, bracing for a tongue-lashing and preparing to counter the verbal assault with the feeble excuse that the rags were all that was available.

"Good job, friend," said January. "You just might have saved this man's life." He looked back at Simons's wounds and nodded approvingly as very little blood oozed from them now. "Yes, sir. A right good job. Pretty much stopped the bleeding. Save the blood, save the life. That's the way it was taught to me. Like I said before, you just might have saved this man's life, friend. Now I just might kill him."

"How's that?" asked Creed, curious on the one hand and startled on the other.

"If I go to digging in those holes for that buckshot now, I'll start him bleeding all over again. If I don't, he might die from the poison all that lead is putting in him right now." He looked at Creed, then at Simons. "You tell me, friend. Do I dig now? Or do I put clean bandages on you now and dig later when it's going to hurt a helluva lot more? You tell me which way I should go."

"You're saying he could bleed to death," said Creed, "if you operate on him now, or he could die of lead poisoning if you don't operate now. Is that it, Doctor?"

"That's it precisely," said January.

Creed looked down at Simons and said, "I know you're hurting bad, Bill, but if I were you, I'd let the doctor bandage me up for now and then let Dr. Bennett take that buckshot out of you when we get back to Hallettsville."

"Bennett?" queried January. "Dr. Mason Bennett?"

"That's him," said Creed. "You know him?"

"I know he's a yellow-bellied Yankee-lover," said January, spitting the words.

"Well, he's not the only doctor in Hallettsville," said Creed a little defensively. "We could take him to someone else."

"I'm afraid it wouldn't be wise to move your friend just yet," said January. "If he was to travel now, that buckshot might do more damage and his bleeding might start up again. That would kill him for sure. My advice is to leave him here with me. I've got a room in the back he can stay in, and my niece can tend to his wounds for me. As soon as I see that he's getting stronger, I'll start digging out that buckshot a few at a time. It might take me a week or two to get it all—and there's no guarantee that I will get it all—but it's the best chance I can give him to live."

Creed stared hard at Simons and said, "Then I think that's the best way to go, Bill."

Simons shifted his eyes from Creed to January and said, "You do with me whatever Creed tells you, Doc. He's more to be trusted with my life than I am."

January stared at Creed, who was the youngest man in the room, and said incredulously, "Is that a fact?"

"Yes, sir, it is," said Flewellyn firmly.

"All right, Mr. Creed," said January. "Do we wait a few days or do I operate now?"

Creed scanned the faces of Flewellyn and the Reeves brothers, then said, "We wait, Dr. January."

"Wise decision," said January. "Now tell me about this bushwhacking you boys just went through while I bandage up your friend here."

Creed quickly related the tale, then finished up by saying, "We didn't stick around to bury the men we killed. We left that up to their friends."

"You say you killed four of them?" asked January.

"That's right," said Flewellyn. "Four."

"Did you tell anyone about it?" asked January.

"No, sir," said Creed. "We came straight here. Why do you ask?"

"Yankees," said the doctor. "They run things here now. At least for the time being, they do. But never mind all that now. You boys best get on out of here now and let me tend to your friend. You can come back tomorrow morning if you like. In the meantime, you'd be wise to avoid any Yankees who might cross your path, and don't go telling everyone in town what happened out there today."

"Don't you think we should tell the law?" asked Creed.

"I thought you were listening to me, son. The Yankees *are* the law around here. Do you want *them* butting into your affairs, Mr. Creed?"

"I think I get your drift, Dr. January," said Creed. He turned to the others and said, "Come on, boys. We'd better find us a place to stay the night."

"Best to stay clear of town," said January. "Too many Yankees with prying eyes."

Creed nodded, said, "Thanks for the advice," then followed the others outside.

"What now?" asked Flewellyn.

"We do like the good doctor says," said Creed. "We stay clear of town."

"And all them Yankees," said Flewellyn.

Creed looked grim and said, "Right."

3

After leaving Bill Simons under Dr. January's care, Creed and the others decided to camp at the edge of town instead of checking into a hotel. They bought some provisions at a grocery, then found a suitable spot in the Guadalupe River bottom north of the bridge and the riverfront district. They chose this location because the area south of the boat landings was the site of Shantytown, the makeshift village of several hundred former slaves who had forsaken the countryside and their former masters and come into Victoria believing the Yankees were going to give them forty acres and a mule of their own. To camp nearer to Shantytown was to invite trouble, and the men from Lavaca County had already had enough of that.

The Reeves brothers made a fire and set a pot of coffee to simmering. While Clark sliced up a slab of bacon and opened two cans of red beans, Kent mixed up a batch of biscuits and set them to baking. Flewellyn and Creed tended to the horses, and the Golihars sort of sat around and did nothing except bellyache about how hungry they were and how they'd rather sleep in a real bed instead of on the hard ground again that night.

"That's all just fine," said Flewellyn as he helped himself to a cup of coffee. "You boys can just go ahead and rent yourselves a nice clean hotel room in town if you want. Won't make no matter to us."

"Now you know we can't do that," said Charlie. "We ain't got no money left for that."

"Then quit your calf bawling about the way things are," said Flewellyn. "Be grateful we're here at all and not back at that creek bottom having our innards being picked over by the buzzards."

"Jake is right," said Creed, thinking of the irony in Flewellyn's statement. Like most Texans, Creed had a deep sense of history. Twenty-nine years earlier over three hundred Texans had been murdered in cold blood and left for the vultures by the Mexican army under General Urrea. The massacre had occurred near the very spot where the men from Lavaca had been waylaid. But returning his thoughts to the present, he said, "Just think about poor Bill laying up there in that doctor's office with his leg and ribs full of buckshot. I'd bet he'd trade places with either one of you right now except that he's not the kind of man to wish injury on anyone if he can avoid it."

"That's right," said Flewellyn.

"Hell's bells, Creed," said Crit, "we didn't mean nothing by it. It's just that I know we'd all be more comfortable in a hotel sleeping in real beds and not having to be out here sleeping on the cold ground and eating camp food again tonight."

"Is there something wrong with my cooking?" complained Kent.

"Or mine?" asked Clark.

Crit flinched when he saw the anger in their eyes. There was no way he wanted to tangle with either of them. Both were big everywhere except around the waist, and each was muscled like a Greek statue, and just as hard, too.

"No, your cooking's fine," stammered Crit. "Ain't it, Charlie? Just fine, right?"

"That's right," said Charlie, who was equally frightened of the Reeves brothers. "Best camp cooking I ever et. How about you, Crit? Don't you think so?"

"Sure do, Charlie. Sure do. Best I ever et, too."

Clark smiled at Kent and said, "Hear that, little brother? Best camp cooking they ever et. How about that?"

Kent nodded and said, "Well, if it's the best they ever et, then maybe they'd like to show their appreciation for us being such good cooks by washing up the utensils tonight."

"Good idea," said Clark. "Hey, do you think they might really want to show their appreciation by doing up the utensils every night till we get home?"

Kent got a gleam in his eye and let it sparkle on the Golihars. "How about that, boys? Would you be that appreciative of our cooking?"

Both Golihars blanched at the thought, but they went along with it.

"Sure, Kent," said Crit. "We'd be glad to do up the utensils for you till we get home. Ain't that right, Charlie?"

"Anything you say, Crit."

"Good," said Clark. "Then it's settled. We'll keep doing all that great cooking Crit and Charlie love so much, and they'll do up all the utensils for us as our reward. Now ain't that a nice arrangement?"

"Sounds like a natural to me," said Flewellyn, smiling like a drunk holding a full house. "How about you, Creed?"

"Anything that will keep you boys from jawing at each other will suit me just fine," said Creed a bit grumpily. He picked up his plate and cup and helped himself to the coffee and some beans, bacon, and a biscuit. He sat down on a fallen tree trunk and went to eating while the others followed his example. After swallowing a few bites, he said, "I was thinking that we've come a long way from Mexico, but we're only a couple of days from home now. We could just go on home, but I know I wouldn't feel right about leaving Bill in Victoria all by himself. I should think he'd appreciate one of us staying behind to sort of keep him company, you know, sort of look in on him every day until he can travel again. Crit, you and Charlie might not want to hang around until then, and I wouldn't blame you none if you rode on without us. Jake, you and Bill served together, and I know what good friends you are, and I know Clark and Kent are his good friends, too. And that's why I know Bill wouldn't mind none if you were to ride on without him."

"Are you saying we should go on home?" asked Flewellyn uneasily.

"Not all of us," said Creed. "Just you boys. I'm staying here until Bill can travel again, then I'll bring him home."

"Sounds all right to me," said Charlie.

"Not to me, it don't," said Flewellyn. "Not after what we've seen around here. All those Yankees in town and all. I don't like it, Creed, and I don't think Bill is as safe as Dr. January said he was. Not around here."

"That's especially why you should go," said Creed. "Stick around here and you'll just be asking for trouble."

"And you won't?" queried Flewellyn.

"One man is less a worry than six," said Creed.

"Creed's right," said Charlie.

"No, he ain't," said Flewellyn, glaring at Charlie. "It's better for all of us if we stick together. Creed knows that, too. He's just looking out for us first like a good officer does when it comes time to fight a battle. Ain't that right, Creed?"

"Yes, I am thinking of all of us," said Creed. "Especially Bill. I got him into this mess, and it's my duty as a friend to stick around and see that he's all right and such."

"We're all in this together," said Crit, surprising everyone, especially Charlie. "I go along with Jake. I think we should all stay here until Bill can go home with us."

Creed finished the last of his biscuit and said, "Well, I can plainly see that it won't pay to argue with you boys on the matter, so we'll all stay, I guess."

He didn't feel exactly comfortable with the thought, but he saw no other alternative. Maybe they would be better off if they stayed together. Maybe not. Who know? Not Creed. Not then.

4

The next morning, Creed rode into town to pay a visit to Bill Simons at Dr. January's in-home hospital. The doctor wasn't in when he arrived, but his niece was. She greeted Creed at the door.

"Good morning, sir. May I help you?"

Startled by her presence, Creed stammered, "Yes, ma'am. I'm here to see my friend. Bill Simons." Then, remembering his manners, he removed his hat and introduced himself. "My name is Slate Creed."

"Won't you come in, Mr. Creed?" she said politely, then moved aside in order to allow him entrance. "I am Dr. January's niece, Miss Catherine Ramsdale. I am also his nurse when he has a patient staying here." She closed the door behind Creed. "Your friend is resting comfortably."

Creed hardly heard her words over the pounding of his heart, the excitement brought on by the general similarity he felt Miss Ramsdale bore to his Texada. Like the girl back home that he was so eager to see and hold again, Miss Ramsdale was female, blond, and blue-eyed, and that was where the real likeness to Texada ended as far as anyone except Creed would ever notice. Miss Ramsdale was also tall and lithe, with a slender neck, a throat so lovely and angular that it seemed made for sensuous kissing, especially since it was adorned by a black velvet choker, with an ivory cameo, outside a ruffled white lace collar. The tone and texture of her face stated plainly that she spent much of her time out of doors and in the sun. When she smiled, her eyes sparkled like sapphires, but when she wasn't smiling, she gave the appearance of being quite prim and proper, almost bookish, maybe even a little dull. Her hair was a bit wavy and curly, having the aspect of fine wire instead of silken thread, and she styled it rather austerely. Altogether, though, she seemed older and more mature than Creed, a fallacy encouraged by the fact that she wore the wire-rimmed spectacles of the day. But even so, out of his loneliness, he saw her as being attractive, attainable, and quite provocative in almost every way, making him desirous for her gentle touch.

When she had first seen Creed on the landing outside the office door, Miss Ramsdale wasn't able to see his features distinctly because of the bright sunlight behind him. But once he was inside and her vision adjusted to the dimmer, softer light, she saw him clearly and liked what she saw. A giddy physical infatuation for him put a blush in her tan cheeks. She felt the crimson glow but hoped that he couldn't see it. She bowed her head to hide it, then straightened up in the next instant as an inner strength regained control of her senses.

"I just finished changing Mr. Simons's dressings, Mr. Creed," she said firmly, "and he's had a dose of laudanum for the pain. However, he should still be awake." She went to the door to Simons's room, opened it, and peeked inside. Turning back to Creed, she said, "Yes, he's still awake." She opened the door widely and said to Simons, "You have a visitor."

Creed brushed against Miss Ramsdale as he stepped through the doorway. He liked the contact and sensed that she did, too. In fact, he suspected that she had actually forced it by not making any attempt to move out of his way. He was right.

"If you need anything," she said, "I'll be here in the office."

"Thank you, Miss Ramsdale," said Creed.

She closed the door behind her.

"If I'd known about that pretty nurse back at Coleto Creek," said Creed, "I might have been tempted to shoot myself in the foot just so she could take care of me, too."

Simons wasn't seeing Miss Ramsdale in the same light as Creed, but he laughed at the joke anyway, more so because of the laudanum than out of politeness.

Creed pulled up a chair and sat down beside Simons. He related how he and the others had found a campsite near the river and assured him that no one was going anywhere until he was well enough to go with them. Simons thanked him for that but said it was unnecessary to stay on his account, especially since they were so close to home and he knew how anxious all of them were to get home for Christmas.

Funny, but Creed hadn't thought about that at all.

Home.

For Christmas.

He hadn't enjoyed a Christmas in Lavaca County since before the war. He'd almost forgotten what it was like to spend the holidays with anyone except comrades-in-arms.

His mind fought to recall images of his family on Christmas Day. He found it downright difficult to remember them.

So much had happened to Creed—and everybody, for that matter—since his last Christmas at Glengarry Plantation. His grandfather, Dougald Slater, had passed away. His widowed mother had remarried and moved north to some place called Weatherford, where her new husband, a Yankee named Howard Loving, was in partnership with his cousin Oliver Loving in a cattle ranch. His brother, Denton Slater, had been murdered when rustlers tried to steal their cattle on a drive to New Orleans. His best friend, Jess Tate, had also been murdered on that trip. His sister, Malinda, had become engaged to a Yankee officer named Lucas Markham. And Creed? He had been accused of, tried for, convicted of, and sentenced to hang for a crime that he hadn't committed; in fact, he hadn't even been in Mississippi when several ex-Confederates raided a Federal wagon train, killed a few guards and a teamster, and stole an army payroll. After the trial, he had escaped the hangman's noose, changed his name from Clete Slater to Slate Creed, and ridden to Mexico in search of some of the men who had murdered his brother. While below the Rio Grande, he had gotten himself and four good friends tangled up in the civil war down there, but as soon as he was able to extricate himself and his compadres from that mess, they all headed home to Texas.

All of these events had changed Creed's life, but none of them had impacted it so much as that moment when he fell in love with Texada Ballard. Creed had known her as a skinny tomboy when they were growing up before the war, and he hadn't given her a single romantic thought during all that time. But when he returned home after four years of fighting and saw how she had blossomed, he forgot about those simpler days when they both wore breeches and went barefoot most of the year, and he saw her as the woman of his dreams. From the instant he realized that he loved her and wanted to spend the rest of his days with her, his life had a purpose. Before that moment, he hadn't been sure of what he wanted out of this world, especially since he had been disinherited by his grandfather—who had done so reluctantly, Creed told himself. Until learning that disheartening fact, he had always thought that he would become the master of Glengarry Plantation on his grandfather's death and that he would marry a young lady of wealth and position and they would live out their lives contentedly raising cotton, cattle, and children. He had assumed this would be the natural order of his life, and he was satisfied that it would be so.

Now it seemed that none of that was to be. No Glengarry. No plantation or ranch of any kind. No wife, no children. Nothing until he could clear his name and could once again be Cletc Slater.

But that was still far in the future. For now, he was stuck in Victoria County waiting for a friend's wounds to heal so they could go home for Christmas together.

By the time he left Simons to rest, Creed had forgotten about Miss Ramsdale and how she had affected him. The memory lapse was only temporary because she was waiting for him in Dr. January's office.

"I hope you had a nice visit," she said.

"Yes, we did," said Creed. "He looks to be getting the best care possible, Miss Ramsdale. I thank you for that."

"Don't thank her," said Dr. January as he entered the room from the hall that led to the rest of the house. "Thank me. I'm the boss around here."

"He just thinks he's the boss," said Miss Ramsdale with an indulgent smile.

January feigned shock as he said, "You mean I'm not the boss?"

"No, Uncle, you aren't," she said gaily.

January struck a grumpy pose and said, "I beg to disagree, girl. Now off with you while Mr. Creed and I enter into a manly discussion of politics and the like."

Miss Ramsdale pecked January on the cheek and said, "Yes, Uncle, if you insist."

"I do."

She turned to Creed and said, "By your leave, sir?" and curtsied as a good Southern lady should.

"It was an honor to make your acquaintance, Miss Ramsdale," said Creed as he offered her a gentlemanly half bow.

"Thank you, sir." And she left through the doorway that January had used to enter the room.

The physician offered Creed a chair beside his desk, which Creed accepted. January then sat down behind the desk and said, "Mr. Creed, it is my observation that you and your friends are birds of my feather. That is to say, that you are former members of the Confederate army, fighting men like I was for the first three years. Would I be correct in this assumption, sir?"

"Yes, sir, you would," said Creed.

"Then please allow me to give you some sound advice, Mr. Creed. Leave this county as soon as you can and go home as fast as you can. This is not a decent place for any man who wore the gray."

"Why do you say that?" asked Creed.

"I say it because it's true," said January. "In fact, your own county may not be a decent place for you."

Creed snickered lightly and said, "You got that right. At least as far as I'm concerned. Not so my friends though. They haven't got a Yankee—" He caught himself before saying "noose," and instead he stammered, "Uh, colonel, uh, who's taken a personal dislike to them like the one who—how should I put this—who thinks of me as a fish bone in his craw."

"Very aptly put, sir," said January. "I have my own Yankee albatross here in Victoria. Colonel Isaac Rose. He commands all the troops in Victoria County. His own unit is from Pennsylvania, and they're camped across the Guadalupe west of town. Colonel Barry commands a nigger regiment from Michigan that's camped on the plain east of here, but you can see them standing guard on every street corner in town." He slid open the bottom drawer of three on the left side of his desk and took out a bottle of whiskey. "Would you care to join me, sir?" he asked, holding up the quart container for Creed to inspect the label.

"I'm not one occasioned to indulging in hard drink with any sort of frequency," said Creed, "but I think it would be rude of me to refuse your gracious hospitality, sir." As always, Creed displayed good Southern manners.

January took two shot glasses from the same drawer and poured each of them a drink. He handed one to Creed, then picked up his own, saying, "To the Confederacy," as he raised the glass in toast.

Creed made no attempt to join in the salute. Instead, he lowered his glass, then sat motionless, looking at the floor.

January stayed his own hand, cocked his head at Creed, and asked, "Is there something wrong with drinking to the Confederacy?"

"Since you asked," said Creed, setting his eyes on January's nose, "I am forced to reply truthfully. Yes, there is something wrong with drinking to the Confederacy. At least as far as I am concerned, sir."

"And what might that be, sir?" asked January, readying for a verbal charge at Creed.

"The Confederacy is dead, Dr. January," said Creed matter-of-factly. "Dead and buried. Dead and buried in a hundred thousand graves from Gettysburg to Vicksburg to Petersburg and Atlanta and places I've never even heard of yet. The graves of good men who died for the Confederacy, sir. Good men who believed we were fighting for our freedom. That we were fighting the tyranny of the North over the South."

"We were," said January, picking up the gauntlet.

"No, sir, we were not. We were fighting to preserve a way of life that was morally wrong, that was a mote in the eye of God, sir." Creed could hear himself saying the words, but he was having a hard time believing they were his. He was not one to wax eloquent, to expound anything in the manner of religious parlance; yet here he was doing so. "Slavery, Dr. January. That was our cause. Slavery. Not the supremacy of the states over the national government or over other states. No, sir, we fought for the preservation of slavery in the South and the spread of it to the territories. We weren't fighting for our freedom, sir. We were fighting to keep the Negro in bondage."

"So what, pray tell, was wrong with that?" demanded January, glaring at Creed. "The Negro is our inferior, and God placed him here on earth to be in our care."

"Our care, sir?" queried Creed. "Forcing him to work under threat of the lash is caring for him? Depriving him of his freedom is caring for him? Selling him or his wife and children against their will is caring for him?"

"One must take the bad with the good," said January. "Our slaves were clothed, fed, and housed at our expense, not theirs. And for this, they were required to work."

It suddenly occurred to Creed that he was wasting his breath. Dr. January had his views of slavery, and probably nothing would ever change them. At least not Creed at this time.

"Dr. January, we could debate the question for days on end," said Creed, "and when we finished, we might be enemies. I would prefer that not to be, sir."

January was taken aback. He was miffed and sat rigidly in his perplexity.

"Just let me say this, Dr. January," said Creed. "The Confederacy is dead, in the past, and I wish to forget it and all it stood for. If you choose to think otherwise, that is your prerogative, and I will respect it only in your right to believe so, not in the belief itself. As for me, I am here today, looking forward to tomorrow and whatever it might bring."

"Yes, of course," said January amicably. "Your paraphrase of the great French philosopher Voltaire is noted and accepted, sir. I take it that you would prefer that I choose another toast."

Creed didn't know who this Voltaire was, but he wasn't going to let January know that. He simply said, "That's about the size of it, sir."

January smiled warmly, raised his glass again, and said, "Then to Texas. May heaven be as beautiful."

A smile broke out on Creed's face, and he acknowledged the salute by saying, "To Texas," and by downing his drink. The whiskey lit a fire all the way down his gullet, but it was a good feeling all the same.

"Now, sir," said January, "as I was about to say before our conversation was momentarily diverted, Victoria is not a peaceful place. It is overrun with Yankees and Yankee-lovers.

Our Yankee-loving governor, Mr. Andrew Jackson Hamilton, has appointed good men to govern us and enforce our laws, but the Federals have usurped these roles. All except that of county judge, the post held by Sam White, who is also the publisher of our newspaper, *The Victoria Advocate*."

January slugged down the rest of his whiskey, then continued. "These Yankees balance the scales of justice with silver dollars as the counterweights. Every Unionist who left the county during the war has returned now, and they have decided to exact a heavy price on those of us who favored secession. It seems that any man who sided with the Confederacy and who now has a single dollar in hard cash to his name is suspected of fomenting and continuing the rebellion, as the Yankees are wont to call our late war for independence. I am considered by them to be the ringleader of this rebellious faction because of my outspoken ways and education." January chuckled at the thought, then continued. "The irony of the whole matter is that there is no organized resistance to the Yankees, although I should think that there should be. The wicked wrongdoers of this world are always wont to point an accusing finger at others in order to hide and disguise their own degeneracy and guile."

He poured himself another shot of liquor, then offered to refill Creed's glass, although it wasn't empty yet.

"I'm still pleasuring this first one, sir," said Creed.

"Well, just help yourself when you feel the need," said January, placing the bottle on the desk within easy reach of both of them. He leaned back, looked pensive for a moment, then said, "As I was about to say, sir, that is not my point, that Yankees and Yankee-lovers are evil and wicked people. God knows that evil and wickedness know no borders. But that is not my point either, Mr. Creed. My point is this. You and your friends are strangers here and are thus in danger, to which you can already attest by the assault on you yesterday. In this county, we have those in power—the Yankees and their supporters—and those who are not in power—former Confederates, like myself, and those who served the Confederacy—and we have those who are caught in between, like Sam White—the people who remained here during the war but who did not actively support the Confederacy. The Neutrals, I call them. If our Yankee lord and master, Colonel Rose, learns of your presence and that you were soldiers in the Confederacy, he will immediately place you on the opposite side of the law and do something that will either drive you away from this county or put you before his Yankee justice of the peace, who will then put you in the custody of his Yankee jailer. If the latter should become the case, you will be incarcerated in their county jail, where you will be guarded by niggers. Any property that you might have in your possession at the time of your arrest will mysteriously disappear, and you will be left with no legal recourse to recover it. Upon your release, you will be afoot, penniless, and possessing only the clothes on your person. You will be given a day, possibly two, to either find work or to leave the county. If you do neither, then you will be arrested again and put through the same system all over."

"You paint a pretty bleak picture of matters in this county," said Creed. "Surely, it can't be that bad."

"These Yankees mean to have their pound of flesh from us, sir," said January. "If you remain here while your friend is recovering from his wounds, you will learn the truth of what I say and you will learn it in a most distasteful manner. Please accept my word of caution and leave this county now. I will send you word of when your friend can travel again and you can come for him then. Until then, he will be under my care and thus my protection from Colonel Rose and his nigger soldiers."

Creed finished his drink, set the glass down on the desk, then said, "I appreciate the advice, Dr. January. I'll tell the boys what you said, and we'll decide from there what we'll do." He stood, put his hat on, tipped it, and said, "I'll be back tomorrow and let you know what we've decided to do." Feeling more than a little uneasy, he left and headed back to the camp along the Guadalupe.

5

After conferring with his friends on Dr. January's advice to leave the county immediately, Creed returned to town the next day to visit Simons and tell January about their decision. That was on the surface. Beneath that shallow purpose was his hope to see Miss Ramsdale again. He did.

January's niece greeted Creed at the office door with much of the same ladylike courtesy that she had given him the previous morning, but on this day she added a certain sensuality to her voice that fanned the embers of passion glowing deep within him. Acting on Creed's senses, in concert with the subtle tone of her speech, was a rosewater perfume that accentuated that subliminal feminine essence emitted by all erotic women when aroused. He relished the scent of her, not really knowing why, but not questioning the feeling either. Instead, he responded to her every gesture, every syllable in kind, and the more he did, the more enticing she became.

"Uncle said he advised you and your friends to leave Victoria County," said Catherine. "Have you come to tell him that you are accepting his advice?"

"On the contrary, Miss Ramsdale," said Creed. "My friends and I have no intention of leaving Bill behind, although we know he'll receive the best of care in this house as long as he's here. No, ma'am, we intend to stay until Bill can travel home with us."

"I'm glad to hear that," said Catherine with a sigh of relief. Then realizing how she must have sounded, she added, "For Mr. Simons's sake, of course."

"Of course," said Creed, hoping to relieve the lady of her slight embarrassment. "Is your uncle about, Miss Ramsdale?"

"Not at the moment, Mr. Creed, but I do expect him soon because it's nearly dinnertime, and he never misses dinner. Unless, of course, there is some medical emergency that has drawn him away for the noon hour."

"Yes, of course. Well, if I shouldn't see him, would you tell him of our decision to remain in this vicinity until Bill is well enough to travel?"

"Why don't you stay for dinner and tell him yourself, Mr. Creed? I'm certain he would be delighted if you did. Stay for dinner, I mean."

Creed looked down the length of his person, then back at Catherine. "I don't think I'm properly attired for dinner in a house this fine, Miss Ramsdale."

"Nonsense, Mr. Creed. Your attire is more than appropriate for this house, I assure you. Uncle and I are not ones to stand on ceremony, sir."

"In that case," said Creed, "I accept your gracious invitation, Miss Ramsdale."

Catherine took him by the arm and started to lead him toward Simons's room. "I'll show you in to Mr. Simons," she said, "then I'll go downstairs and tell Lavinia to set another place at the table." She opened the door to the sickroom and more or less pulled him through it. "Mr. Simons, Mr. Creed is here to see you, but he won't be able to stay too long because it's almost dinnertime. I'll leave you two alone for now, but I'll be back in a few minutes with your noon meal, Mr. Simons."

The two men watched her leave, then Creed asked the initial question everyone asks when visiting an ailing person. "How do you feel today, Bill?"

"Same as yesterday," said Simons. "With my fingers." He laughed at his own joke.

Creed chuckled politely at the homespun witticism, then said, "Now tell me serious how you're feeling."

"Lots better, Creed. Especially since you were here yesterday. Just what did you do to that gal?"

"Now what are you talking about?"

Simons grinned and said, "Aw, come on now, Creed. This is Bill Simons you're talking to. You know what I mean."

"No, I don't, Bill."

Simons nodded toward the door and said, "You know. That gal. Miss Ramsdale. What did you do to her yesterday that lit her up like a dry Christmas tree when the candles burn too low?"

"I swear I don't know what you're talking about, Bill."

"All right, have it your way then," said Simons, leaning back in bed and looking away in mock anger. "Makes no difference to me lying here with my ass chock-full of buckshot. No, sir. Makes no never mind to me. You go ahead and keep your little secret, if you want. I don't care."

"Honest, Bill—"

Simons rolled back toward Creed and interjected, "Honest, my foot! You're sparking that girl, ain't you?"

"Are you crazy?" asked an astounded Creed.

"No, sir, I ain't. And I ain't blind neither. Ever since you was here yesterday that girl's been prancing around here like she was the belle of the ball. And why? Because you done something to her, that's why. Now what was it?"

"I swear, Bill, I didn't do nothing."

"Then what did you say to her? Did you sweet-talk her or something?"

"Not a word, I swear."

Simons glared at Creed, then said, "Now don't tell me that you just showing up here did it. We all know Miss Texada thinks you're mighty purty, Creed, and I know that *muy bonita* señorita down to Matamoras was sweet on you, too. Those two can be excused because one's a wildcat what don't know no better and the other's a Mexican who'd pick any Texas longhorn over all the shorthorn greasers in all of Mexico. But hell, man! This girl wears specs, so she ought to be able to see what an ugly cuss you really are."

Creed finally realized that Simons was pulling his leg, but he didn't think the joke was all that funny. The remark concerning his looks had no effect on him at all, and the digs at Texada and Silveria were forgivable. But the unkind inference that Miss Ramsdale was less than a whole person because she wore glasses was uncalled for and downright mean. Even for Simons.

"Bill, how many times have you bit into an apple that looked perfectly good on the outside and found only half a worm on the inside?"

Simons didn't understand the question at first, and his face said so. Then the gist of it struck him, and he was embarrassed by what he'd said. "Sorry, Creed. I didn't mean nothing by that bit about her glasses. I was just trying to fun you, is all."

"I know you were, Bill, and I know you didn't mean anything by it. But next time you try taking potshots at someone, make sure there's no one else in the way."

Simons nodded seriously and said, "Yeah, sure, Creed." Then after a short pause, he said, "I suppose you've come to tell me you're going to heed Dr January's advice and get the hell out of this county before the Yankees do something to you."

"No, that's not what I came here to tell you."

"Then why are you here?"

"Well, to see you, of course, and see how you're feeling today."

Simons perked up and said, "I ain't buying that, Creed. You came to see Miss Ramsdale more than to see me."

Creed blushed a bit, unable to disguise his feelings completely. "Well, she's easier on the eyes than you or that bunch back at camp."

"I'll go along with you there," said Simons, "but don't you think you're being a mite unfair to her by encouraging her the way you're doing?"

"I'm not encouraging her to do nothing, Bill," said Creed defensively. "I just came to see you and to tell Dr. January that we'll be sticking around here until you can travel again."

"You told him that yesterday, didn't you?"

"Not after he told me how things were around, I didn't. I said I'd talk it over with the boys what he said, and together we'd decide whether to go on home now or wait until you're ready to go."

"Well, I told you yesterday and I'll tell you again today," said Simons. "Go home. Now. Before there's trouble with the Yankees here."

"To hell with these Yankees, the same as to hell with those Yankees back home," said Creed. "As long as we don't break any of their damn laws, we've got no reason to walk around like whipped dogs dragging our tails in the dust. Even if that's how they want us to act."

"I guess there's no arguing with you then, is there?"

"No, there isn't, Bill. We're staying until you can go home with us, and that's final."

The door opened and Miss Ramsdale stepped into the room, carrying a serving tray with Simons's dinner on it.

Creed stood up, and Simons straightened up.

"I must apologize for the lack of meat in your diet, Mr. Simons," said Catherine as she placed the tray on his lap, "but Uncle hasn't been able to butcher any of his cattle lately and the larder is close to being empty right now. Even so, Lavinia was able to put a little bacon in the beet greens today. I hope you like beet greens, Mr. Simons."

"Raised on them, ma'am," said Simons. "They'll suit me just fine. Thank you."

"Now if you don't mind, Mr. Simons," said Catherine, taking Creed by the arm, "I'm going to drag Mr. Creed downstairs to have dinner with Uncle and me."

"I do mind," said Simons. "Not so much that he's leaving but that you're not staying, Miss Ramsdale."

She looked at Creed, feigning worry, and said, "Poor man. He must be delirious. Don't you think so, Mr. Creed?"

Creed heaved a sigh as he looked over his shoulder at Simons, who was grinning back at him like the proverbial cat that had just swallowed the canary. Then he said, "I only wish he was, ma'am."

6

At dinner, Dr. January told Creed that he thought Simons was strong enough to withstand a little probing of his wounds for the buckshot embedded there. Creed was glad to hear this news. January said he was planning to operate early the following afternoon, and then he related how he thought Creed and the others should stop by and visit Simons a bit later in the day, because having company would help Simons take his mind off his pain. Creed was quite agreeable to this idea; they would do just that.

"And if all goes well and I am able to get all the buckshot out tomorrow and there is no serious loss of blood, then you should be able to take Mr. Simons home a few days later."

"That would be fine," said Creed.

"Yes, it would," said Catherine, although she didn't really mean it.

January noted the disappointment in his niece's voice, but the tone escaped Creed because he was thinking of home and Christmas and Texada at that very moment. Of course, he was forgetting the risk that he was taking by returning to Lavaca County before clearing his name, but right now he didn't care. All he wanted was to be with Texada.

Catherine had other thoughts. She wanted Creed to remain there, to become part of her life on a permanent basis. Other men had affected her emotions before Creed, but none of them had been able to awaken the woman in her. And he had done this simply by— How had he done it? She wasn't sure, but she knew that she was feeling things for him that she hadn't ever felt for anyone else. Was this love? Another good question for her to answer—somehow.

With the meal at an end, Catherine said, "I suppose you will be joining Uncle for a cigar in the drawing room, Mr. Creed, so I'll just go upstairs and look in on Mr. Simons. If you'll excuse me, sir?"

Creed and January rose from the table as Catherine left the room.

"Yes, Mr. Creed," said January. "Won't you join me in the drawing room for a smoke?"

"I'll join you in the drawing room, Dr. January, but not for a cigar. I don't indulge in the weed, sir."

"You don't smoke, Mr. Creed?"

"No, sir, I don't. I've never been able to acquire a taste for it. I don't chew either."

January moved toward the doorway, saying, "Well, all I can say is there's nothing like a good cigar after a good meal. And brandy, too. You do drink, I know this for a fact. So you'll join me in a glass of brandy. Yes?"

Creed chuckled and said, "Yes, sir. A glass of brandy."

The two of them removed to the drawing room in the front of the house. January poured the liquor for them, then lit up his cigar. He raised his snifter in toast and said, "To your health, sir. May you live a long and prosperous life."

"And the same for you, sir," said Creed, returning the gesture.

January smiled, and they drank.

"Now, sir," said January, "about Catherine." He drew on the cigar, savored the smoke, then tilted his head back and blew it out again. "She appears to be smitten with you, Mr. Creed. What do you intend to do about it?"

This was a turn Creed hadn't suspected. Certainly he felt something for Catherine; exactly what, he was unsure. And he had allowed his ego to whisper to him that she was attracted to him; exactly how deeply, he was unsure. But to have Dr. January say that she was smitten with him? Was this true? And so what if it was? It wouldn't be all that serious. Not to him anyway. But what about January? For that matter, what about Catherine?

Creed was suddenly a bit nervous, but he disguised the feeling with innocence. "I am unaware of any such notion, Dr. January. Certainly, Miss Ramsdale is a lady who is merely displaying good manners and good breeding by entertaining me in your home, sir."

January waved off Creed's feeble attempt to dismiss his question and said, "Of course, she is that, but can't you see that she's quite taken by you?"

"No, sir, I can't say that I can."

"Well, sir, I can. The girl is quite taken with you, sir, and as her guardian, I am quite concerned about it. She's the closest thing I have to a daughter, and I worry about her considerably, Mr. Creed." He inhaled on the cigar again, then exhaled. "She isn't the most attractive girl in this county. In fact, she's downright plain to look at. Certainly, she cuts a decent figure, but she'll never be the belle of the ball."

Odd, thought Creed, that January should use the same expression that Simons had.

"I've seen her around other young men before," said January, continuing, "and she's been giddy and schoolgirlish with them, but I've never seen her this way before."

"What way, sir?"

"Dammit all, Creed! Are you blind? She waltzes around you like a woman preparing for a wedding."

Creed forced a laugh, intentionally trying to settle January's feelings. "Doctor, I think you're exaggerating a bit."

"No, sir, I am not!"

"But we only met yesterday," said Creed.

"So what? Don't you know anything about women, Creed? Young women? Especially young women. Young women who aren't practiced in the ways of courtship. Like Catherine. You smile at them and say a kind word or two, and the next thing you know they're picking out lacy dresses for a wedding."

"I assure you, Dr. January, that I have absolutely no designs set on your niece. She is a charming woman, and I find her company to be most agreeable but strictly in a cordial way."

"That's what I suspected," said January. He frowned. "Too bad. You're the first decent fellow she's ever taken an interest in." He waved off his statement and added, "Oh, not that the others were bad or anything like that. It's just that you're the first one that I thought was man enough to handle her. She can be awfully headstrong, you know."

"No, sir, I didn't," said Creed. "In fact, I would have thought her to be a very genteel lady."

"Sure she can be, but she can also be as stubborn as a mule. And vindictive, too."

Creed thought the doctor had to be wrong on that score, so he laughed out loud and said, "Vindictive? Miss Ramsdale? Dr. January, I think you're pulling my leg now."

January's face scrunched up in total seriousness as he said, "Mark my words, son. You cross Catherine, and you'll pay for it. I guarantee it."

The doctor had thrown down quite a gauntlet, and Creed wasn't sure whether to pick it up or not. He toyed with the idea for a second, then chastised himself for even considering it.

"You need not worry yourself on that account, sir," Creed heard himself saying. "I have no intention of misleading Miss Ramsdale and crossing her, as you so aptly put it."

January started to speak his mind a bit more but held his tongue because Catherine could be heard approaching. Instead, he told himself to keep closer watch on Creed and his niece so that neither of them should suffer from the sting of Cupid's arrows.

Catherine entered the room and said, "Uncle, you have a patient waiting for you upstairs. Mr. Cunningham."

"What's his complaint?" asked January.

"From the sounds of him, I'd say he has the croup."

"Croup, eh? Well, I'd better tend to him right away. If you'll excuse me, Mr. Creed?"

"Certainly, sir. I should be going anyway."

"Nonsense, Mr. Creed," said Catherine. "Why, we've hardly had time to visit."

January glared at Creed but said nothing. He didn't have to. Creed knew what he was thinking.

"I really should be going, ma'am."

"No, sir. I won't hear of it. You simply cannot eat at our table, then run off as soon as you've finished." She smiled mischievously and added, "You have to pay, Mr. Creed. With some polite conversation."

"Better give in, Creed," said January grudgingly. "I know this girl. She won't take no for an answer. Now I must see about Mr. Cunningham. Good day, sir."

"Good day, Doctor," said Creed, resigning himself to his fate.

"Now, Mr. Creed," said Catherine, taking Creed by the arm again and directing him toward the sofa, "tell me all about Lavaca County."

7

After spending a quiet afternoon with Catherine Ramsdale, Creed returned to the camp on the Guadalupe and told his friends about January's plan to operate on Simons the next day and how if all went well, they just might be leaving Victoria in a few days. This was cause for celebration, but Creed said they should heed January's warning and stay out of town as much as possible; there would be ample time for celebrating once they were back in their own territory.

The next day, Creed, Flewellyn, and Kent and Clark Reeves stopped up to see Simons before the surgery, then they joined Crit and Charlie Golihar at Bill Scanlan's Gem Saloon to pass the time while January operated.

An on-and-off drizzle had driven most folks indoors for the day, especially the local men who worked outside. They used the foul weather as an excuse to go to town for a toddy or two and confer with the boys on just about any subject that touched their fancy. Scanlan's was a favorite watering hole for these men, and more than a dozen of them were standing at the foot of the L–shaped bar, not saying much of anything to each other, because their tongues weren't loosened up enough yet by the liquor, when Creed and the others entered the establishment. The locals fell totally silent, their fear of strangers holding full sway over their emotions as they suspiciously watched the newcomers troop by them single file to the upper end of the bar.

Bill Scanlan, the Irish bar dog and proprietor, was tall and thin, and he was bald, but he hid this fact under a black plug hat. He was the proud owner of a handlebar mustache that needed very little wax to keep its curls. He wiped his long hands on the clean white apron tied twice around his waist, then casually strolled behind the bar, toward the new customers. "What'll it be, boys?" he asked.

"Beer," said Creed.

"A glass of San Antone," said Crit Golihar, specifying his favorite brand.

"San Antone for me, too," said Charlie.

"San Antone all around," said Creed, clarifying his own order.

"I don't carry San Antone here," said Scanlan.

"Well, then," said Creed, "any old lager will do. Right, boys?"

They all agreed.

Scanlan dipped a little as he reached under the bar, then straightened up, magically producing six glass beer mugs and putting them on the counter. Before filling a single one, he said, "That'll be five cents each," saying it as if he didn't expect any of the strangers to have the coin with which to pay.

Creed dug a silver dollar out of his watch pocket and gently placed it on the bar. "Take it out of here," he said.

Scanlan smiled warmly at the sight of the cash, nodded, then started filling the mugs and passing them out. With the beers served, he picked up the cartwheel and took it to his cash box in the middle of the bar to get change. By the time he returned, all but Creed were ready for a second round.

"Set them up again," said Creed as he slid a quarter back to Scanlan. "But not me. Just my friends."

Scanlan pocketed the money, then filled the order. "Haven't seen you boys in here before," he said. "New in town?"

"Just passing through," said Creed.

"We were passing through," said Flewellyn bitterly, "until some wild ass bushwhackers shot a friend of ours the other day."

Creed waggled a knee against Flewellyn as a reminder that Dr. January had warned them against talking about the incident. Flewellyn frowned at his friend for making the gesture but knew Creed was right.

"Oh, I see," said Scanlan, playing dumb as if he hadn't

noticed Creed's movement: "You mean the fellow Doc January has got up in his hospital?"

"Hospital?" queried Flewellyn.

"Well, I guess it ain't a real hospital," said Scanlan, "but he calls it that and it's the closest thing we got to one around here."

"Yes," said Creed, "our friend is Dr. January's patient."

"I heard about the shooting," said Scanlan. "It was that bunch that hangs out down to Coleto Creek, wasn't it?"

"We don't know who they were," said Creed, "but that's where it happened. A pretty bummy looking bunch. You know them?"

"Only know of them," said Scanlan. "Veterans, every one of them. Served under Captain Ruply in the 6th Texas Infantry. You boys fight in the war?"

"Not all of us," said Flewellyn, referring to but not pointing out the Golihars, who had successfully evaded the draft and the Home Guards as they sat out the war at Somer's Thicket. "The rest of us fought under Terry."

Scanlan's eyebrows shot up his forehead and almost disappeared beneath the rim of his hat as he said, "Terry, you say?"

"That's right," said Flewellyn. "Except Creed here. He only served under Terry for a short time at the start of the war. After that, he fought for Morgan and Mosby."

"Morgan? And Mosby, too?"

"And Mosby, too," said Flewellyn.

"My name is Bill Scanlan," said the proprietor, extending his hand to Creed expectantly.

"Mine's Creed. Slate Creed." He shook Scanlan's hand, then introduced the others. "We're on our way home for Christmas."

"And where do you call home?" asked Scanlan.

"Lavaca County."

"Hell, you boys are practically neighbors. You figure to be here long?"

"Only as long as it takes for our friend to heal enough to travel," said Flewellyn.

"Hurt bad, was he?"

"Bad enough," said Creed. "He took a load of buckshot in the side and lost a lot of blood. Dr. January is taking out some

of the lead today, and he hopes Bill will be able to travel soon
so we can all go home together."

"Well, he's in good hands," said Scanlan. "Doc January has
been mending folks around here since the days of the Republic.
Resigned his commission and came home in '64 when we had
a yellow fever epidemic here. Good man, Doc January."

"That was my impression," said Creed.

"Your friend isn't the first man shot up by that bunch down
to Coleto Creek. I don't understand those boys. Shooting their
own kind. It ain't right. You'd think they'd rather be shooting
some of these Yankees or some of these damn Yankee-lovers
we got around here."

"Or maybe a few of these uppity niggers we got around
here," said a man in a gray planter's suit at the other end of
the bar.

Creed looked down the bar at him, saw the hate in his eyes,
and chose to ignore the remark.

Scanlan leaned forward and said, "It's all right, friend. Every
man in here already knows about the shooting scrape you were
in the other day. Doc January told us. We just didn't know you
were the ones he was talking about when you walked in here."

"I don't understand that, Mr. Scanlan," said Creed. "Dr.
January warned us not to tell anyone about it, and now you tell
me he's told you and all these men here. Why is that, sir?"

"Yankees," said the same man who had made the remark
about the former slaves in town. "That is why, sir." He picked
up his beer mug and moved closer to Creed. "We try our best
to exclude the Yankees from everything we do around here,
sir, because if we don't, they will run us all into early graves."
He offered his hand to Creed and said, "I am Colonel Benjamin
Hill, sir."

"Proud to meet you, Colonel Hill," said Creed, accepting
the handshake. Creed was quite sincere and impressed because
he recognized Hill as the former military adjutant general for
Texas. To meet a man such as Hill was quite an honor.

"And you are, sir?" asked Hill, his blue eyes a bit glassy
from imbibing.

"Pardon me, Colonel. I am Slate Creed from Lavaca County." He introduced the others with him, and Hill smiled and
nodded at each man in turn.

"Creed?" queried Hill. "I don't believe I know that name, sir. At least not in connection with Lavaca County. Has your family been there long, Mr. Creed?"

"I have no family there, Colonel," said Creed. "I've only been there for a short time myself."

"I see," said Hill. "And before that, where did you reside, sir?"

Creed smiled patronizingly and said, "Wherever Colonel Mosby had us make camp for the night."

"I thought I heard you say that you rode with Mosby, Mr. Creed. I must say that I am quite impressed, sir."

"I was just doing my duty, Colonel," said Creed, now beginning to be annoyed by this line of conversation.

"That's all any of us were doing, Mr. Creed, but let me ask you this, sir. Do you think our duty to Texas ended when General Lee or General Smith surrendered to those damn Yankees?"

"Our duty to Texas, Colonel?"

"Yes, sir."

"No, not to Texas, Colonel," said Creed.

Hill smiled broadly and twisted one half of the mustache of his vandykeed beard. "So I thought," he said.

"But, Colonel, my idea of my duty to Texas just might be a bit different from yours."

"And what would your idea of duty to our glorious state be, Mr. Creed?" asked Hill.

"I'm not sure, Colonel," said Creed, "but I know that it starts with obeying the law."

"But whose laws, Mr. Creed? Ours? Or those being forced on us by our Yankee oppressors?"

Creed looked hard at Hill, then said, "Colonel, my mother used to drag me to prayer meeting every Sunday when I was a boy, and the one thing I learned from all that churchgoing was that if you want to get along in this world, you don't hurt anyone unless you want to get hurt yourself."

"The Golden Rule," said Hill.

"Something like that, Colonel."

"I see, but don't you think that we are being oppressed by these Yankees just as we feared we would be when we chose to separate ourselves from them four years ago?"

Creed was really annoyed now. He glared at Hill and said, "Colonel, I had a conversation similar to this one the other day with Dr. January. I don't like repeating myself, but I guess I'll have to. When we Southerners started that war, we did it to keep our slaves. We fought, and we lost. Doesn't that tell you something, Colonel? That maybe we were wrong? I recall our preacher spouting a sermon at the start of the war that said God was on our side because He had placed the black man on this earth for us white folks to care for and in return he was supposed to serve us."

"I believe I heard a sermon similar to that one on more than one occasion," said Hill, "and I never once doubted the sincerity with which it was delivered."

"Oh, I don't doubt the sincerity of it either, Colonel," said Creed. "I just think the preacher was wrong, that God wasn't on our side. If anything, God was helping the Yankees, Colonel. He helped them at Shiloh, at Vicksburg, at Petersburg, and I do believe that He was riding with Sherman all the way across Georgia. And why was He on their side, Colonel?"

Hill was near to being apoplectic and was unable to answer the question.

"I'll tell you why, Colonel," said Creed, continuing. "Because those Yankees were fighting for something a little more honorable than we were. They were fighting to free the Negroes, while we were fighting to keep them as slaves. It's that simple, Colonel. Slavery is, or was, evil in the sight of God, and He punished us for it, and He'll probably keep on punishing us for it until we learn to treat the black man better."

Through clenched teeth, Hill said in a low growl, "Sir, you have spoken blasphemy. You have desecrated the graves of all those brave boys who gave their lives to preserve our freedom in the—"

"Our freedom?" queried Creed, interrupting Hill. "We were already free, Colonel. That was one thing we didn't have to fight for."

Hill lashed out with a backhand, slapping Creed on the right cheek with it. "I will not stand for your insults to the Confederacy one more minute, sir," he growled. "I demand satisfaction, Mr. Creed."

Creed ignored the rising pain in his face and looked Hill

straight in the eye with the cold stare of a coiled rattler preparing to strike. "All right, Colonel, I'll give you your satisfaction." And without further words, he slammed his left fist into Hill's solar plexus, driving the wind from his chest and doubling him up. In the next instant, his right crushed Hill's cheek, knocking him unconscious and flattening him to the floor.

The men with whom Hill had been drinking glared at Creed and started toward him. Flewellyn produced a skinning knife from his boot and stepped up alongside Creed. The Reeves brothers flanked Creed's other side, and the Golihars moved up close behind him.

"Wait a minute, boys," said Scanlan. "We'll have none of that in here." He produced a shotgun from beneath the bar and lowered it at a point midway between the two factions. "The first one to cross the path of this bird gun gets a load of buckshot in his gizzard."

Every man in the saloon froze in place.

"Mr. Scanlan," said Creed, "my apologies, sir, for disturbing the peace in your fine establishment. With your permission, my friends and I would like to take our leave now."

"Apology accepted, Mr. Creed," said Scanlan. "You can use the back door, if you like, to take your leave."

"Thank you, sir," said Creed. He put a quarter on the counter, then led his friends out into the rain.

8

"You struck Ben Hill?" queried Dr. January, his face animated with incredulity and amazement simultaneously. He was sitting at his desk, looking up at the six men from Lavaca County who stood in a half circle before him.

"He slapped Creed first," said Flewellyn.

"I'm not sure of what to think of this," said January. "Ben Hill is my friend. I've known him a lot of years, but I've also known him to be a hothead. The damn fool never knows when to shut up. He'll push a man to the brink of murder just for the sake of argument. I sometimes think he does this intentionally, as if he wished to cause an altercation. From what you tell me, he was doing it again." He snickered, then added, "Serves him right, the damn fool. I only wish I'd been there to stop him." He looked Creed straight in the eye. "Ben Hill is not a man to be taken lightly, my young friend. He won't soon forget this. Most likely, he'll come after you again, and next time, he won't just slap you. He carries a pocket revolver. One of those little pepperboxes that shoots four shots. Best steer clear of him, Mr. Creed. At least until I can smooth things over for you with him."

Creed heaved a sigh and said, "I'm sorry it happened, Dr. January. I'd heard of Colonel Hill, and I was proud to make his acquaintance this afternoon. I sure didn't think it would end up like this."

"Don't fret any over it, my young friend," said January, rising from his chair and patting Creed on the shoulder. "We'll look in on Mr. Simons, then we'll go over to Scanlan's and have a word with Ben. He'll understand."

Bill Simons was still groggy from the heavy dose of laudanum that January had given him before the operation, but he was alert enough to recognize and converse coherently with his friends. They visited for several minutes, then Simons fell asleep.

On their way over to Scanlan's saloon, January explained that he had removed four pellets from Simons's thigh and hip but that he hadn't attempted to remove any of the shot in Simons's side due to the severe loss of blood while probing the leg. They would have to wait a few days until Simons was up to having another operation.

Colonel Hill wasn't at the Gem Saloon when January and the Lavaca men entered the premises. A quick inquiry and Scanlan informed them that Hill and the rest of the men with him had gone down the street to Napoleon Lytle's Smile Saloon. January led the way there.

Again on the street, he looked both ways before remarking, "Seems to be more than the usual number of nigger soldiers in town today. Hmm! I wonder what Rose is up to now." Then he waved off the thought and said, "Never mind that now. Let's go find Ben Hill."

Creed noted that the scene inside the Smile was much the same as the one he had seen in the Gem earlier in the day. Hill and his contingent of heelers dominated one end of the bar, while the far end remained vacant. The way Hill was haranguing his minions it was plain to see that he was highly agitated. Seeing January in Creed's company only infuriated him all the more.

"My dear Dr. January," said Hill rather formally for one old friend to another, "am I to assume that you have sided with this upstart who had the audacity to strike me?"

"Shut up, Ben," said January calmly. "It's barely the middle of the day, and already you're half in the bag. And over what? Because this man spoke his mind and you didn't agree with him."

"He insulted the Confederacy," said Hill indignantly.

"I know that," said January. "And he had every right to do it, too. Isn't that part of why we were fighting the Yankees? Our freedom. Weren't we fighting for the right to speak our minds when we wanted to and any way we wanted to?"

"But he insulted the Confederacy," stammered Hill.

"Dammit all to hell, Ben. Haven't you been listening to me?"

"Well, yes."

"Then what did I just say?"

"He still doesn't have the right to insult the Confederacy," grumped Hill.

January heaved a sigh and said, "I thought you said you'd been listening. If you had, then you'd know that I said he had the right to insult the Confederacy or anything else he wants to for that matter. Every man has the right to express his opinion on something. It don't make him right, but he has got the right to talk. Now don't you agree with that?"

"Well, yes, but—"

"Dammit, Ben, will you give it up? You slapped the man, and he socked you in the jaw. I don't think he would have done that if you hadn't struck him first."

Creed stepped forward and said, "That's right, Colonel. I would never strike a man of your stature without being provoked."

"Are you apologizing, Mr. Creed?" asked Hill.

Creed's backbone stiffened as he said, "No, sir, I am not."

Hill glared at Creed for a brief second, then a smile broke out on his face. "Mr. Lytle!" he called out over his shoulder to the proprietor of the saloon. "Set up a round of beers for Mr. Creed and his friends. On me, of course." Then to Creed, he said, "Won't you join me, sir, in a bit of libation?"

Creed knew an apology when one was being offered. He grinned and said, "I'd be proud to, Colonel."

"And as for you, January," said Hill quite sternly, "you may buy your own drink." He turned a cold shoulder on the doctor but didn't really mean it. They had been friends far too long.

"All right, I'll do just that," said January, also trumping up his hollow anger, "and next time you need a doctor you can go to that Yankee-loving Goodwin for all I care."

Creed stepped up to the bar beside Hill, and January did likewise on the other side. The remainder of the Lavaca men spread out down the counter and began quaffing the brews placed before them by Napoleon Lytle. All was quite jovial until the front door swung open and a very large man entered the premises. That in itself wasn't unusual, but the fact that this giant was of African ancestry was.

Six months prior to this day no one would have thought much about a Negro coming into the saloon, because only slaves seeking their masters for one reason or another would dare do so. They would come in, bare their heads, keep their eyes lowered, and wait for some white person to speak to them before they stated their business. If the master was there, the slave would speak with him, then depart immediately, leaving the white gentlemen to enjoy their privacy.

That was six months ago. Before the Federals showed up. The Negro company from Michigan and the white company from Pennsylvania. Each and every one of them ready to assist the freed slaves in obtaining their new rights. Exactly what those rights were, no one really knew yet, but the soldiers were ready to protect them, especially if protecting them meant an affront to former Confederates.

Nap Lytle wanted to challenge the Negro for coming into his saloon, but he knew that if he did, the man just might run to Colonel Rose and complain. That would surely result in the Yankee colonel revoking his beer license and having his store closed until Lytle softened his stance a bit.

No one else offered to challenge the Negro until he stepped up to the far end of the bar and ordered a drink. Then it was Colonel Hill who took exception to the man's presence.

"Hey, boy, this saloon doesn't serve niggers," said Hill, almost spitting the words.

Lytle made no move to get the man his drink.

"It do now," said the man rather happily. He slapped a silver dollar on the counter and said, "Caesar Blair always pays, Mr. Bartender, so set me up. I is dry as a mule fart in a dusty field of cotton."

"Don't you serve that foulmouthed nigger nothing," said Hill to Lytle. "Just throw his black ass out of here, Nap."

Blair appeared to look up and down the bar, then started chuckling loud enough for everyone in the place to hear.

Creed had watched the man's eyes and seen them glance past everybody in the saloon to focus on something or someone outside on the street. Creed turned, spied out the window, and saw a knot of Negro soldiers staring intently in the saloon's direction. They seemed to be waiting for something or someone. Creed didn't have time to ask himself what that might be, as his attention was drawn back to the scene inside the Smile.

"Lordy," said Blair, "y'all sure do talk bold, sir. Why, there ain't three of you white trash peckerwoods big enough to throw Caesar Blair out of this here saloon or any other saloon for that matter."

"Why you mouthy nigger!" swore Crit Golihar, who then reached down in his boot and pulled out a hunting knife. "I think I'll cut your black ass to ribbons and use them to hog-tie the rest of you so it'll be easier to throw you in the nearest shit hole where you belong."

"Come on, boy!" invited Blair with a waggle of fingers on a hand that appeared big enough to engulf Golihar's entire head. An evil smile creased Blair's face.

Golihar hesitated when he realized that he was challenging Blair alone. The pause was long enough for Creed to step between them.

"Put that knife away, Crit," said Creed, holding up his hand in front of Golihar. "We don't need any more trouble in this town, especially with all these Yankees around here."

Golihar stared at Creed, not knowing whether to be angry or glad that Creed had intervened.

"Outta the way, boy," growled Blair, "and let that white trash come on. I's ready for him."

Creed turned to Blair and said, "Now look here. . . ." Then he realized the real size of the man. His eyes rolled up and down, awed by all six feet eight of Blair; but he showed no fear, only respect for a man who was probably powerful enough to break every one of his ribs with a not-too-gentle hug of his massive arms. "Uh, Mr. Blair, there's no need to be causing any trouble here."

"I ain't the one causing the trouble, peckerwood," said Blair angrily. "I just come in here wanting to wet my whistle the same as y'all. That's all. Just let me have my drink, and leave me be in peace. That's all. Just leave me drink in peace. Ain't that what I'm doing for y'all?"

"Look, Mr. Blair," said Creed, again addressing the man respectfully in the hopes that it would make him see reason, "these gentlemen—"

"What gentlemens?" interrupted Blair. "I don't see no gentlemens. All I sees is a bunch of white trash stinking up the place." He sniffed the air and made a sour face. "Yessuh. Sure do stink in here."

"I've had just about enough of you, nigger," said Hill, darting forward past Golihar and Creed. "You'll either walk out of here this instant or we'll drag your dead black ass out of here later."

Blair's first thought was to laugh in mockery of this cocky bastard, but he didn't. Instead, his eyes bulged in disbelief. He reached for a ceramic pitcher on the bar, grabbed it, and drew it back to heave it at Hill.

Creed reacted to Blair and didn't see the derringer in Hill's hand. He took one step forward before Hill raised his arm and fired the first ball in Blair's direction. The flash of exploding gunpowder stayed Creed's feet, and the pop of the pepperbox caused him to lean aside, to hesitate long enough for Hill to shoot again.

Blair couldn't deliver his missile. The first ball had bored into his chest just above his heart, and the second struck only a few inches below the first. The big man stumbled backward, clutching the ewer as if he still intended to throw it. He fell against the bar, gasping for air and holding his free hand over his wounds. His legs gave out, and he crashed to the floor. As did the pitcher. Both of them dead.

January was the first man to react. He rushed forward to check Blair's condition. He knelt down beside the body, felt for a pulse on the victim's neck, and found none. He turned, looked up at Hill, and said, "You've killed him, Ben."

"Serves the dirty nigger right," said Crit Golihar.

Hill said nothing, because suddenly the consequences of this act struck him. He had murdered a man. Whether he liked it or not, he had murdered a man. Not a slave. Not a nigger. Not now. Not in December 1865. Not when the town, the county, the state, the whole South were being ruled by Abolitionist Black Republican Yankees and their regiments of Negro soldiers. Never mind that Blair was a Negro. He was a man in the eyes of the law, Abolitionist Black Republican Yankee law, and Colonel Benjamin Hill had murdered him. And for this, he could hang. He would hang, if his fate were left in the hands of the Yankees.

Everyone in the bar crowded around to see the dead man. "Good shooting," said some. "Served him right," said others. None of them said a thing when two Negro soldiers from the Michigan regiment burst into the saloon.

"Out of the way!" commanded one as he led the other through the knot of men.

The crowd parted to let them pass. Only those standing close to the victim remained still. A cloud of gunsmoke hung over them like a shroud.

The first soldier stopped short of Blair's body, his eyes wide with disbelief.

"He's dead!" exclaimed the second man, also disbelieving what he was seeing. "This wasn't supposed to happen, Marcus."

"Shut up, y'all!" snapped Marcus. He looked around at all the Caucasian faces that were looking at him. "Go get Captain Spaulding, Rafe. Go get him now!"

Rafe didn't understand the reason for the command, but he obeyed it. He turned, bolted through the crowd that parted for him almost magically, then burst through the door and outside to the street, hollering for Captain Spaulding at the top of his lungs.

Marcus leveled his Springfield at Hill, who was still holding the derringer at his side. "You do this?" he asked.

"Aim that rifle in another direction, nigger," said Hill defiantly.

Marcus thumbed back the hammer of his gun and said, "Mister, I ain't got but one bullet in here, but it's all I needs to send y'all to hell."

"He's only one man, nigger," said Crit Golihar. "What do you plan to do to the rest of us when you've finished him?"

"Back off, Crit," said Creed, stepping between Golihar and the soldier. "You'll only get us all in trouble if you keep spouting off like that."

"What's the matter with you, Creed?" asked Crit. "I knew you were partial to Mexicans, but I didn't think it carried over to niggers, too."

Creed didn't have to answer Golihar because Flewellyn did

it for him by slamming his fist into the side of Golihar's head and knocking him unconscious to the floor. "Loudmouth son of a bitch!" swore Flewellyn as he stood over Golihar. He looked up at Charlie and said, "Your mammy didn't teach you boys much about manners, did she, Charlie?"

Charlie was too scared to answer.

"That's uncalled for, Jake," said Creed. "When Crit comes around, maybe you'd better apologize for saying anything about his mother." He turned to the soldier and said, "There won't be any more trouble here, Sergeant."

Before anything else could happen in the saloon, Captain Spaulding and a squad of Negro soldiers burst through the door with their guns ready for action.

"All right, you men," said Spaulding, brandishing his Colt's New Army .44, "line up against the bar. Sergeant Jones, search these men for weapons and arrest every man who's carrying even the smallest carving knife."

Creed knew that Spaulding's order would include him and his friends as well as Colonel Hill, but there was no sense in trying to stop the search. Not when Spaulding had more men coming in every second and every one of them was a former slave or the son of slaves who hated Southern whites more than a bad case of the skitters. The wise thing to do was to go peacefully and hope for the best. Or so he thought.

9

For some odd reason, Creed wasn't arrested with the other men from Lavaca County and Ben Hill. He was searched by Sergeant Jones just the same as they had been, but Jones told his captain that Creed wasn't carrying a weapon, not even the smallest carving knife. Jones was lying, of course, because Creed kept a hunting knife in his right boot, and Creed knew the man had felt it when his hands passed over Creed's shanks. Whatever Jones's reason for lying, Creed was a free man that afternoon.

"This is not a good situation," said January. He had returned to his office with Creed and a few other men in the community who had joined them to discuss the arrest of Ben Hill and Creed's friends. January was doing most of the talking. "We may have the beginnings of real trouble here, boys. Those nigger soldiers will be aching to get at Ben pretty damn quick, not to mention your friends, Mr. Creed."

"Don't you have any civil law in this town?" asked Creed.

"We have a town marshal and a justice of the peace," said January, "but they only do what the army lets them do and that isn't much. Mostly, they stick to local matters. You know. Like when two white boys get in a tussle over something stupid. But when it concerns a nigger, the army steps in and decides what's what. Of course, they do this within the system, but Colonel Rose determines what the system is. If you get my drift."

"What about your county judge?" asked Creed. "Is he a Yankee or a Yankee-lover like the one up in Lavaca County?"

"Nope. Sam White has been in these parts since the days before the Revolution. He's one of our own. Can't say that he was real sympathetic to the cause when the war was on, but he sure wasn't a Unionist. Pretty much a middle-of-the-roader, if you ask me. I guess that's why he's the judge now."

"Well, doesn't he have any power around here?" asked Creed.

"Some, but not much with all these Yankees hereabouts."

"Well, why don't we see how much power he does have?" said Creed. "Leastways, he might let my friends out of jail."

"All right, let's go over and see him."

Everyone stood up and started for the door at the same time.

"Now wait a minute," said January. "We can't all go over there at once. We do that, and the Yankees will get suspicious or something. Whatever, they won't like it, and they'll get in our way, and before you know it, there'll be more trouble. Mr. Creed and me only. We'll go. The rest of you just leave here one at a time or so. Don't leave all at once or the Yankees will get suspicious about that, too." He chuckled and added, "They'll think we're fomenting another rebellion."

"They'd be right, wouldn't they?" said Andy Cunningham, a former captain in the 6th Texas Infantry. Unlike January, he was quite serious.

"No, they'd be wrong," said January, glaring at Cunningham. "Now look here, boys. I don't like the Yankees any more than any of you do, but we lost the war and that's all there is to it. They got the might—"

"But they ain't got the right," said Creed, anticipating January's next line of words.

"Maybe not," said January. "Maybe not, but who's going to tell them that? You?"

"If I have to," said Creed firmly, evenly.

Cunningham grinned, nudged the man next to him, and said, "I'd like to be there when you do, mister."

"Never you mind that kind of talk now, Andy," said January. "It's loud boasting like that what got us into the fix we're in now. Ask your daddy sometime about what happens to them that boast too boldly then can only back it up in a half-assed way. He can tell you."

Cunningham appeared to be properly chastised. He knew

exactly what January was referring to: the military fiasco of 1842 when a Texan army marched foolhardily into Mexico against the advice of wiser counsel—including that of Major John Cunningham, Andy's father—and met total defeat.

"Now, the rest of you," said January, "do like I told you. Leave here one at a time and go about your business. Leave this affair to Mr. Creed and me."

January and Creed walked down Liberty Street to Constitution, then turned west and walked to the center of town at Main Street. In the next block was the home of the local newspaper, *The Victoria Advocate*, formerly *The Texan Advocate*, the name having been changed by its present owner, Samuel Addison White, a Texas hero in his own right, having fought in the Battle of Velasco in 1832, served in the Texican army as a captain during the Revolution, and fought the Comanches at Plum Creek in 1840. The building was a modest one-story wooden structure with a false facade rising above a roofed porch that stretched across the entire front. A sign in the large square window advertised job printing.

When January aimed his path toward the newspaper, Creed said, "I thought we were going to see the judge."

"We are," said January, without breaking stride. "Like I told you the other day, Sam White isn't just the county judge. He's a newspaper publisher, too. And a planter and a stockman."

They marched up the three steps at the side of the porch, and January opened the plain wooden door for Creed to enter first. Always cognizant of his elders, Creed insisted that the doctor precede him inside.

The interior was like any other newspaper office of the day. A short counter separated the business area for customers from the working area of the editorial staff, and behind the latter was the printers' space, which was dominated by a Washington printing press. Silver-haired, lanky Sam White sat at one desk, and his youthful-looking reporter, Victor Marion Rose, was busy writing at the other. Both men looked up at the visitors, but only one spoke.

"January," said Judge White, "I thought I'd see you before long. I already heard about the shooting, and I'll tell you right now that there's not a thing I can do about it." He fixed his view on Creed. "And who are you, sir?"

"This is Mr. Slate Creed of Lavaca County," said January, stopping in front of White's desk.

"Lavaca County, you say?" queried White.

"Yes, sir," said Creed.

"You with that bunch the Yankees arrested with Ben Hill?"

"Yes, sir, I am."

"And I suppose it's them that you came to see me about," said White. Then back at January, he said, "And I suppose you were going to demand that I let Ben out of jail, weren't you, January?"

"That's pretty much it, Sam," said January.

"Your Honor, my friends and I just happened to be in the same saloon as Colonel Hill when the shooting occurred," said Creed. "We didn't have anything to do with it."

"In fact, Mr. Creed was trying to prevent trouble," said January. "Ben was just too quick with his pepperbox."

White shifted his eyes from January to Creed and asked, "Why weren't you arrested with your friends?"

Creed shrugged and said, "Your guess is as good as mine. I was carrying a knife just the same as they were, but the soldier who searched us didn't tell his captain that I had one." As an afterthought, he added, "And I don't know why he didn't tell him either."

"I know why," said January. "Mr. Creed here stopped what might have been a riot, Sam. One of his boys started after the nigger who was holding his rifle on Ben, and Mr. Creed stopped him. If he hadn't, that nigger would have shot Ben, and the next thing you'd know we would have been fighting Yankees all over town."

"Oh, I don't know about that," said Creed.

"I do!" snapped January. "You don't know these Yankees, Mr. Creed. This Colonel Rose who's in charge of them is a real Black Republican in every sense of the term. If he had his way, he'd line up every Texan who fought for the South and shoot us dead just the same way that Santa Anna ordered Urrea to do it at Goliad. And what's more, he'd have his nigger boys do the shooting for him. I'll tell you this, too, Creed. Once the shooting starts there won't be time to stop and choose up sides. Those black bucks will be on us in a cat's wink, and when they've finished with us, they'll be after our women.

Mark my words, son, that's exactly what will happen."

Creed could hardly believe he was hearing this. He'd heard this sort of farfetched drivel before the war and while the tragic conflict raged, especially after the Yankees had started putting together Negro regiments to fight for them. He'd heard other officers tell their men that if they didn't kill every nigger they saw in a blue uniform, those black bucks would run wild and rape every white woman in the South. When nothing like this occurred anywhere in the conquered states, Creed knew that his superiors had either imagined this out of fear of reprisal or had machinated this ugly piece of propaganda as a way of frightening the troops into continuing the fight against what were becoming more overwhelming odds every day the struggle lasted.

"Well, I don't know about that," said Creed, not willing to tell January that he was so full of shit a bucket of November prunes would be needed to get him regular again.

"Nor do I," said White. "I'll admit that Colonel Rose is a real horse's ass, but I don't think he or his men would allow the Negroes to get out of hand like you say, January."

"Well, I, for one, sure as hell don't want to find out if they can control their niggers or not," said January.

"As I've already said, January, there's nothing I can do about Ben Hill. He shot a man, and he'll have to stand trial for it. You can bet Colonel Rose will more than insist on that. As for your friends, Mr. Creed, the Yankees haven't charged them with anything yet, as far as I know, but it's my suspicion that they'll be charged with being accessories to the shooting."

"Your Honor, we didn't have anything to do with it," said Creed. "As much as I hate to say it, Colonel Hill had his gun out already when he walked up to that man. I don't think he intended to shoot Blair until Blair picked up the pitcher."

"Mr. Creed, you can save your testimony for the trial," said White. "Right now, let's see what we can do about your friends. Have you retained a lawyer yet?"

"A lawyer?" queried Creed. "I didn't think I'd need one."

"My advice to you is that you retain John McClanahan," said White. "January knows where to find him. McClanahan will take care of the legals, and we'll do what we can for your friends."

"Thank you, Your Honor," said Creed.

"Thanks, Sam," said January with a nod. Then he led Creed outside and around the corner to McClanahan's office on Main Street. McClanahan was expecting them, or so he acted when they entered the premises. January introduced them, then told McClanahan the problem.

"So you want me to get the wheels of justice turning for your friends?" queried the lawyer. But before Creed could answer, he added, "Easy as one-two-three." He took a piece of paper from his desk drawer and began writing on it. Then he asked, "What are your friends' names?"

Creed recited them, and McClanahan wrote them on the paper. The lawyer blotted the ink, then stood up.

"Gentlemen," said McClanahan, grabbing his plug hat from the hat tree in the corner, "to the courthouse."

The trio marched up Main Street to the plaza and cut across it to the Victoria County Courthouse, a wooden two-story structure that was painted white, had a cupola, was situated on a block by itself, and was surrounded by a split-rail fence also painted white. They went right in to the clerk of the court, to whom McClanahan presented the paper he had written, a writ of habeas corpus that needed the judge's signature. The clerk looked it over, nodded, and said, "The judge just came in." He took the writ immediately to His Honor, obtained the proper autograph, then promptly returned it to McClanahan. With a wink, McClanahan told Creed and January to follow him to the jail.

At the lockup, matters didn't proceed as smoothly as they had at the courthouse. The trio was met at the door by Captain Spaulding, the same sandy-haired young cavalry officer who had arrested Hill and the men from Lavaca County.

"Something I can do for you, gentlemen?" he asked.

"I have a writ of habeas corpus, Captain," said McClanahan.

"Who for?" asked Spaulding, scowling.

McClanahan looked at the paper he had written and read, "Jacob Flewellyn, Kent Reeves, Clark Reeves, Charles Golihar, and Cristobal Golihar. You do have these men in your charge, do you not, Captain Spaulding?"

"I do."

"Then you are to present them to the court of the Honorable Samuel A. White posthaste, sir," said McClanahan.

"Let me see that," said Spaulding, snatching the writ from McClanahan's hand. He read it, then, glaring at the trio, said, "It looks legal enough. All right, I'll have them over there within the hour."

"Not good enough, sir," said McClanahan. "The writ states a specific time." He pulled his pocket watch from a vest pocket and said, "I believe the writ states three o'clock post meridiem on this very day, sir, and by my watch that gives you less than fifteen minutes to present them before the court or risk being held in contempt."

"All right," snapped Spaulding, "we'll bring them right now." Over his shoulder, he shouted, "Sergeant Jones!"

Jones came forward and popped to attention. "Yes, sir."

"Jones, get those five men we arrested with Hill and take them over to the courthouse immediately."

"You had better come along, too, Captain," said McClanahan. "After all, you were the arresting officer."

"Get the prisoners, Sergeant," said Spaulding, "and get a squad together to guard them."

Jones did as ordered, and in less than two minutes, the parade to the courthouse was under way. The prisoners were each flanked by two soldiers. Spaulding marched alongside the detail, and Jones brought up the rear. McClanahan, Creed, and January walked casually along behind, and after them came several more Negro soldiers, a few Negro civilians, and several local white businessmen who had quickly locked up their shops and stores when they saw or heard about what was happening in town. This throng soon filled Judge White's courtroom.

The bailiff called the court to order, and the audience rose when Judge White entered the room. He sat down behind the bench and said, "Be seated, everyone." Then he looked out over the crowd and added, "I didn't know this case was so important to so many that half the town would close up shop just to be here." He set his eyes on McClanahan, who was sitting alone at the defendant's table. "I understand you have some business before this court, Mr. McClanahan."

"That is correct, Your Honor," said McClanahan, rising to his feet. "I represent five gentlemen from Lavaca County,

Your Honor, who have been incarcerated in our local jail by the occupying army of the Union but who have not been charged with any crime. I have presented a writ of habeas corpus to the arresting officer in this case, Your Honor, uh, Captain Spaulding, who has forthwith delivered his prisoners to this courtroom."

White turned his gaze on Spaulding, who sat at the prosecutor's table, although the county attorney wasn't present. "Why did you arrest these men, Captain Spaulding?" asked the judge.

Spaulding stood to reply. "They were carrying concealed weapons, Your Honor."

"Is that the only reason?" asked White.

"They were also part of a mob that murdered a man in the Smile Saloon just a few hours ago, Your Honor."

"Are you positive of this fact, Captain?" asked White, looking a bit cockeyed at Spaulding.

"I am positive that a man was murdered in the Smile Saloon, Your Honor," said Spaulding.

"And how was this man murdered?" asked White.

"He was shot, sir."

"How many times?"

"Well, just twice."

"By two men?"

"No, sir. One."

White stroked his chin and said, "I see. And all these men pulled the trigger together?"

"Well, no, sir," said Spaulding, a blush beginning to show in his clean-shaven cheeks.

"Then how did a mob commit this murder, Captain?"

"Well, I guess a mob didn't commit it, Your Honor, but these men were caught with concealed weapons."

"Your Honor," said McClanahan, "is the captain charging my clients with carrying concealed weapons?"

"I don't know, Mr. McClanahan," said White. "What say you, Captain Spaulding? Is that the charge against these men?"

Spaulding glared at the floor for a second, then looked up at White and replied, "Yes, sir, it is."

"Then, Your Honor," said McClanahan officiously, "I would request the court to hear this case as soon as possible so that my clients might enter a plea."

"No time like the present," said White, "seeing that we got everyone here except the county attorney. Anyone know where he's at?"

Heads shook all around.

"This does present a problem," said White. "Unless, of course, you'd like to do the prosecuting yourself, Captain."

"I think I can handle that chore, Your Honor," said Spaulding. He turned to Sergeant Jones and said, "Bring the prisoners before the bench, Jones."

Jones gazed around the room, looking rather perplexed, then said, "Which bench does you mean, sir? The one they's sitting on or some other bench?"

This brought a roar of laughter from most of the Caucasian onlookers in the courtroom. Creed, Spaulding, Jones's fellow soldiers, and the Freedmen in attendance failed to see any humor in the sergeant's ignorance, all of them remaining rather stolid until the merrymakers ceased their guffawing.

Through gritted teeth, Spaulding said, "Take them up before the judge, Sergeant."

Jones's brow furrowed for a second before he fully understood the command. Then he realized that the bench and the judge were synonymous. Now he understood why they had laughed at him, and he made a silent promise to work harder at learning to read and write and figure numbers.

"Get up, y'all!" snapped Jones angrily at the prisoners.

"Your Honor," said McClanahan, "could I confer with my clients before we approach the bench?"

"Go right ahead," said White.

Jones led the five men over to the defendant's table, where McClanahan huddled with them.

"Gentlemen, I think it would be expedient if we were to enter a plea of guilty to the charge," said McClanahan.

"Why?" asked Flewellyn.

"Because the judge will probably fine you some minor amount for such a minor offense," said McClanahan, "then let you all go."

"What does Creed think?" asked Flewellyn.

McClanahan turned away from them and said, "Mr. Creed, would you please join us?"

Creed rose from the first bench and stepped forward to confer with the lawyer and his friends.

"Mr. Creed," said McClanahan, "I have advised your friends that a plea of guilty should be entered because I expect the judge to levy a small fine, which he will no doubt suspend, then allow you and your friends to be on your way. Your friends wish to know your feelings on my recommendation."

"Yeah, what about it, Creed?" asked Flewellyn. "Do we plead guilty or what?"

"You do what Mr. McClanahan recommends, boys," said Creed. "The judge is on our side in this."

"All right, we'll do it," said Flewellyn. He looked at the others, and everyone nodded in agreement.

Creed returned to his seat.

McClanahan approached the bench ahead of his five clients. "Your Honor, my clients wish to enter a plea of guilty to the charge of carrying concealed weapons in the city of Victoria."

White looked over the defendants and said, "Is that right, boys? You plead guilty?"

"Yes, sir, we do," said Flewellyn. The others nodded.

"Then so be it," said White, rapping his gavel on the table. "This court fines each of you one dollar. Pay the clerk and you can all go free. If you can't pay up, then you'll have to sit in jail until someone else can or until you've served three days. Court is adjourned." He banged his gavel again, then left the courtroom amidst a sudden peel of thunderous applause from much of the crowd.

"I thought you said he'd suspend the fine," said Flewellyn to McClanahan.

"I thought he would," said the lawyer.

"Now what do we do?" Flewellyn asked Creed as he joined them again.

"Don't worry, boys," said Creed. "I've got enough money to cover it. You just take it easy until I can get things settled." He took McClanahan's hand and shook it. "Thank you, sir. How much do I owe you for your services?"

McClanahan looked at him and said, "Five dollars will do. You got that much?"

"Not on me," said Creed, "but I can get it quick enough."

"Fine. Just bring it by my office before you leave town," said the lawyer.

Creed turned to January, shook his hand as well, and said, "Thank you for your help in this matter, Dr. January. How can I repay you for this service?"

January looked around them, then said, "Let's talk about that at some other place a little later when there aren't so many ears around."

Creed wasn't sure what January meant by that, but he didn't have time to worry about it now. He had fines to pay first and then a lawyer. He would concern himself with January later.

10

While in New Orleans at the end of the War Between the States, Creed had had a lucky streak at the roulette wheel in Monsieur DuMorney's Bourbon Street casino, Le Bijou Rouge, and he won two hundred dollars in hard cash before calling it quits. He then sewed his winnings, ten twenty-dollar gold pieces, in a fold of his bedroll until he needed them again. The first time he'd needed them had been when he was buying cattle to drive to market in New Orleans that past summer. After selling the herd, he replaced a like amount of funds in the same hiding place and since then had removed only one coin at a time on three different occasions. Now came the fourth.

With a twenty-dollar gold piece in hand, Creed returned to John McClanahan's office and presented payment in full to the lawyer.

"I'm sorry, son," said McClanahan, "but I can't make change for that double eagle. We'll have to go around to the newspaper office to change it."

Upon entering the *Advocate* building, Creed was surprised by the number of men gathered in the rear of the establishment. Prominent among them were two he knew now: Dr. January and Judge White. By the way they were huddled together, he surmised that they were engaged in some sort of intrigue, especially when they fell silent upon seeing him and McClanahan enter the office.

"Good," said White loudly when he noticed the two newcomers. "McClanahan, glad you could join us. You, too, Mr. Creed."

"We aren't exactly joining you," said McClanahan from where he and Creed stood at the front counter. "We just came by to see if you might be able to break up a double eagle."

White's bushy, silvery eyebrows pinched together over his prominent nose, and his blue-gray eyes zeroed in on Creed. "You got that much hard cash, son?"

"Yes, sir," said Creed, taking note of how the others stared at him with the same question that White had asked.

"Well, we can break it down for you all right," said the judge. "I suppose you need it to pay the court and McClanahan here, too."

"Yes, sir," said Creed, his aspect telling the others to mind their own business.

White nodded, stepped away from the circle of men, and made his way to his desk. He removed a key from his vest pocket and unlocked the drawers. He pulled out the bottom one of three and bent over it in such a manner that he prevented anyone from peering inside. He reached into it. A squeak of a tin box's lid was followed by the clinking of silver and gold coins and the rustle of the new paper specie that the Federal government had only recently begun issuing. In a minute, White finished the counting and reversed his earlier actions, closing the money box, closing the drawer, straightening up, and locking the desk. He placed two five-dollar bills on the desk, then made two stacks of five silver dollars each atop the folding money.

Creed walked around the counter and handed the double eagle to White, who gazed at the coin avariciously as he accepted it.

"Twenty Yankee dollars," said White, nodding at the money on the desk while looking up at Creed. "Care to count it?"

"No, sir," said Creed.

"You don't mind the paper money, do you?" asked White.

"No, sir, it'll do," said Creed as he picked up the money. He turned to McClanahan and asked, "Would you prefer silver or paper, Mr. McClanahan?"

"Silver, if it's all the same to you."

"Makes no difference to me," said Creed as he handed over five cartwheels to the lawyer.

"Would you like a receipt for that?" asked McClanahan as he accepted the payment and pocketed it.

"That won't be necessary," said Creed as he stuffed the bills and remaining coins in a pants pocket, "but I'd be obliged if you would accompany me to the courthouse again and make sure everything is done proper to get my friends out of jail."

"I'd be pleased to," said McClanahan.

"When you're done over there," said White, "come back here, will you? Both of you. And bring your friends, Mr. Creed. We could have use for them, too."

"What are you up to here, Sam?" asked McClanahan, both curious and a bit annoyed because there was plotting going on and he hadn't been invited from the start.

White stroked his chin, glanced over his shoulder at the men in the rear, then said, "Come on into the back now, and we'll tell you all about it."

McClanahan looked askance to Creed, who answered with a shrug that said it made no difference to him.

"Your friends can wait a few more minutes," said White.

"What do you think?" asked McClanahan.

"I suppose so," said Creed.

Then both men turned to the expectant White, who nodded his approval. He stood up, then led the lawyer and Creed to the knot of men in the rear.

Creed recognized a few more faces besides January's but could only put names to two of them: Andy Cunningham and Vic Rose. The others had been at January's earlier in the afternoon, but they hadn't been introduced.

"I asked John and Mr. Creed to join us, gentlemen," said White. "I think we'll need all the help we can get."

"Ten good men is all we'll need," said January, his eyes burning with defiance.

White made a quick head count and said, "Well, that's how many we've got here right now."

"Ten men for what?" asked McClanahan.

"To guard Ben Hill," said January.

"But the Yankees are guarding him," said McClanahan.

"Yes, but which Yankees?" said Cunningham.

McClanahan thought about it for a second, then realized what Cunningham was implying. "You don't think those niggers will do him harm, do you?" asked the lawyer.

"That's exactly what we think," said January.

"He killed one of them, didn't he?" said Cunningham.

"I didn't hear that," said White, the judge.

"Well, didn't he?" repeated Cunningham.

"That's for a court of law to prove," said McClanahan, the lawyer, rebuking Cunningham for bypassing the basic right of all Americans, that one is innocent until proven guilty beyond a shadow of a doubt.

"He won't get to a court of law if we don't protect him now," said January. "As sure as the sun's going to rise tomorrow, those nigger soldiers aim to do Ben in as soon as they can. You can bet on that, John."

McClanahan stroked his chin as he thought over what January had said. He looked up at White and said, "What do you propose to do about this, Sam?"

"Well, for one thing," said White, "I'm too old to be carrying a gun—"

January jumped in with, "And you're the county judge, Sam, so you shouldn't be carrying a gun anyway."

White glared at January and continued, "As I was saying, I'm too old for this, but men like Vic and Andy here aren't. You, too, Mr. Creed. You're all veterans of the Confederacy. You're the ones who should be standing guard over Ben Hill."

"I'm not so sure about that," said Creed. "Leastways, not about me being a part of this."

"Why not?" queried January. "We need you, Creed. And your friends. With men like you guarding Ben, those nigger soldiers won't dare do a thing against him."

"But what if they do?" asked Creed. "Then what?"

"Then you do your duty," said January, "and shoot the bastards down dead!"

Creed tried to keep his smile under control but was only partially successful as he said, "Ten men against a whole regiment, sir? We start shooting those men, and they'll burn this town to the ground . . . *after* they've hung every man in it first. No, sir. I want no part of that."

"Now let's not be hasty," said White. "As I was saying before, I'm too old to be carrying a gun, and I am the county judge, which carries some weight in these parts, even with the Yankees. I say we go to Colonel Rose and demand that he turn Ben over to our civil authority at once and that he send all his Negro soldiers across the river until this all cools down."

"That sounds like the sensible thing to do," said McClanahan. "We go to Colonel Rose and get Ben out of their hands first. Then we can decide how to protect him."

"I think we'll need a show of force to convince him," said January. "If he sees that we're armed and prepared to defend a fellow Texan to the death, he's most likely to go along with our demands."

Suddenly, the eyes of all the locals fell on Creed as White spoke for them. "What say you to that, Mr. Creed? Would you be willing to come along to see Colonel Rose, and to bring your friends, too? Just as a show of force? A little poker bluff, you might say."

A chill ran down Creed's spine, but he didn't twitch a single muscle. Something was telling him not to go along with them, but he knew he had to do it. These men were Texans, the same as he was. They had befriended him and helped him. Now all they wanted from him in return was a little moral support. It was the least he could do, although he felt certain it would lead to more trouble in the end.

11

When the Union army first occupied Victoria County in July, 1865, General David Stanley requisitioned the house of merchant and financier Abraham Levi on the southwest corner of Main and Power streets for his headquarters. Levi was away on business in Mexico at the time. Stanley departed the county two months later, leaving Colonel Isaac T. Rose of the 77th Pennsylvania Infantry in command and living in Levi's house. It was to this residence that Judge Sam White led his delegation late that autumn afternoon.

The guard at the entrance to the grounds halted White's small parade and demanded to know what business they were about. As White explained their purpose for being there, Creed had the strange sensation of having been there before. The dreamlike feeling gave him a sense of motion— flight, perhaps—and disjointedness, as if he were actually in another time and place instead of standing at the gate of Abraham Levi's property, confronting a Yankee sentry along with nine upright citizens of Victoria. Creed forcibly blinked his eyes rapidly to make the percipient feeling dissipate, and when it passed he realized that he had actually been in a circumstance similar to this moment. It had occurred when he had first returned to his home, Glengarry Plantation, after the war and found it infested with Yankees. He wondered if Judge White's party would receive the same sort of reception that he had: extremely rude and life threatening.

Captain Spaulding came riding up the street from the business district and reined in his mount at the hitching post in front of the house. "What's going on here, Judge?" he asked. "What are all these men doing here?"

"Captain Spaulding, I'm glad to see you," said White. "My friends and I wish to see Colonel Rose immediately."

"For what reason, Judge?" asked Spaulding.

"It regards Colonel Ben Hill," said White.

"There's nothing you can do about him now," said Spaulding. "I've got him locked up in the jail, and that's where he's going to stay."

"That's perfectly understood, Captain," said White. "We have no quarrel with you on that point."

"Then what is the point of your visit here, Judge?"

"We wish to discuss the security arrangements at the jail," said White. "These men have volunteered to guard the jail against any possible . . . shall we say, intruders?"

Spaulding scanned the faces before him, then dismounted and stepped to the fore. "Maybe you should see the colonel," he said. "Follow me, gentlemen."

Inside the house, Spaulding had the Texans wait in the foyer while he arranged for them to see Colonel Rose. Once he had done this he led them into the library, where General Stanley had set up his office, which Colonel Rose now occupied. The ten Texans entered the room and gathered in a half circle around the table Rose used for his desk. A bottle of brandy and an almost empty snifter sat on a silver tray at one end of the table, and a Colt's army pistol in a black leather holster and belt rested peacefully on the other. Colonel Rose sat behind the desk, leaning sideways, resting an elbow on a wing of a straight-back walnut armchair. His tunic was open at the top, revealing a collarless shirt that was so soiled with sweat and dust it could never be washed to its original whiteness again. Rose's brown eyes were glassy and bloodshot, indicating he had been imbibing that day and probably for several days before that, and his brown hair, mustache, and beard were totally unkempt, in need of trimming, brushing, and a fresh dab of brilliantine.

"What's all this Captain Spaulding has been telling me, Judge?" asked Rose, slurring his words slightly, his tone angry and disrespectful. "You think my men can't guard your precious Colonel Hill well enough, is that it?"

"Not exactly, Colonel," said White.

"Then what exactly?" demanded Rose. "Speak up, man. I haven't got all day." He picked up the brandy bottle and poured two fingers worth in the glass.

"Colonel, there's been talk that your Negro soldiers are planning something with the Freedmen from the river bottoms," said White, "and we think you should turn Colonel Hill over to us, send all your Negro soldiers across the river, and bring your Pennsylvania regiment over here to protect our town from those Shantytown darkies."

Rose glared at White and said, "In the first place, my *negro* soldiers are no threat to you people unless you get out of line with them or you disobey the law like your precious Colonel Hill did today. Secondly, the Freedmen of this locality are under strict orders from this command to obey the law the same as you Confederates. As for your Colonel Hill, he'll remain right where he is along with those other men who were arrested with him this afternoon."

"You can't do that," said White.

"On the contrary, Judge," said Rose. "I can do it, and I will."

"I protest, Colonel," said McClanahan. "Those men were given a fair hearing in a court of law and—"

"To hell with *your* court of law!" snapped Rose, jumping to his feet and leaning both hands on the desk. "It wasn't *our* court of law. It was your goddamned Confederate court of law, and that doesn't count around here anymore, gentlemen. Or aren't you yet aware of the fact that you bastards lost the war?"

"We're quite aware of that fact, Colonel," said White angrily. "You are our constant reminder of that fact."

"Good! Then get the hell out of here and stop bothering me with your petty problems." Rose plopped back into his chair. "I've got enough to do as it is without having to listen to you gripe all the time."

"Colonel," said McClanahan, "I am a licensed attorney, and the legal representative of those men. I demand that you release them at once. They have been tried in a *legal* court by a *judge* who was appointed by *your* Yankee governor. How much more *legal* do we have to be?"

Rose was suddenly struck with a momentary sense of sobriety, and clear thinking directed his tongue. "All right, I'll grant you that much. You were appointed by the governor of this state, and I guess that does make you legal, Judge. You fined them, right?"

"That is correct, sir," said White.

"And has their fine been paid?" asked Rose.

"Not yet, Colonel," said Creed, leaning forward, "but I've got the money right here." He produced the five silver dollars from his pocket and held them out for Rose to see.

"Who the hell are you?" asked Rose, trying to look Creed in the eye but missing the mark as the momentary lucidity passed.

"My name is Slate Creed, sir. From Lavaca County."

"Lavaca County? What the hell are you doing here?"

"Just passing through."

"Just passing through, you say?"

"Yes, sir."

Rose strained to focus on Creed's eyes, even tilting his head forward to get a better look. "So what are these men to you?" asked Rose, indicating the Victorians with a waggle of his head.

"These men here are just acquaintances, Colonel," said Creed, indicating the others in the room with a slight wave of his hand. Then, figuring he might as well tell Rose everything now, he said, "The men you have in your jail are my friends and traveling companions. We were on our way home when some bushwhackers jumped us south of here and wounded one of my friends. We came into town to find a doctor and met up with Dr. January here. My friend was hurt bad, and Dr. January put him in his hospital. We decided to stay around until he was well enough to travel again. We just happened to be in the same saloon as Colonel Hill when the shooting took place. Your captain arrested my men by mistake."

"There was no mistake, Colonel," said Spaulding. "Those men were carrying concealed weapons, and that's why we arrested them."

"I thought you said they were part of a mob that killed that Negro fellow?" queried Rose. "What was his name again?"

Spaulding cleared his throat, then said, "Blair, sir. Caesar Blair."

"And this man's friends were part of the mob that killed him, right?"

"That's what we thought originally, sir," said Spaulding, eyeing the judge, "but we were mistaken on that point. Only Colonel Hill fired any shots."

"But they were with him, weren't they?"

"Yes, sir."

"Then they were part of it," said Rose. "Keep them locked up until they can be tried for taking part in killing that man."

"Colonel, those men have already been tried and convicted in my court," said White.

"Convicted of what?" asked Rose. "Murder? Then hang them."

"No, not murder," said McClanahan. "For carrying concealed weapons, and for that they were properly sentenced to pay a one-dollar fine each or spend three days in jail."

"Well, I'm changing their sentence," said Rose.

"You can't do that," said White.

"I can do any damn thing I please with you Rebs," said Rose. He drew his Colt's from its holster and wagged it at White. "I can even shoot you in the balls, and there won't be a thing you or any of your goddamned Reb friends can do about it, Judge." He cocked the hammer and aimed at the judge's groin, his hand surprisingly steady.

Everyone shrank away from White except Creed, who moved to stop Rose, and Spaulding, who moved to stop Creed.

BANG! The explosion was deafening in spite of the fact that the library was quite capacious. The ball and a tongue of flame spewed from the barrel toward White's crotch. The ball lodged harmlessly in the wall behind White, not having touched any flesh but having pierced his trousers just inches below his testicles. The flash of gunpowder set the cloth on fire, and the sexagenarian judge danced backward, trying to squelch the glowing embers in his pants leg and hoping to make himself a lesser target as Rose took aim again.

Creed and Spaulding struggled for a few seconds, then Creed's right fist slipped out of Spaulding's grasp and smashed the Yankee between his left temple and ear, knocking him senseless and crumpling him to the floor temporarily.

BANG! Rose fired again, putting a second hole in White's trousers, this one near his left hip, setting the cloth to smoldering there as well. White danced all the more as he tried to smother the second fire.

"Damn you! Stand still!" swore Rose as he took aim for the third shot.

BANG! Same gun. Same shooter. Same result.

Creed grabbed Rose's arm with his left hand and jerked it upward so that the Colt's was aimed at the ceiling. With his right, he punched Rose in the right side of his face, breaking the man's cheek and knocking him unconscious but not before Rose squeezed off one more round, which shattered the plaster overhead, bringing a shower of white dust down on everyone.

As the colonel slumped in his chair, Spaulding recovered enough to grab Creed around the legs and spill him on the floor. By this time, the guards from outside were pouring into the library, their Springfields ready for action. They forced every man against the wall at gunpoint, and two of them joined Spaulding in subduing Creed.

Realizing that further combat was futile, Creed released his hold on Spaulding and relaxed, raising his hands in surrender although he was flat on his back.

Spaulding scrambled to his knees beside Creed, aimed a punch toward Creed's jaw, but only nicked his chin. He backed up and tried again, but the second attempt never got there. Creed caught Spaulding's fist with his left hand and twisted it aside. With his right, he grabbed Spaulding by his blouse and jerked him downward until their faces were only inches apart. No words passed between them, but the animal ferocity in Creed's eyes issued a warning that Spaulding's primeval instincts clearly understood. The captain tried to pull away from Creed, not to resume the fight but to escape; and when Creed realized this, he released the Yank.

"Sergeant Hirsch!" snapped Spaulding as soon as he was on his feet. "Arrest these men and put them all in jail!"

Hirsch scanned the room. His view fell on White, and the judge's fiery look caused him to swallow hard. With disbelief in his eyes, the soldier shifted his gaze to Spaulding and said, "The judge, too, sir?"

Spaulding stopped straightening his uniform, enraged that his order was being questioned, and shouted, "All of them, dammit!"

12

Somewhere it was written that a wise man minds his own business and keeps his nose clear of everybody else's affairs. That's all Creed was trying to do that day—mind his own business. But somehow he'd been drawn into a peck of trouble that landed him in jail.

Captain Spaulding arrested Creed, Judge White, Dr. January, Lawyer McClanahan, Andy Cunningham, and the other five men who had gone to see Colonel Rose about the situation concerning Colonel Ben Hill's safety. The captain locked the ten protesters in the cell next to the one occupied by Colonel Ben Hill and Creed's five friends.

"As God is my witness," said White upon being incarcerated, his voice in full rage, "I will not stand for this for one minute more, Captain Spaulding! I am the chief justice of this county, and I demand that you release me and these other men this very instant!"

"You can demand all you want, Judge," said Spaulding smugly as he stood in the corridor outside the cells with his hands planted firmly on his hips, "but no one is going anywhere until Colonel Rose orders it."

"You are breaking the law, Captain!" roared White.

"No, sir, I am not!" retorted Spaulding angrily. "I am enforcing the law, Judge. I am obeying Colonel Rose's orders, sir, and as far as you should be concerned, Colonel Rose is the law in this county for as long as he is in command of the occupying forces posted here." He paused as if to allow White a chance to rebut his argument, but when that didn't happen, he added, "Now I will tolerate no further outbursts from you or any of you other Confederate troublemakers." Feeling a bit bolder, he glared at Creed and added one more item. "And that goes especially for you, mister."

Creed turned his Choctaw face to Spaulding, confusing the captain with his passive, stoic aspect. No way would he allow this Yankee to see into his head or his heart.

Mentally disarmed, Spaulding could think of nothing else to say and exited the cell block. The guards followed him, leaving the Texans alone to ponder their plight.

"This is an outrage!" said White.

"What happened, Sam?" asked Colonel Hill from his adjoining cell. "What are all of you doing here?" He saw the bullet holes in White's trousers, noting how they were severely singed around the edges. "What happened there, Sam?"

"I am near to being apoplectic, gentlemen," said White as he sat down on the bottom bunk. He wiped the sweat from his face on his coat sleeve and more calmly said, "I can't believe this is happening, my friends. Here. In Texas."

"You better believe it's happening here in Texas," said Creed, who was standing near the cell door. "It's happening now, and it's going to continue to happen here for some time to come. It will keep happening as long as we resist the Yankees and their law, gentlemen."

"Are you saying we should give in to them, Mr. Creed?" asked January. "Bow down to them as if they were our new masters from the North? Subject ourselves to them and their nigger vassals? Is that what you are saying, sir?"

"No, sir, not exactly," said Creed.

"Then what are you saying?" demanded Hill. "We've already given up our fight to determine our own sovereignty. Do we have to give up our rights as men, too? The Yankees have robbed us of our chattel by setting the niggers free and have thus bankrupted us to the point that we may never recover financially. Does this mean we have to allow the niggers to be our equals, too?"

"Why not?" said Creed. "They're human, aren't they? You have to admit that much, Colonel Hill."

"Gentlemen, gentlemen," said White. "This is not the time to start a debating society. We are in jail, gentlemen, or haven't you noticed that fact recently?"

"I am all too cognizant of that fact, Sam," said Hill. "And for what? For killing an uppity nigger?"

"It's your fault we're all in here, Colonel," said Flewellyn from the corner of their cell. He stepped forward and said, "If you hadn't shot that buck, we'd all be fixing to have supper about now."

"You had best remember your place, sir," said Hill.

"Maybe you'd best remember yours, Colonel," said Creed angrily. "We're not in the army anymore. We're all civilians now, and every man here has a right to speak his mind. None of us has to agree with him, but he does have a right to speak."

Hill glanced around at the other men, then said, "I will grant you that much, sir."

"Gentlemen, we are getting off the track again here," said White. "We are incarcerated here, and we must do something to gain our freedom from this place."

"Your Honor," said McClanahan, a sly smile curling his lips as he addressed White in the formal manner of the courtroom, "I have a thought. Why don't you order Captain Spaulding to deliver prisoner Sam White to the courtroom of Justice Samuel A. White and force him to show just cause for holding prisoner White in jail?"

White smiled and said, "I like the notion of that, John. Yes, I believe I'll do just that." He rose and walked over to the cell door. "John, do you still have that writ of habeas corpus you wrote up for Mr. Creed's friends?"

"Yes, I do," said McClanahan, producing the document from an inside coat pocket.

"Good! Scratch off their names and put ours on it." He watched McClanahan make the changes, then called out, "Guard! I wish to speak with Captain Spaulding this instant! Do you hear me out there? I wish to speak to Captain Spaulding this instant. Send him in here immediately."

The cell-block door opened, but instead of a guard or Spaulding stepping through it, Colonel Rose staggered forth, followed by Spaulding, the sergeant-of-the-guard, and four soldiers carrying Springfields with bayonets locked in place. Rose's cheek was swollen and already very discolored where Creed had struck him.

"Colonel Rose," said White who was quite surprised to see the commander. He regained his composure and said, "Precisely the man I wish to see."

"Shut up, Judge," said Rose. "I don't care one iota about anything you have to say."

"Colonel, I demand that you execute this writ of habeas corpus at once," said White. He took the paper from McClanahan and held it out for Rose to see.

"What the hell is this?" queried Rose as he took the writ from White. He glanced at it, then threw it on the floor. "You can take your goddamned writ, Judge, and go straight to hell with it. You and your friends . . ." He scanned the faces before him until he saw Creed, to whom he pointed. " . . . all except that son of a bitch who hit me—all of you are being moved to another jail."

"Another jail?" queried White. "We don't have another jail in Victoria. Where are you taking us?"

"Just you never mind, Judge," said Rose. "You're going. You and all your friends except that murdering son of a bitch Hill and the son of a bitch who hit me. What was your name again?"

Creed stepped forward boldly and said, "Slate Creed, Colonel Rose, from Lavaca County."

"Yes, you, you son of a bitch! You're staying here with Hill to pay the same price as he'll pay. Captain, get them moving now. It's getting dark already." Rose staggered out of the cell block, leaving Spaulding and the guards to carry out his orders.

The Texans looked around at each other, unsure of what Rose was talking about; but every one of them knew it was not good, whatever it was.

"All right, you men," said Spaulding as he approached Colonel Hill's cell first, "stand back away from the door. Sergeant, unlock the door." The sergeant did as ordered. "All right, everyone except the colonel come out of there. You just make yourself at home, Colonel. You aren't going anywhere yet."

Before the men from Lavaca County would step out of the cell, Flewellyn and the Reeves brothers looked at Creed with a question in their eyes. He recognized it, then answered them with a slight shake of his head that only they noted. No, they were not to jump the guards and Captain Spaulding and make a break for it. They should wait, wait until force was the only option left to them. For now, they should go along with the Yankees. He would remain in jail with Colonel Hill to meet whatever fate should come their way, whether it came that night or not.

The Lavaca men moved out peaceably, as did the Victorians when they were taken from their cell. But before he would allow himself to be pushed through the doorway to the office, January offered one final word of encouragement to Hill and Creed.

"Don't worry, boys," he said. "We'll get you out of this. Be patient. We aren't the only loyal men in this town." And with that, he was gone with the others.

Spaulding and the sergeant were all that remained behind. The captain drew his pistol and casually pointed it in Creed's direction. "All right, Sergeant," he said, "put Creed in the same cell as Hill. Creed, I wish you'd make a move to escape about now."

"And give you an excuse to shoot me?" said Creed, raising his hands high over his head. "Not me, Captain. I like it here." He winked at Spaulding. "Nice and quiet in here, and I could use a night in a bed instead of sleeping on the ground."

The sergeant unlocked the cell door, and Creed came out and walked over to Hill's cell.

"Stand back, Colonel," said Spaulding. "I wouldn't want to shoot you for escaping. Colonel Rose wouldn't like that. He's looking forward to seeing you hang."

Hill backed away, and the sergeant unlocked his door. Creed went inside, and the sergeant locked up behind him.

"Don't bother getting better acquainted now, gentlemen," said Spaulding with a wicked grin. "Something tells me you'll have all of eternity to do that." He laughed at his own sadistic joke, then followed the sergeant out of the cell block.

Hill and Creed looked at each other but said nothing. They knew what Spaulding was insinuating, but neither of them wanted to think about it. Not yet. Not while there was still hope for help from outside.

13

News of the arrest of Judge White and the contingent of men who had called on Colonel Rose that afternoon spread through Victoria faster than a hurricane come inland. Whites, Negroes, Mexicans—everybody was talking about it, but only a few were doing anything about it—at the moment.

As the sun settled on the horizon and the moon rose over Victoria, Catherine Ramsdale was calmly setting the supper table in her uncle's house. She had heard about Colonel Hill shooting a Negro in a saloon and how he had been arrested with Creed's friends, but she was yet unaware of the current plight of her uncle and the others.

Much to her chagrin, she was only setting two places, one for herself and one for her uncle. She looked wistfully at the chair across from her seat and wished she was setting a third place—for Creed. But, alas, she thought, she hadn't had the opportunity to invite him to supper that evening, when she saw him briefly during his first visit to Bill Simons that morning.

As Catherine was putting down the last fork, Lavinia, the cook and housekeeper, burst into the dining room from the kitchen. Lavinia had been a slave in the January household during the days of slavery, but unlike many other domestic slaves, who left their masters as soon as freedom came, she had stayed on, because she had no family except Dr. January and Miss Catherine.

Catherine looked up and saw the agitation in Lavinia's face. She thought to ask her why she was so upset but didn't get the chance to speak the words.

"Miss Catherine! Miss Catherine!" said Lavinia, quite excitedly. "Them Yankees done locked up Dr. January and a whole bunch of other men, including Judge White and Mr. McClanahan, the lawyer! They's got them in the county jail house right now!"

"What are you going on about, Lavinia?" queried Catherine.

"Dr. January, Miss Catherine. The Yankees has got him locked up in the county jail."

Catherine gasped, then her hand instinctively covered her mouth as if to hide her shock. "This is terrible news, Lavinia," she said, lowering her hand. "Are you sure about it?"

"That ain't all of it, Miss Catherine. Cleo say the judge's done been shot by that Yankee colonel."

"Judge White shot? Is he hurt badly?"

"Don't know, Miss Catherine. Cleo didn't say outright, but she did say something about the judge's private parts being—"

"Lavinia!" gasped Catherine, interrupting the former house slave who was now a paid servant. "Ladies do not discuss such things or even mention them!"

"Yes'm, I knows," said Lavinia, "but I's only repeating what Cleo done said. She say the judge's gonna have to sit down when he go to the outhouse now and he ain't gonna have no trouble hitting the high notes at prayer meeting no more. Yes'm, that's what she said."

"Lavinia, I won't have that kind of talk in this house."

"Yes'm, I know, but that's what she said."

"Never mind what Cleo said," said Catherine. "You know you can't believe half of anything she says. What makes you think she's telling the whole story this time?"

"Ain't sure that she is," said Lavinia. "I's hoping you'd go over to the courthouse and find out yourself though."

"This is all politics, Lavinia. That's men's business, and ladies do not involve themselves in politics."

"Cleo also say that nice young Mr. Creed was arrested and that Colonel Rose is gonna hang him with Colonel Hill because Mr. Creed done struck Colonel Rose up side the head and he punched Captain Spaulding in the jaw."

Catherine gasped at this last bit of the tale. Her uncle, Judge White, and the other men of Victoria landing in jail was merely bad news, but Creed's arrest was catastrophic.

"Are you sure Cleo said Mr. Creed was arrested with Uncle and the others?" asked Catherine once she collected herself.

"Yes'm, that's what she said. He's in the jail house, too. Waiting for the hangman the same as Colonel Hill."

"I can't believe this, Lavinia. I'll have to go find out the truth for myself."

"Yes'm, you do that. You go next door and ask Cleo yourself, and I'll stay here and keep your supper warm."

"I have no intention of asking Cleo anything," said Catherine. "I'm going to the jail house to see for myself."

Shocked, Lavinia said, "Miss Catherine, you can't do that."

"I must do what I must do," said Catherine. "I'll be all right, Lavinia. You just stay here and keep supper warm. I'll be back before you know it."

"But it ain't safe for a lady to be out by herself in the night," said Lavinia weakly. Then, as Catherine disappeared into the other room, she said under her breath, "Especially a white lady."

Catherine went to the closet beneath the staircase. The sun was down now, and the evening air outside was quite damp and chilly. She tied on a warm bonnet that covered her ears, then threw a cape over her shoulders, tying it snugly at the neck. She put on long gloves to keep the chill off her fingers. Satisfied that she would be protected from the elements, she thought to do something about the other hazards she might face that night.

Hanging on a hook in the corner of the closet was the pistol and holster her uncle had bought when he fought in the Mexican War. When she was a teenager January had taught her how to handle the Colt's Walker .44 with proper respect. She took it down, verified that it was loaded, then strapped the holster tightly around her waist where it would be out of sight beneath her cape.

Now feeling quite safe against any danger, Catherine marched out of the house to be about men's business.

14

The fall of twilight seemed to be a signal for the Freedmen of Shantytown to wander into town. Most of them had been slaves on the ranches and plantations of Victoria County before the coming of the Yankees, but some of them had moved to the area from Louisiana and other parts of the Confederacy on the rumor, begun and embellished by whites from both the North and the South, that the Federal government would give every male Negro forty acres and a mule and tools to work the land, and that most of this free land was in Texas. The truth was they were supposed to make contracts with their former masters or other owners of the land to work the fields and share in the crops that were produced. These sharecropping contracts were supposed to be introduced, written, witnessed, and enforced by the Freedman's Bureau, whose overall duty it was to supervise the peaceful assimilation of Negroes into the mainstream of American society. Because the South was too vast and Negroes so numerous, establishing a civilian agency was impractical. Therefore, President Johnson chose to use the army to fill the void.

Each county in the occupied South was assigned a military unit. Its commander was in charge of the local Freedman's Bureau, and his troops were his police. In theory, it was a practical system, but in December 1865 it was too soon to see if it was workable in every area. One thing for certain was it hadn't worked in Victoria County yet, and the fault for that lay directly at the feet of Colonel Isaac Rose.

By the time the Yankees arrived in Victoria County, the

cotton had long since been planted for the year, but it still wasn't too late to establish the new system of sharecropping. The Negroes were supposed to be kept on the plantations by the army, and their new "partners" were supposed to be kept from cheating the Negroes by the army. The first was meant to go with the second, but in Victoria County the first never happened because Colonel Rose actually encouraged the Negroes to leave the plantations and the ranches and come into Victoria. What they did in town was their business as long as they didn't bother him or his troops. Until Caesar Blair walked into the Smile Saloon, the Negroes had pretty much kept to themselves, and the whites in Victoria had tolerated their presence peacefully. Blair's murder shattered that status quo, and no one knew exactly what would happen now, especially Miss Catherine Ramsdale, the niece of the outspoken Dr. January, as she marched from her uncle's house to the county jail several blocks away.

Catherine met no one on the street until she came to Main. To her surprise, that thoroughfare was also fairly empty of people. Conspicuously absent were the soldiers. The few men that she did see were young Negroes in ragged civilian attire. She ignored them as she hurried toward the plaza, but they didn't ignore her.

Sitting on the boardwalk in front of Abraham Levi's store were a knot of Freedmen from the area, along with Cassius Pembroke and Pompey Gilmore. Pembroke and Gilmore had left a plantation in Alabama and walked to Texas to get some of that free land they had heard about, but they had been bitterly disappointed. Both of them had been cruelly treated while they were slaves, and the cruelty had continued since being set free. Now they figured the government, meaning the white folks, had lied to them with the intent of luring them west so they could starve to death or could be killed by Indians. Whichever, Pembroke and Gilmore figured the whites aimed to get rid of them. They no longer trusted whites. Their distrust had turned to bitterness, and their bitterness had become hatred. This, combined with empty stomachs, meant they were apt to do anything.

"Who's that white lady strutting down the street there?" asked Pembroke.

"Can't be no lady," said Gilmore. "A lady wouldn't be out here at this time of night all alone by herself."

"Then if she ain't no lady," said Pembroke, "she must be one of them whores the white soldiers is always talking about."

"I ain't never seen a white whore before," said Gilmore. "Not close up, anyways. Saw one in New Orleans though. Remember that, Cassius?"

"Yeah, I do," said Pembroke. "Wanted me one of them white whores then but didn't have no money. And I wants me one again."

"But you still ain't got no money," said Gilmore.

"This is Texas. Maybe I don't need none here. Come on, let's go find out."

The two of them stood up, but the locals remained seated. They looked down at the others, and Pembroke said, "Y'all coming or not?"

"I thinks not," said Hector Venable, a former slave of a Victoria County planter. The others said nothing, looked away.

"And why not?" demanded Pembroke.

"This is Texas, man," said Venable. "You go to messing with white women down here, and y'all gonna wind up like Caesar Blair did this afternoon."

"That's cowshit, and y'all know it," said Gilmore. "Your ass is yellow, that's all."

"Maybe so, but I ain't gonna go near no white woman," said Venable. "Not tonight. Not ever."

"Come on, Pompey," said Pembroke. "Let's go on and leave these yellow niggers to play with themselves."

Pembroke and Gilmore ran across the street and disappeared in the shadows of the trees in the plaza.

Catherine was well past the center of the square on the northeast-to-southwest walk when Pembroke and Gilmore suddenly stepped into her path, startling and stopping her.

"Evening, missy," said Pembroke, the bolder of the two. "Y'all going somewheres in a hurry?"

"Out of my way, boy!" said Catherine angrily.

"Now lookey here, missy," said Pembroke. "Y'all shouldn't be talking to us like field hands no more. We's free now, and y'all gots to talk to us like we's citizens. Ain't that right, Pompey?"

Catherine had been walking with her arms folded in front of her as a way to keep off the chill. She let her right hand slide down to the Colt's grip.

"That sure is," said Gilmore. "We's as good as white now. The law say so."

"I said to get out of my way," said Catherine as she fondled the pistol beneath her cape.

"Now lookey here," said Pembroke. "We knows y'all is one of them white whores and we aims to get us a taste—"

Catherine didn't wait for him to finish. Her left hand joined the right in drawing the revolver, cocking the hammer, and raising the gun straight out in front of her, taking aim at Pembroke's nose.

"If you don't get out of my way this very instant," she said in a low snarl, "I will shoot you dead." She waved the pistol at Gilmore for good measure. "Both of you."

From birth, Pembroke and Gilmore had been taught that guns were absolutely forbidden to them and that when they saw one in the hands of a white person it usually meant that there was killing about to commence and the prey was usually some runaway slave. Their mammies had told them how bugaboos carried guns and shot bad little colored boys. With this fear of guns so ingrained in them, both men backed away without further ado.

Moving cautiously at first, Catherine stepped past Pembroke and Gilmore. As soon as she felt she was safe again, she replaced the Colt's in its holster, and her step became more lively as she continued on to the jail house.

Colonel Rose was riding away just as Catherine walked up. January, Judge White, and the other prisoners who were being removed from the jail to be held elsewhere were being loaded into wagons. Catherine recognized her uncle in the dim, flickering torchlight.

"Uncle!" she shouted.

January turned toward her, knowing her voice but totally surprised to hear it now. "Catherine?" he queried.

She ran up to the wagon. "Uncle, what's going on here?"

"Catherine, what are you doing here?" said January, ignoring her question. "Don't you know the danger you're in?"

"Hey, what's going on here?" demanded a guard. "What are you doing here, ma'am?"

"I am Dr. January's niece," said Catherine proudly, "and I am conversing with him."

"Catherine, you should go home immediately," said January.

"Yes, Miss Catherine, you should," said Judge White.

"You'd better stand back away from the wagon, ma'am," said the guard.

"I will not go home until I find out why you have been arrested," said Catherine adamantly, ignoring the guard.

"Captain Spaulding!" shouted the guard. "Someone get Captain Spaulding. We got trouble brewing here."

"Catherine, go home!" snapped January a bit angrily.

"Judge White, are you all right?" asked Catherine. "I was told that you were severely injured by that Yankee colonel."

The judge turned sheepish and said, "Only my pride and my trousers were hurt, Miss Catherine."

"Was anyone else shot?" she asked.

"No," said January, "now go home!"

"What's going on out here, soldier?" asked Spaulding as he came out of the jail house.

"It's this lady, Captain," said the guard.

Spaulding walked up to Catherine, smiled, tipped his hat politely, and said, "Good evening, ma'am. Is there something I can do for you?"

"Who are you?" demanded Catherine.

"I beg your pardon, ma'am. I am Captain Linus Spaulding of the 18th New York Cavalry. At your service, ma'am."

"Well, at least you're a polite Yankee," said Catherine. "I am Miss Catherine Ramsdale, Captain Spaulding, and Dr. January is my uncle. I demand to know what is going on here."

"Well, Miss Ramsdale, your uncle and these other men are under arrest for assaulting an officer of the Union army."

"I see," said Catherine, looking over the men in the wagon and not seeing Creed. "All of these men assaulted one Yankee officer, Captain?"

"Well, not exactly, Miss Ramsdale—"

"Of course not exactly," interjected January.

"Uncle, I am conversing with Captain Spaulding. Would you kind'y refrain from interrupting?" She turned back to Spaulding and said, "You were saying, Captain?"

"I was saying, Miss Ramsdale, that not all of them struck Colonel Rose and myself, but they were all together in Colonel Rose's office when it happened and none of them did anything to aid either the colonel or myself. Therefore, they are accomplices to the man who did strike us."

"And which one of them did it, Captain?"

"He isn't with this bunch, Miss Ramsdale. His name is Creed, and we're keeping him here in the jail along with Colonel Hill."

Catherine didn't like the sound of that, but she didn't want Spaulding to know it. "I see," she said. "So where are you taking my uncle and these other men now?"

"They're going across the river to the encampment of the 77th Pennsylvania Infantry so we can better protect them."

"Protect them, Captain? From what, pray tell?"

Spaulding stammered, "Did I say protect, Miss Ramsdale?"

"You most certainly did."

"Well, I meant guard them better over there, ma'am," sputtered Spaulding. "The jail here is too small for this many men. There is more room for them with the 77th."

"I see," said Catherine, "but why aren't you taking Colonel Hill and Mr. Creed, too? Won't it be easier to guard all of them together instead of divided into two groups?"

"The Michigan regiment will be guarding the jail, Miss Ramsdale," said Spaulding, evading the question. "They will protect Creed and Colonel Hill well enough. Now if you'll forgive me, Miss Ramsdale, we must be on our way." He tipped his hat and added, "Good evening, ma'am."

"One more thing, Captain, please. May I speak with Uncle for just a moment before you take him away?"

"Well—"

"In private, of course," said Catherine.

Spaulding frowned and said, "All right, but only for a minute, then we must really be going, Miss Ramsdale." He left them, to attend other business.

"Catherine, you must go home now," said January.

"I will, Uncle, but first tell me what I can do to help."

"You can help by going home and staying clear of these Yankees," said January.

"Wait, January," said Judge White. "There is something more that Miss Catherine can do for us."

"It isn't us that I'm concerned about," said January. "It's Ben and Creed that I'm worried about. Those nigger soldiers are sure to do them evil tonight if they aren't stopped."

"Yes, I know," said the judge. "That's why I want Miss Catherine to find Sherman Goodwin and get his help."

"Not that Yankee-lover!" snapped January. "I'd just as soon hang than ask him for a single ounce of aid."

"Yankee-lover or not," said White. "Sherman Goodwin is a Texan, the same as you and me."

"Maybe the same as you, Sam," said January, "but not me."

"We need Goodwin to help Ben and Creed," said White. "They're the ones in the gravest danger."

"What do you want me to do, Judge White?" asked Catherine.

"Catherine, I forbid you to involve yourself in this affair," said January.

"Oh, hush up, Uncle!"

January was too astounded by her words and her tone to reply. He simply sat back and observed and listened.

"Go find Dr. Goodwin, Miss Catherine," said White, "and tell him he must stop Colonel Rose, that we must be allowed to return to the jail—armed, if necessary—to protect Colonel Hill and Mr. Creed."

"Yes, sir, I'll do it."

"Catherine, be careful," said January, finding his tongue and his common sense again.

"Don't worry about me, Uncle," said Catherine. She parted her cape enough for him to see the revolver and said, "I've got your Colt's to keep me company."

15

As a youth, Creed had been taught by his grandfather, Dougald Slater, to question authority, not obey it blindly, to seek the reasons behind any commands that weren't clear to him. Of course, this led to many angry, unsettling arguments with his grandfather, but only in the earliest years of Creed's life, when he was inexperienced in the fine art of debate, a major pastime among men of all walks of life. As he grew older, he grew wiser and more practiced in the intricacies of speech, often taking the part of the other side in a discussion, if for no other reason than to give opposition. When he did this, he sometimes found his own mind being changed by his skillful argument.

This had been the case in his feelings about Negroes. He had been raised to accept them for what they were at the time: slaves, servants of whites. He had been told that they were inferior to whites as well, but his firsthand knowledge of them said differently. When some whites argued that Negroes weren't even human, he immediately crushed that theory with one simple fact: whites and Negroes could interbreed, thus they weren't apes as some ignoramuses contended. No one could dispute that point, especially not those men who had bred slave women themselves. Yes, Negroes were human, these same ignoramuses would admit, but were they equal to whites in every way? This was a question Creed couldn't completely answer with facts, although he felt in his heart that the answer was positive, that Negroes were every bit as capable of deep thought and high intelligence as whites. There had been slaves on his grandfather's plantation who had displayed greater intelligence than their taskmasters; he had seen this and knew it to be a fact, but he was unable to convince those bigots who were dead set in their belief that Negroes were inferior to whites and would always be inferior.

Standing on the other side of the cell from Creed was Colonel Ben Hill, a man who saw the Negro as his footstool instead of as a person. Creed looked at Hill and wondered why anyone with his intelligence could not accept Negroes as people. Negroes loved, hated, feared, felt sorrow and happiness, and they could be as bold and as brave as any white. They could be sympathetic and apathetic, but could they be empathetic? This was a good question that applied to white and black, Creed had told himself on more than one occasion, when his mind considered such possibilities while he was on the trail alone. How could blacks and whites be empathetic with each other when neither had the same life experience as the other? This question had remained unanswered in Creed's mind and would probably stay that way for some time to come. For certain, it wouldn't be answered this night in the Victoria County jail. Not by Ben Hill anyway.

"So you struck that nigger-loving Yankee," said Hill, his smile filled with satisfaction. "I wish I could have been there to see that. That son of a bitch needs a good horsewhipping, if you ask me. What caused you to hit him, son?"

"He was shooting at Judge White," said Creed.

"Is that how Sam got those bullet holes in his trousers?"

"You guessed it."

"What was Rose aiming at?"

"His crotch."

Hill laughed and said, "I'll bet that set old Sam to dancing. Jump high, did he?"

"High enough."

"Whoo-ee! I wish I'd been there to see that. Yes, sir, I truly do wish I'd seen that."

Hill fell silent, and so did Creed, who hadn't felt like talking all that much in the first place. His thoughts were centered on their predicament. Maybe the colonel didn't realize it or maybe he chose to ignore it, but the fact was they were in mortal danger as long as they were Colonel Rose's prisoners.

And hadn't the Yankee commander said something about how they were about to pay the same price? What exactly had he meant by that?

As Creed pondered this question, the cell-block door opened and Nap Lytle from the Smile Saloon came in carrying a tray of food. "Supper time, Colonel," he said as he approached the cell. "It ain't much. Just a loaf of bread and some cold beef. Got a couple of hard-boiled eggs here, too. And a pitcher of beer to wash it down with."

The sergeant-of-the-guard stepped into the cell block after Lytle. "Stand back there," he said to the prisoners. "Away from the door." He waved a large metal ring with four keys on it at them to emphasize his order. As soon as they complied, he moved past Lytle and opened the cell door. "Set it down on the floor," he said to Lytle, and the saloonkeeper obliged him. "When you're finished with that, give a holler."

"I sure am sorry to see you in this fix, Colonel," said Lytle. "I wish there was more that I could do to help."

"You've done plenty," said Hill. "Thank you, Nap."

Lytle stared at the bread and said, "I certainly hope so, Colonel. For your sake." Then he glanced at Creed and added, "For both of your sakes."

"Come on, Lytle," said the sergeant. "You ain't allowed to visit with them. Just give them the food was all you were supposed to do."

"Good luck, Colonel," said Lytle.

"Come on, Lytle. Let's go now."

Lytle and the sergeant departed, leaving Hill and Creed to eat in peace. Hill picked up the tray, set it on the bunk, then sat down beside it. Creed remained leaning against the wall.

"Better come and eat," said Hill. "There won't be any more food until morning." He picked up the loaf of bread and started to break it open but stopped in the middle of the action.

"What's this?" he muttered.

Creed was watching Hill. He saw him tear at the bread, then stop. Why? he wondered. Then he knew, when he saw the blade protruding from the end of the loaf.

Hill glanced at the cell-block door, then at the window behind Creed. As soon as he felt certain that no one was watching them, he pulled the knife from the bread and slipped it under the folded blanket at the foot of the bunk.

Creed crossed the cell, sat down at the other end of the bed, and helped himself to the food. "That thing only means trouble, Colonel," he said softly.

"It means we can get out of here if we put our minds to it," retorted Hill, his voice conspiratorial.

"Haven't you ever heard of prisoners being shot while trying to escape?"

"Certainly, I have," said Hill, "but I don't intend on it happening to me."

Creed sighed heavily, then said, "Colonel, you don't know when you're licked, do you?"

"No, sir, I do not. This knife came from friends. They obviously thought it would help us to escape."

"Why do we have to escape from here, Colonel?" asked Creed. "Have you asked yourself that question?"

Hill glared at Creed for a second, then realized what Creed meant. "You don't think we're in danger here, do you?" he asked.

"Yes, I do," said Creed quite exasperated. "You killed a man today, Colonel. A Negro. A Negro in a town full of Negro soldiers who hate us just because we're Texans who fought for the South. Don't you see it, Colonel? We're everything those people hate. We stand for every white plantation owner, every white overseer, every white Southerner who ever laid a lash on the back of a single slave. I don't know what's been happening around here before today, but from what I can tell, this town is a powder keg with a short fuse. And you, sir, just put a torch to that fuse. Just how long do you think it will be before this place explodes in a bloody riot?"

"Nothing will happen," said Hill. "Our fellow Texans won't permit it."

Creed was incredulous. He stood up and peered down at Hill. "Colonel, our fellow Texans are under arrest in another part of town. There is nothing they can do about anything."

"Someone has done something," retorted Hill. "Someone put this knife in this loaf of bread, didn't they?"

"But why, Colonel?"

"To help us escape, I would suspect."

"Or maybe for protection," said Creed. "Maybe something's going on outside that door that we don't know about, but everybody else in town does. Listen. What do you hear out there?"

Hill cocked an ear and listened for a few seconds, then said, "I don't hear a thing."

"That's it exactly, Colonel. Neither do I. I don't hear anything. Not a horse or a wagon on the street. No laughter or music from one of the saloons. Not even a dog barking at a cat somewhere in town. It's too quiet out there, Colonel, and that scares me."

"Pshaw! You're afraid? You weren't afraid when you struck me this afternoon, and you certainly weren't afraid when you struck Colonel Rose. So why should you be afraid now?"

"I could see you when we had our little row, and I could see Colonel Rose, too. I don't fear what I can see, Colonel. It's what I can't see that puts the willies in my spine, and right now I can't see what evil might be lurking beyond that door. If I could, I might know what to expect, and I could deal with it, Colonel. It's not knowing what I'm up against that troubles me in times like this."

"You sound like a man who is afraid of the dark," said Hill.

"It isn't the dark, Colonel. It's what hides in the dark that makes me cautious, and right now I can't help but feel that there's something out there just waiting to pounce on both of us."

"Nonsense! I've already told you that there is nothing to fear. Not while we're in this jail being protected by white soldiers."

"That's it!" said Creed as if he'd just discovered the answer to a mystifying riddle. He rushed over to the cell door. "There's no noise coming from out front, Colonel. We're in this building all by ourselves. Guard!" he yelled. "Guard! Guard!"

No answer. Dead silence. Too dead, for Creed's liking.

16

Dr. Sherman Goodwin came to Victoria in 1850 from Sandusky, Ohio. He brought his family down the next year. Since that time, he had become one of the county's leading citizens and had done so in spite of the fact that he was an Abolitionist and a Yankee sympathizer during the war. Of course, he wasn't alone in his loyalty to the Union. Several other transplanted Northerners had remained opposed to slavery and secession, but few were as outspoken about it as Goodwin had been. It was this opposition to the Confederacy that had made January his enemy.

Goodwin's medical practice had proven quite profitable over the years, and he had invested his money wisely enough to build himself a mansion in the Diamond Hill district of the town. It was to this house that Catherine Ramsdale hurried that fateful December night.

The doctor had just returned home from a long day's work in the country, delivering a stillborn child and saving a young woman's life. He was tired and cranky and totally unaware of the day's events in Victoria. Reluctantly, he received Catherine.

"What is it you want, Miss Ramsdale?" he asked bluntly.

Catherine had seen Dr. Goodwin on many occasions, and always she had viewed him with awe and respect, possibly even a bit of fear, because he had the sort of countenance that made him tend to dominate those around him by his mere presence. His hair and long beard were quite white. When he was about his business of medicine, he always wore a long white coat, and when his work took him away from his home, he wore a white hat and rode a white horse, giving him the confident appearance of the legendary hero, the knight in shining armor. To his patients, he was exactly that, a white knight going about the countryside doing good deeds and saving lives.

"Dr. Goodwin, there's much trouble afoot in Victoria today," said Catherine very calmly.

"There's trouble afoot in Victoria every day, Miss Ramsdale. What makes today any different?"

"Colonel Hill shot and killed a Negro in a saloon early this afternoon," said Catherine, "and he is now locked up in the county jail house."

Goodwin frowned more than his fatigue had been making him frown before this announcement. "May I assume that Colonel Hill was intoxicated when this occurred?"

"I don't know, sir, but I do know that five other men were arrested with him."

"Five others? Was there some sort of riot at the time?"

"No, sir."

"Who were these men?"

"Strangers to Victoria, sir. They are friends of the man Uncle is caring for."

"Oh, yes, the wounded man. I heard about that. Some of those Rebel bushwhackers down on Coleto Creek jumped him and his friends last week, wasn't it?"

"Yes, sir, that is quite correct."

"So what have these men to do with Colonel Hill?"

"Nothing, Dr. Goodwin, but their other friend, Mr. Slate Creed, has since been arrested and thrown in the county jail."

"And what was his crime?" asked Goodwin, who was becoming a little annoyed by the conversation.

"He struck two Yankees," said Catherine, and then, realizing that the term might be offensive to Goodwin, she corrected herself by saying, "I mean, two army officers."

Goodwin squirmed a little in his chair and asked, "Which two did he strike?"

"Colonel Rose and a Captain Spaulding."

Goodwin bolted upright. "Rose and Spaulding? Are you certain of this?"

"Quite certain, Dr. Goodwin."

"What was his cause?"

"From what I understand, Mr. Creed was trying to stop Colonel Rose from killing Judge White, and when Captain Spaulding tried to stop Mr. Creed, Mr. Creed and he fought."

"Rose tried to shoot Sam White?" Goodwin leaped to his feet, now quite excited over her tale. "This is incredible, Miss Ramsdale. Was Sam hurt?"

Catherine blushed as she recalled Lavinia's version of the incident, but she said, "No, sir, he wasn't. Colonel Rose only managed to shoot a few holes in the judge's trousers before Mr. Creed stopped him from shooting any holes in the judge."

"So what else has happened in my absence?"

"Colonel Rose had Mr. Creed and the judge and my uncle and several other men arrested and put in jail as well."

"All Rebels, I suppose."

Catherine took a turn now at being annoyed. "Dr. Goodwin, the war is over, and we're all back in the Union again. Don't you think it's time we stopped thinking of each other as either Unionists or Confederates and started thinking of ourselves as Texans?"

"Are those your words, Miss Ramsdale?" queried Goodwin, eyeing her with a certain respect that he usually reserved for men of his own ilk. "Or are they your uncle's?"

"Does it make a difference, sir?"

Goodwin studied her for a moment, then said, "No, I suppose not." After a short pause, he asked, "All right, what do you want from me?"

"Judge White said to come to you for help," said Catherine. "The soldiers have taken him and Uncle and all the others except Colonel Hill and Mr. Creed across the river to their encampment over there. Uncle thinks they've done this because the Negroes are planning to do some sort of evil to Colonel Hill and Mr. Creed tonight."

"Didn't you say Colonel Hill and this Creed fellow were in the jail house?"

"Yes, sir, I did."

"Then I see nothing to worry about, Miss Ramsdale. Colonel Hill and this Mr. Creed are perfectly safe there."

"That's just the point, Dr. Goodwin. They aren't safe there, because the Negroes are the ones who are supposed to be guarding them."

"So what do you want me to do about it?" asked Goodwin.

"I was thinking that you might go to Colonel Rose and prevail upon him to remove Colonel Hill and Mr. Creed to the other side of the river, with Uncle and the others, until matters have time to settle down."

"I suppose I could do that," said Goodwin. "But in the morning. After I've had a good night's rest. I'm quite exhausted now, Miss Ramsdale."

"But the morning might be too late, Dr. Goodwin," pleaded Catherine. "The Negroes could do them harm tonight."

"Not very likely, Miss Ramsdale. Colonel Rose has been very good about keeping his Negroes in their proper places. I'm certain he'll have them under tight control tonight as well."

"But, Dr. Goodwin—"

Goodwin raised his hand to stop her from making any further argument, then he said, "In the morning, Miss Ramsdale. I promise you. First thing in the morning." He pushed himself erect and added, "I'll see Rose first thing tomorrow and get him to do the right thing then. But tonight I am simply too tired to move another muscle. Unless, of course, one of my patients needs me." He smiled patronizingly at Catherine. "Of course, you'd understand all about that, wouldn't you, Miss Ramsdale?"

"No, sir, I would not," said Catherine after rising. "The lives of Colonel Hill and Mr. Creed are at risk, Dr. Goodwin, and all I understand is that you aren't willing to help them one iota."

"Miss Ramsdale," said Goodwin sternly, as if he were speaking to one of his own children, "I have already said that I would tend to this matter in the morning, and I have nothing more to say to you on the subject tonight. Good evening, Miss Ramsdale."

And with that the interview was over. But not so the night and all the evil that it might hold.

17

Waiting can be maddening, especially when one doesn't know what's coming or when it will come.

It was already dark when Nap Lytle delivered supper to Creed and Colonel Hill, and as the two prisoners discussed their plight, heavy clouds blocked out the moonlight, completely enveloping Victoria in darkness. The only light in the cell block came from a single kerosene lantern suspended from the ceiling of the corridor, and the flame in it was still turned down low for daylight hours.

Creed had called for the guard periodically in the hour that had passed since Lytle's visit, but no one came or even answered him. Either he and Hill were alone in the building or the guards were simply ignoring them. Creed didn't like either possibility. When he wasn't at the cell door calling for the guards, he was at the window listening. For what, he wasn't certain, but he knew instinctively that he should continue to listen.

"Why don't you relax, Mr. Creed?" whined Hill. "You're starting to get on my nerves."

"I'd be more worried about my neck than my nerves, if I was you, Colonel."

"My neck is perfectly safe in here."

"No, it isn't," said Creed. "Do you hear that, Colonel?"

"I don't hear a thing," said Hill.

"Then maybe you'd better come over here and have a listen because they're talking about us."

"What are you talking about?"

"That," said Creed.

Hill listened, and now he heard it.

Voices. Several of them. All men. All Negro. Growing louder with each second. And coming closer to the jail with each second. Angry voices. Drunken voices.

"The niggers!" gasped Hill.

"That's right, Colonel. And they're coming here. For us."

Hill leaped from the bed with the knife in his hand. "I'll carve up the first one that comes through that door," he boasted.

"It isn't the first one that I'm worried about, Colonel," said Creed. "It's the dozen or more that will come after him that scare the hell out of me."

The voices were louder now. They passed the rear of the jail and faded around the corner. Then they were in front of the building and soon inside.

Creed stayed standing beneath the window, his body turned sideways toward the cell door, his hands stuffed in his trouser pockets. He made his face go limp, to appear as if dead, an effect enhanced by half-open eyelids. Some ancient Cherokee instinct told him this was the most passive pose he could strike.

Hill stood tall in the center of the cell, the knife in his hand but with the blade turned upward and hidden behind his forearm. His face was angry and defiant.

The cell-block door burst open, and the men behind the voices spewed forth, filling the corridor. Their faces were barely discernible because of the dim light and because they were all quite dusky in pigmentation. The strong odor of moonshine permeated the air. This wasn't good, thought Creed. They were drunk, and that placed them beyond reason. Damn!

Creed's blood was racing through his veins. He'd faced death before, but always before he had been armed or had had an avenue of escape. In the jail, he had neither, and he felt out of control of his own fate. This, more than anything, frightened him, but he refused to show his fear. He would die, if that must be, but he would die like his ancestors, like Scotsmen, like Cherokee and Choctaw warriors.

"Someone get the keys!" said a leader.

Creed recognized the voice as that of Sergeant Marcus Jones, one of the two soldiers who had been the first ones to come into the Smile Saloon that afternoon, right after Hill had shot and killed Caesar Blair.

"Man, it's dark in here," said another. "Someone turn up the lamp." The voice belonged to Cassius Pembroke.

"There it is," said a third, Pembroke's compadre, Pompey Gilmore. "Hanging from the ceiling."

"The ceiling ain't high enough to hang him from," said Jones as more men crowded around him. "We's gonna have to take him outside and hang him."

"You aren't taking anyone anywhere!" said Hill defiantly.

"You murdering peckerwood!" snapped Jones.

"Here's the keys, Marcus."

"Give 'em here," said Jones, snatching them from the man and making a loud jangling.

Someone turned up the flame on the kerosene lamp.

"Don't you niggers come in here!" growled Hill, brandishing the contraband blade at them.

"Look out, Marcus! He gots a knife!"

"I sees it," said Jones. He stuck the key into the lock and said, "You best put that knife down, Colonel, and come along peaceable like. Make this a whole lot easier on all of us. You peckerwoods gots to learn we's free now, and y'all can't be treating us bad no more."

"Amen, brother!" said Pembroke.

"Tell him, Marcus," said Gilmore.

"I'm not going anywhere with you, nigger," said Hill as he lunged toward the door.

"No, Colonel!" shouted Creed as he tried to stop Hill. He caught the colonel by the shoulder and spun him about.

Hill lashed out at Creed, cutting him across the upper left arm. "Leave me be, nigger-lover!"

Creed reacted to his wound, covering it with his free hand and backing away from Hill.

Jones threw open the cell door and rushed inside. Several others followed. The sergeant grabbed Hill in much the same way that Creed had.

Hill responded in the same manner except that he intended the blade to cut Jones's throat. It would have, too, if another soldier hadn't gotten in the way.

"Ai-ee!" the man screamed.

Jones grabbed Hill by the wrist of the hand that held the knife. Another soldier took hold of the colonel's other arm.

"Unhand me, nigger!" Hill broke free and began swinging both arms wildly, flailing with one and cutting and stabbing with the other.

"Get outta the way, brothers!" yelled the man who had retrieved the keys for Jones.

Creed hadn't recognized the man's voice, but he knew his face. He was Rafe Moon, the soldier who had been with Jones in the saloon that afternoon. Creed also recognized the weapon in Moon's hands. "Don't do it!" he screamed, still holding his bleeding arm. He started forward, but a soldier who had gotten behind Hill intercepted him.

Maybe a bullet between the eyes would have stopped Moon, but the sound of Creed's voice and the words he shouted had no effect on him whatsoever; he was that crazed with hate for Hill. Moon swung the axe at the colonel, and the dull blade found its mark in the side of Hill's neck.

Hill let out a short scream, then collapsed on the floor. The knife fell from his hand as he reached for the gory wound in his neck. His eyes were wide with fright and disbelief. His legs began kicking and jerking involuntarily, spasmodically. Just as suddenly as the thrashing had begun, it stopped. Colonel Ben Hill was dead.

Moon drew back the axe and prepared to deliver another blow.

"No, Rafe!" said Jones as he reached out to stop his friend. "He's dead, fool!"

Moon held back the swing, looked at Jones, then at Creed, and said, "Then it's your turn, peckerwood." He started toward Creed.

Creed made no move to retreat. He stood straight, holding his wounded arm, waiting for the blow to be delivered.

"No, Rafe," said Jones, stepping between Moon and Creed. "Not him."

"But, Marcus, the colonel said we could take both of them."

"No, not this man, Rafe," said Jones.

"But, Marcus—"

"I says no, and I means it." Then, raising his voice, he said, "Y'all hear that?" He glanced around the room at the others to make certain they were paying attention to him. "We's leaving this one. Y'all hear that?"

"How come, Marcus?" asked Pembroke. "He's just another peckerwood, ain't he? So how come we ain't gonna kill him, too?"

"Never mind how come," said Jones. "I says we leaves him be, and that's all there is to it. Come on now. We come to hang this peckerwood, and that's what we's gonna do." He kicked Hill's body. "So let's get to it, y'all. Get the rope, and let's get to it."

"But, Marcus, he's dead already," said Moon.

Looking at Moon, Jones said, "I knows he's dead, but we's gonna hang him anyway. Now give me that axe, boy, before y'all hurts yourself."

Reluctantly, Moon handed over the axe. He glared at Creed and said, "Count yourself lucky, peckerwood."

"Shut up, Rafe!" snapped Jones. "And help get that body out of here."

Moon complied. He and three others carried Hill's lifeless form out of the jail.

"Everybody out!" shouted Jones. "Outside for the hanging."

The men who had forced their way into the cell now filed out of it in an orderly fashion. They went down the corridor and exited through the cell-block door.

Jones hung back, the axe still in his hands. He turned and looked at Creed and saw the question in the Texan's eyes. "You done right by me, Mr Creed," he said. "I can't forget that. Even though y'all is white, I can't forget that." He turned away and followed the others outside.

18

Upon leaving Dr. Goodwin's house, Catherine heard the shouts of men in the distance, coming from the business district. They only served to hasten her feet.

Catherine was quite out of breath when she arrived at the front gate of the Levi mansion. The two sentries posted at the gate eyed her with greatly different looks: one leered quite lasciviously, while the other's face was flooded with concern for her condition.

"Are you all right, ma'am?" he asked.

"Yes, I am fine," she gasped. "I wish to see Colonel Rose. Immediately."

The soldiers made eye contact, then the concerned one said to the other, "You'd better go get the sergeant."

"Why should I go?" complained the man.

"Because I can whup your ass and I said so," said the first angrily. Then remembering that a lady was present, he turned back to Catherine and said with lowered eyes, "I'm sorry, ma'am. I forgot myself there for a moment."

"That's quite all right," said Catherine, accepting the man's apology with sincerity. "My uncle, Dr. January, often employs much fouler language while in the presence of gentler folk."

Still embarrassed, the soldier said, "Yes, ma'am," then turned back to his fellow sentry. "Get going, Caleb!"

Caleb flinched, then nodded and left his post, entering the grounds and running up the walk to the front door. He spoke to the guards stationed there, then entered the house.

Catherine noted that the tumult she had heard on her way to the Levi mansion had subsided, almost as if the mob had been swallowed in toto by some ogreish leviathan. This disturbed her greatly.

In a minute, Caleb came outside again and was followed by the sergeant-of-the-guard. They hurried down the walk to the gate, where the sentry resumed his post.

Tipping his hat politely and smiling, the sergeant said, "I'm Sergeant Hirsch, ma'am. What can I do for you?"

Having collected her thoughts now as well as her breath, Catherine replied, "I wish to see Colonel Rose immediately, Sergeant Hirsch."

"On what business, ma'am?"

"On the matter of the men he has locked up in the jail."

"And who shall I say is calling, ma'am?"

Standing a bit stiffer with her Southern pride, she said, "I am Miss Catherine Ramsdale. Dr. James P. T. January is my uncle."

Hirsch tipped his hat again and said, "One moment, ma'am. I'll be right back." He turned and went back into the house.

As she waited, Catherine's worry over the fate of Creed and Colonel Hill grew. The shouts of men could be heard coming from the area of the jail house. This was an angry mob, she knew, and with each passing second, her anxiety continued to build.

At last, Hirsch returned. He tipped his hat again and said, "I'm sorry, ma'am, the colonel doesn't wish to see anyone at this hour."

"I must see him," said Catherine urgently. "It's a matter of life and death." She started to step past Hirsch, but he blocked her way. She glared defiantly into Hirsch's Germanic blue eyes and said, "Out of my way, Sergeant Hirsch!"

"I'm sorry, Miss Ramsdale, but I can't let you go in. Colonel's orders, ma'am."

"Sergeant, if you don't let me pass, the blood of two men will be on your hands."

Hirsch looked sternly at Catherine. Up to this point, he had been playing the soft-spoken gentleman that his mother had always taught him to be when conversing with a lady. But now Catherine had raised his hackles with the mentioning of blood.

"Miss Ramsdale, I have killed several men," he said in a low, steady voice. "I don't know exactly how many. It's a score I never wished to keep. And I have seen hundreds of my comrades killed while fighting you Rebs. I've seen their innards hanging out of them, and I've seen their faces ground into sausage meat by grapeshot. They were men I knew. Fine men. Friends. Fellow Unionists. Brothers . . . in spirit if not in flesh. They died fighting you Rebs. They were good men who didn't deserve to die. Not when they were so young, with most of their lives ahead of them yet. They were killed by you Rebs, so I killed a lot of you Rebs in return." He held up his hands. "There's already plenty of blood on these hands, ma'am, so I suppose the blood of two more Rebs won't make any difference when my time comes to face my maker."

Catherine could see quite plainly that Hirsch wasn't about to budge. Further argument was useless. This man meant to keep her from seeing Colonel Rose, and that was that. She felt the weight of her uncle's Colt's beneath her cape and thought of using it to force her way into seeing the colonel, but she quickly discarded that idea as being rather foolhardy, as the kind of alternative a man would choose in this situation, but not the sort a woman would elect to follow.

"No, I suppose not," said Catherine. "You Yankees cared little about us before the war, and you care even less now. I should have known better." She held her head high, turned, and started to walk away, only to be stopped by the sight of Captain Spaulding and a squad of mounted soldiers coming up the street. She recognized Spaulding even in the dimness of the evening, and although he had been a mite hostile—and only a mite—at their first meeting earlier, she felt that she might fare better with the captain than she had with Hirsch.

Spaulding halted his mount and with a raised gloved hand ordered the squad to do likewise. Seeing Catherine sent a ripple of excitement through him, starting at his heart and ending in his loins. There was something about this Texas lady—something provocative in her eyes, in the way her lips curved, in the way her chest heaved when she spoke—that stirred him deeply, and he wasn't sure whether he enjoyed the bittersweet sensation or not. He alighted and approached her.

"Miss Ramsdale," he said, tipping his hat and offering her his best smile.

"Captain Spaulding," said Catherine, dipping ever so slightly, as a lady should when greeting a gentleman.

"I thought you had gone home," said Spaulding.

"No, sir, I have not."

"Yes, I can see that," said Spaulding. "What brings you by this house at this hour?"

"I have come to see Colonel Rose," said Catherine, now a bit more businesslike, "but this sergeant refuses to let me in to see him."

Spaulding looked at Hirsch, who said in his defense, "Captain, it's not me. It's Colonel Rose, sir. He's . . . he's not seeing anyone tonight."

Spaulding knew exactly what Hirsch meant: Rose was drunk and was in no condition to see anyone.

"What did you want to see the colonel about, Miss Ramsdale?" asked Spaulding.

"Mr. Creed and Colonel Hill. I believe they are in grave danger, Captain."

"We've already been over this earlier this evening, Miss Ramsdale. I assure you that they are in no danger whatsoever. Both of them are safe and sound in the jail right this very minute."

"I don't believe you, Captain," said Catherine.

Spaulding was affronted but held his temper. Instead of challenging her accusation, he simply smiled and said, "What must I do to convince you that they are fine, Miss Ramsdale?"

"Take me to the jail so that I might see for myself that they are all right," said Catherine.

"That wouldn't be advisable, ma'am," said Spaulding.

"And why not, pray tell?"

"Because there are many men about town this evening, Miss Ramsdale, and I fear that most of them are not in a condition that a lady would find pleasant. If you understand my meaning."

"I understand you perfectly, Captain, and I thank you for your consideration. However, I still wish to know that Mr. Creed and Colonel Hill are safe."

"Miss Ramsdale, if it will please you, I will take this squad of men to the jail," he said, indicating with a wave the men behind him, "and see for myself that they are quite safe, and I will double the guard on them so that they will have a peaceful night."

Catherine surveyed Spaulding's face for any sign of deceit, and when she saw that none was positively discernible, she said, "All right, Captain, if that's the best you can do."

"It is, Miss Ramsdale." Spaulding tipped his hat again and added, "By your leave, ma'am?"

"I shall wait here until you return," said Catherine.

"I won't be long," said Spaulding. He mounted up and gave the order for the squad to follow him.

Catherine watched them ride off into the darkness, and as they did, she noted that the town was again filled with the shouts of men bent on making mayhem. Evidently, the beast she had imagined before to have swallowed the tumultuous mob had found them foul to its taste and spewed them forth to rend the peace of the night once more.

19

Night was upon Victoria. A darker night than any other that the town had ever known. And in the darkness was a terror that the townspeople hadn't experienced since the days of Santa Anna.

The Victoria jail was a two-story affair with a balcony across its front. The builders had wrapped a ribbed banister around the balcony, then covered the whole thing with a wooden shingle roof. Originally, the building was intended to be used as a kind of fort in case of attack by Indians or Mexicans, the paranoia behind the design having been precipitated by the Great Comanche Raid of 1840 and the ill-fated invasion of Texas by Mexican troops in 1842.

When Sergeant Jones and the other lynchmen emerged from the jail, they chose the balcony railing to be Colonel Hill's gallows, doing so only because there was no place higher for them to tie a rope. After swinging a line over the banister, they hung his bloody corpse with triumphant shouts of approval.

Creed watched this horror scene from a window. It sickened him on the one hand but also made him quite aware that this was no ordinary mob of men; they had become a pack of animals with an insatiable lust for blood. And now that they had had a taste they would want more. But whose? He wasn't about to stick around to find out.

Colonel Hill had cut Creed badly, and although he had wrapped a cloth around the injured limb, he knew that he should have a doctor attend to it immediately. The only doctor he knew in town was January, but January was in

Federal custody. That left Catherine as his next alternative.

Cautiously, Creed crept downstairs in the jail house. The lower level was dark, the lynchmen having taken the lanterns outside with them. Creed could see the mob through the window. It was growing larger and louder by the minute. He figured it would not be long at all before they overruled Sergeant Jones and came storming back into the jail for him. At the foot of the stairs, he halted and listened and watched.

As soon as the grisly deed of hanging Hill's body was completed, the lynchmen were joined by several dozen more torch-carrying Freedmen from Shantytown. They seemed bent on avenging 250 years of wrong in a single night.

"Let's hang every Rebel in this town!" shouted Cassius Pembroke above the din of drunken voices.

"That's right!" shouted Pompey Gilmore. "We know who they is! Let's hang 'em all! Tonight!"

"Let's do it!" chorused others.

"Hang 'em, hell!" yelled a soldier. "Let's burn 'em out! Let's burn 'em all!"

"Yeah, let's burn 'em all!" cried Gilmore.

Jones jumped up on the railing around the jail's lower porch, steadying himself by holding on to a post. "Hold on, y'all!" he shouted above the roil of angry words. "Ain't nobody else in this town hurt us! We ain't got the right to hurt none of the other folks in this town."

"Yes, we does, Marcus!" yelled Rafe Moon. "We only killed one murdering peckerwood so far. We gots lots more to kill yet."

"Yeah, that's right!" said Pembroke. "We already done in one of 'em, so let's git the rest!"

"No, sir!" screamed Jones. "We ain't gonna do it!"

"Git your yellow ass down from there, nigger!" shouted Gilmore. "Y'all ain't the man just 'cause y'all got them three stripes on your sleeve!"

"No, I isn't!" retorted Jones. "I's just a nigger who fought to be free and to be treated the same as white folks. That's all I is. I ain't no murdering son of a bitch like this peckerwood we killed tonight." He pointed at Hill's corpse. "The Good Book say an eye for an eye and a tooth for a tooth. This peckerwood done in Caesar Blair, so we done in him. That's all now. An eye for an eye. A killing for a killing. Now no more killing!"

"Marcus is right!" shouted a soldier that Creed didn't recognize. "No more killing white folks lessen they kills one of ours again."

"We start killing white folks 'round here," said Jones, "and pretty soon our own white soldiers is gonna have to start killing us. Look at yourselves, brothers. We's still just niggers to them white boys. Blue uniforms or not, they is gonna remember they is white first and soldiers second, and when they do, they is gonna start shooting our black asses straight to hell."

As quiet enveloped the crowd, Creed felt a deep admiration for Jones. This man was a leader who could see beyond the horizon, who could stir other men to action—or in this case, inaction. Certainly, he had led the lynching, but as Creed saw it, Jones probably had no other choice. If he hadn't led the mob, someone else—someone less responsible, less dynamic—would have led them and most likely shared their thirst for blood. Better that Jones had been at the front. Of course, Colonel Hill had been murdered, but Hill had committed a murder himself. As Jones had put it, an eye for an eye. Maybe Hill had deserved the dignity of a trial and a formal execution, but he still deserved to die for his crime. That much Creed was certain about.

"So what does we do now, Marcus?" asked Moon.

Jones scanned the faces before him, saw his own hot breath in the chill December air, and said, "Damn cold night, y'all. I don't know about y'all, but I needs a drink or two to warm me up." Then as an afterthought, he said, "I also wants to have one for Caesar Blair. How about y'all?"

"Yessuh! So does I!" said one man, then another and another until their mood had turned from somber to festive.

"That's right," said Moon. "Hanging peckerwoods sure do raise a man's thirst."

"Now wait, y'all!" shouted Jones. "Y'all gits to drinking too much more and y'all just might start forgetting things again. We gots to do right now. No hurting the white folks like I already done said." His eyes darted side to side in his head as he surveyed the crowd. "Y'all hear that?"

"Y'all see any white folks 'round here, Marcus?"

"That ain't no never mind," said Jones. "If we sees any, we leaves 'em be. Y'all understand that? Leave the white folks alone. For now."

"How we gonna get us a drink, Marcus?" asked Pembroke. "All the saloons is closed."

"Then we'll just have to open one up, won't we?" said Jones.

A cheer of approval echoed across the plaza, and in the next instant, Jones was leading the mob toward Main Street and Bill Scanlan's Gem Saloon.

Creed was satisfied that the mob had forgotten about him. He poked around the jail office, hoping to find a gun of some kind, but he was unable to locate one. He would have to chance the dark streets without a weapon.

Exiting the jail house through the front door was a bad idea, and Creed knew it. Someone would be watching. That person might not be someone from the lynch mob, but someone would be watching. And that someone would see him escape. Creed didn't want that. He wanted to get out of the jail and make his way to Dr. January's house without being detected. He slipped out the back door and stayed in the shadows wherever they were available. He could choose one of two routes: either the block north of the plaza or the block south of it. To the north was Colonel Rose's headquarters, which would more than likely have plenty of soldiers on duty around it. To the south were the saloons, and the lynch mob had chosen that direction to go. Creed pondered the problem for a minute, then chose to go south, figuring the lynchmen were carrying torches, which put them in fairly bright light that would make it more difficult for them to see him at a distance.

Creed saw the mob at the front of the Gem Saloon when he crossed Main Street. He didn't stick around to see if they got inside or not. His wound was throbbing, and he wanted to get to January's house as fast as he could to have the injury properly treated by Miss Catherine.

Upon turning the corner of January's block, Creed saw Nimbus and the horses of his five companions still tied up in front of the doctor's home. On the one hand, he was glad of that because his guns were in the saddlebags on Nimbus; he would get them and his powder flask, balls, and caps before going into the house. On the other, he felt sorry for the beasts because they had been without food or water all day. Dr. January had a barn and corral in back of his house. Creed would ask Miss Catherine to put the horses in the corral for the night.

A light shone in the parlor window. This was good. Miss Catherine was probably up, waiting for her uncle, not knowing that he was being held across the Guadalupe by the soldiers. Creed would break this disturbing news to her—or so he thought. He crept onto the porch, carrying the saddlebags, and walked up to the door. He shifted the bags from the hand of his good arm to the other. The movement and the weight of the bags on his arm was painful. With his free hand, he rapped gently on the door frame. No answer came immediately, and no sounds came from within. He knocked louder. This brought results.

"Who's there?" asked Lavinia, January's housekeeper.

Creed had expected to hear Catherine's voice. He figured it was Lavinia, but he couldn't recall her name right off. "I'm Slate Creed," he said, not knowing what else to say.

The door opened wide. Lavinia stood in the doorway, holding a lamp. "Mr. Creed, sir. What y'all doing here? We heard y'all was locked up in the county jail house with Dr. January and the other gentlemens. Miss Catherine got herself all upset and went over there to see for herself. I is here all alone, Mr. Creed." She caught sight of the bloody rag around his arm. "Y'all is hurt, Mr. Creed."

"Yes, I know," said Creed, looking at the wound. "I need Miss Catherine to take care of it for me."

"She ain't here, Mr. Creed."

"Yes, you said that. What was your name again?"

"Lavinia, sir."

"Lavinia, may I come in?"

Lavinia's gaze shifted back and forth between Creed's face and his wound. "Yes, sir. Of course." She opened the door wider and stood aside so Creed could enter.

Creed stepped into the foyer. "How long ago did Miss Catherine leave, Lavinia?"

"Just past sundown, Mr. Creed. She was going to the county jail house to see about you and Dr. January being locked up with the other gentlemens." She closed the door behind Creed.

"Yes, you said that."

"She should be coming home anytime now. I thought she'd be home by now."

Creed looked at the staircase and said, "How do I get up to the doctor's office from here, Lavinia?"

"Right up them stairs and it's the first door on the left."

"Thank you, Lavinia." Creed started toward the stairs.

"Mr. Creed, how'd y'all get out of the county jail house?"

Creed stopped and looked Lavinia straight in the eye. "I walked out the back door."

"Y'all escaped?"

"No, Lavinia, I just walked out the back door."

"What about Dr. January and the other gentlemens? Did they walk out the back door, too?"

"No, Lavinia, they didn't. The soldiers took Dr. January and everybody else except Colonel Hill and me to some other place across the river. Then a lynch mob broke into the jail and murdered Colonel Hill."

Lavinia put a hand to her mouth to cover a gasp of disbelief and terror. "Lynch mob?"

"That's right, Lavinia. They killed him with an axe, then hung his body from the balcony of the jail house. He was still hanging there when I walked out the back door."

"And they didn't hang you, Mr. Creed?"

"Were they supposed to hang me, Lavinia?"

Lavinia flinched, then she became ashen in appearance. Lowering her eyes, she said, "Why, no, sir. I don't know what was supposed to happen down there tonight. My friend Cleo didn't say what was supposed to happen."

"Your friend Cleo?"

"Yes, sir. She's the one that told me about Dr. January and the other gentlemens being locked up with y'all in the county jail house. She didn't say what was supposed to happen down there tonight."

Creed nodded, then said, "And you say Miss Catherine went down to the jail house around sundown?"

"Yes, sir, she did. I is beginning to fret about it, too. She being gone all this time and all."

That thought hadn't entered Creed's mind until that very moment. More than two hours had passed since sundown, and

with conditions as they were, Victoria after dark was no place
for a lady. Damn! What to do!

Creed looked at Lavinia and said, "I'm sure she's all right,
Lavinia. She'll probably be home soon. I'm going to go up to
Dr. January's office and see if I can't find something to put
on the wound."

"I knows where everything's at up there, Mr. Creed," said
Lavinia. "You best let me show you." She hurried over to
the stairs and took the saddlebags from Creed. Their weight
surprised her. "What y'all got in here, Mr. Creed?"

"My Colt's," he said.

That old Negro fear of guns flooded Lavinia's face, and
she unwittingly held the bags away from her. "They's awfully
heavy, Mr. Creed."

"I can carry them, Lavinia," said Creed, reaching for the
bags.

"No, sir, I can do it. Come on now. I can take care of your
wound, too." She took Creed by his good arm and started up
the stairs.

Creed was too tired to argue. He let her take charge of him
for the moment. He would save his strength for later—in case
he should need it then for some urgency. Who knew what the
rest of the night might bring?

20

Bill Scanlan heard the mob approaching, and he prayed that they weren't coming his way. The bang of Jones's fist on the locked front doors told him that his prayers were for naught.

"Open up, Scanlan!" shouted Jones. "Open up or we'll break down your doors!"

Scanlan feared for his life as he crept toward the doors. "I'm closed!" he yelled back at Jones.

"The hell, you say!" shot back Jones. "Y'all either open up these doors or we'll break them down."

"I don't want no trouble!" shouted Scanlan.

"We don't want none neither," said Jones. "We just want to drink. That's all."

Although he didn't know about the lynching, Scanlan suspected the mob of having committed some deviltry that night, and if they hadn't done anything yet, then they were all the more likely to do something after a few drinks. He would have no part in that.

"No, sir!" said Scanlan. "You can't come in. I'm closed."

"Break it down, boys!" shouted Jones.

The mob surged forward, broke down Scanlan's doors, then poured into the saloon.

Scanlan beat a hasty retreat to the rear of the establishment, taking refuge in the private room off the hall that led to the alley exit. He listened at the door, certain that Jones and the rest of the mob would soon be forcing their way inside, intent upon murdering him. When no such commotion occurred immediately, curiosity prompted him to crack the door and peek into the hall. To his surprise, the bar was lined with Negro men, most of them soldiers.

"Come on out here, Scanlan!" shouted Jones. "We gots the money to pay!"

Timidly, Scanlan opened the door and stepped into the hall.

"Come on, man," said Jones. "Ain't nobody gonna hurt y'all. We's just thirsty and we needs us a regular bartender. Now git on out here!"

"Yeah, man!" said Gilmore. "Get your white ass out here and start pouring the whiskey!"

Scanlan skirted the end of the bar and started setting up the drinks. In just a few minutes, every man in the place had a shot of whiskey in his hand.

Jones raised his glass and said, "Here's to Caesar Blair, brothers. May the good Lord have mercy on his soul."

"Amen, brother!" said several men.

Then all drank.

"Keep 'em coming, Mr. Scanlan," said Jones as he slammed his shot glass on the bar.

Scanlan poured, and Jones and the mob drank until every one of them was drunk. Not until then did any of them remember Creed in the jail.

"Marcus, how come we didn't kill that other peckerwood?" asked Gilmore.

"Don't y'all know, brother?" asked Jones.

"If I knowed, I wouldn't ask."

"That man ain't like the rest," said Jones. "Hell, I think he's color-blind."

"He's white, ain't he?"

"Maybe not all white."

"You think he's one of us passing for white?" asked Gilmore.

"No, I think maybe he's part Indian. Something about him that says he knows Indian ways at least."

"Part Indian or not, he's still white," said Pembroke. "Mostly white, anyway, and that means he ain't color-blind. He's like all the others."

"No, he ain't," said Jones. "I just knows he ain't. I's telling y'all now. That man is color-blind."

Pembroke's face turned evil as he said, "Well, why don't we just go back to the jail and see how color-blind he is then?"

"All right," said Jones reluctantly, "we'll do it."

The mob poured out of the saloon and had barely gotten into the street when they were met by Captain Spaulding and the squad of cavalry from the New York regiment.

"Sergeant Jones," said Spaulding, "what are you doing away from your camp at this hour of the night?"

"Just out seeing the sights, sir," said Jones. Then he laughed and said, "Thought I might see someone I knows hanging around town."

The rest of the mob caught the morbid joke and joined Jones in raucous laughter.

Spaulding understood what Jones was getting at, but he didn't like it. Not now. Not since viewing Ben Hill's bloody corpse hanging in front of the jail, not since assuring Catherine Ramsdale that Hill and Creed were safe in the jail.

"Sergeant Jones," said Spaulding, "you are to return to your camp immediately and remain there until further orders are given to you by your company commander. That goes for all of you men in the 3rd Michigan. The rest of you, you civilians, I want you off the streets immediately."

"You go to hell, soldier boy!" shouted Gilmore. "I ain't in your army, so I'll do as I pleases."

"Same goes for me," said Pembroke. "I'll goes home when I's good and ready and not till then."

"You'll do as the army tells you, boy!" shouted Spaulding.

"I done said we ain't in your army," said Gilmore, "so y'all can go to hell with your military shit."

"Disperse!" shouted Spaulding. "Soldiers back to camp, and Freedmen go home!"

"I's had enough of this peckerwood soldier boy telling me what to do," said Gilmore. "Someone give me a gun so I can shoot his white ass offa that horse."

Spaulding drew his revolver and shouted, "Sergeant!"

The cavalry sergeant behind Spaulding knew exactly what to do. He gave the orders to draw weapons and to spread the men so that they flanked Spaulding and confronted the mob.

Jones wasn't so drunk that he couldn't see they were all sitting on the powder keg he had warned his friends of earlier in the evening. He stepped close to Spaulding and said loud enough for everyone to hear, "Captain, we ain't doing no one no harm." He lowered his eyes a bit and added, "Leastways, not now we ain't." Then more boldly, he continued, "We's just out having us a drink or two and then we's going back to camp. By your leave, sir, we'll go when we wants to go and not before."

"Amen, Marcus!" said Moon and several others.

"You tell him, Marcus!" said others.

"I swears it on my mammy's white-haired head," said Jones. "There ain't gonna be no one hurt this night from this moment on. Y'all gots to trust us on that one, Captain."

Spaulding studied Jones's face, then said, "All right, Sergeant Jones. Sergeant Shannon, get your squad back into formation and let's get back to headquarters."

"Yes, sir," said Shannon.

Spaulding leaned down to Jones and said, "Sergeant, a word with you over there." He nodded toward the other side of the street.

"Yes, sir," said Jones. "Y'all stay here," he said to the others, "while I has a word with the captain."

Spaulding and Jones went to the other side of the street, and Spaulding dismounted.

"Sergeant, I've just come from the jail house. I saw Colonel Hill's body hanging out front, and I know you and those other boys are the ones that hung him there."

"So what if we did?" asked Jones.

"Nothing much," said Spaulding. "It's just that I thought we left two prisoners in the jail house, but I only saw Hill hanging outside. What happened to the other man? Creed."

"We let him be, sir," said Jones. "He was still in the jail house when we left it."

"Well, he's not there now," said Spaulding.

"Then he must've run off, Captain."

"And that might mean serious trouble, Sergeant. There's something about that man Creed that tells me he won't let this rest. I've got a feeling that we're in for some serious trouble with that man."

"No, sir, I don't think so."

"What you think doesn't count, Jones. It's what I think and what Colonel Rose thinks that counts around here. Just let me give you a little piece of advice, Jones. The colonel let you boys have your fun with Hill because he killed one of your friends, but I know for a fact that if you harm any of the other citizens of this town, the colonel will turn on you in an instant. Your word that no one else will be hurt tonight better be good, because if it isn't, your people just might lose in one night what it took four years to win."

Jones knew exactly what Spaulding meant, and he became doubly intent on making good his promise to preserve the peace—at least for the rest of that night.

21

Catherine was still waiting in front of the Levi mansion when Captain Spaulding returned. He had hoped that she would have tired of his delay and gone home. That was on the one hand, the soldier side of him. On the other, he was glad in his heart that she was still there.

Spaulding dismounted, tied up his horse, then approached Catherine. He tipped his hat politely and said, "Miss Ramsdale, I'm sorry for taking so long."

"That's quite all right, Captain. Did you see Mr. Creed and Colonel Hill?"

Spaulding averted his eyes and said, "There is no easy way to say this, Miss Ramsdale, other than forthright. Colonel Hill is dead."

"Dead?" she gasped.

Now looking her in the eyes, he said, "Yes, ma'am."

"How?"

"He was lynched."

"Lynched? By whom?"

Spaulding's eyes shifted away from her again as he said, "We don't know. Not yet. I have to report this to Colonel Rose, and I'm sure there will be an investigation."

Catherine's voice was low and controlled as she said, "What about Mr. Creed? Is he . . . dead, too?"

"I don't know, ma'am," said Spaulding, being direct again and a bit annoyed that she was so concerned about Creed. "He wasn't in the jail."

Catherine turned away, not wishing to show Spaulding her relief that Creed wasn't hanged with Hill. She stammered, "How did this happen, Captain?"

"I don't know, Miss Ramsdale. I don't know."

She turned back to him and with an accusatorial tone said, "And you don't know what's happened to Mr. Creed?"

"No, ma'am," said Spaulding rather meekly.

"Captain, I think I'd better be going now."

"Please allow me to escort you home, Miss Ramsdale."

"That won't be necessary, Captain. I think I'd feel safer without any of you Yankees around me, if you don't mind."

Spaulding knew exactly what she meant, and it hurt. He was quite taken by this lady, and that part of him was disgusted by the carnage at the jail. He felt himself to be totally innocent of Hill's murder. He hadn't lifted the axe; he hadn't stretched the rope. But he had taken the jail house guards across the Guadalupe, leaving Hill and Creed unprotected. That had been the plan, and it had worked—almost. Creed was still alive as far as he knew, and he could identify Hill's killers. Not that that would matter all that much. Creed was a Reb, and that meant his word was worthless in a Yankee court. But who knew? The army did strange things. Creed's testimony could be damning enough to convict someone of the heinous crime. Maybe even Spaulding. And if that should happen, then Colonel Rose would have to pay also. Spaulding would see to that. He would not suffer alone. If things should come to that head, of course.

"Please, Miss Ramsdale," said Spaulding. "There are . . . certain men . . . about town who might do you harm if they saw you out alone."

"If you mean the Negroes, Captain, I don't fear them one bit as long as I have this." She showed her uncle's Colt's to Spaulding. "In fact, I have no fear of you Yankees as long as I have this."

"Miss Ramsdale, it's against the law to carry a handgun in this town." He held out his hand as if he were planning on taking it from her.

Catherine cocked the hammer but didn't aim the weapon at Spaulding. "Whose law, Captain? Yours? This is my protection, sir, and I will not surrender it willingly."

Spaulding's eyes widened and locked on the Colt's. "Well, I see no harm in you having it with you tonight, but I do wish you would reconsider my offer to escort you home."

"Would you have me walk or ride one of those horses, Captain?"

"I believe we have a carriage available, ma'am," said Hirsch, who was still standing close by, listening to their conversation.

"Excellent, Hirsch," said Spaulding. "Hitch up a team to it and bring it around immediately."

"No, thank you, Captain," said Catherine. "I can walk home in the time it'll take for your men to get that carriage rigged up. I'll ride a horse."

"Very well, ma'am," said Spaulding. "Sergeant Shannon," he said to the squad leader, "have one of your men dismount and bring his horse forward."

The trooper did as ordered, and Spaulding helped Catherine to mount the animal. "Thank you, sir," she said. Spaulding climbed into the saddle and brought his horse alongside hers. The squad fell in behind them, and they were off at a walk toward Dr. January's home.

Spaulding tried to engage Catherine in conversation during the ride, but she would have none of it. For every question he asked, she gave him a simple one- or two-word answer, usually yes or no. When he made a statement, she either nodded or said, "Is that a fact?" then let him prattle on. Nothing about the ride home was unusual to Catherine until they turned the corner to Dr. January's house and she noticed immediately that the six horses belonging to Creed and his friends were no longer tied up in front of the residence. Catherine made no mention of this fact to Spaulding. When they arrived at the house, Spaulding helped her down from the saddle, then escorted her to the door.

"I see that there's still a light on inside," said Spaulding, fishing for an invitation to stay for a visit.

"Lavinia, our housekeeper, is probably waiting up for me," said Catherine.

"Dr. January isn't married?"

"Widower," said Catherine.

"Sorry to hear that, ma'am."

"Captain," said Catherine in a sigh, "thank you for bringing me home. I am quite grateful, but I must say good night now."

"Yes, of course," stammered Spaulding. He tipped his hat, then as an afterthought, he said, "Miss Ramsdale, may I call on you some other time?"

This was the last thing Catherine expected to hear from him. Surprised by his request, she blurted, "I suppose it would be all right." And no sooner than she had said it, she was regretful.

"Thank you, Miss Ramsdale," said Spaulding, his spirits uplifted at the prospect of seeing Catherine socially. "Good night, Miss Ramsdale." He literally danced off the porch and back to his horse. He leaped into the saddle, spurred the animal, and rode off at a gallop, completely forgetting the squadron of soldiers that had accompanied him.

The sergeant watched Spaulding speed away, gave it some thought, then looked at his men and gave the order to move out—at a walk.

Catherine chastised herself mentally as she opened the door and went inside. Damn! Why on earth had she given that Yankee permission to come calling? No answer now. She'd deal with that question later.

"Miss Catherine, is that y'all?" Lavinia called out from the kitchen.

"Yes, Lavinia, it's me," said Catherine as she went to the closet beneath the staircase to hang up her cape and put away her bonnet and her uncle's gun.

Lavinia came to the foyer and waited for Catherine to emerge from the closet. When she did, Catherine said, "Lavinia, what happened to the horses that were out front when I left?"

"They's in the corral out back," said Lavinia. Then with a coy smile, she added, "Miss Catherine, that nice Mr. Creed is upstairs with the other gentleman."

The news was both wonderful and frightening at the same time. Catherine grabbed Lavinia by the arms and said excitedly, "Mr. Creed? Here? Is he all right? Is he hurt? When did he come, Lavinia? How is he?" Not realizing that she wasn't letting Lavinia get a word in edgewise and desirous of an answer to all of her questions at once, Catherine shook Lavinia violently and snapped, "Answer me, girl!"

Lavinia jerked free of Catherine's grasp, the old slave fear of a beating making her cower and shrink away.

Seeing Lavinia's reaction stirred an equal reaction in Catherine. She felt shame and guilt and said, "Oh, Lavinia, I'm sorry. Did I hurt you?" She reached out to touch Lavinia's hand, but the housekeeper pulled it away. Catherine let her own hand fall to her side as she lowered her eyes and said, "I don't blame you for that, Lavinia. I'm sorry. I had no right to shake you like that. Please forgive me."

Lavinia was no fool. She had been around white folks all her life, having been born and raised in a family of house slaves. She knew when white folks were being taunting, mocking, or condescending, and she knew when they were being sincere and honest. She had known Catherine long enough to know when she was being the latter, and this was one of those times.

"It's all right, Miss Catherine," said Lavinia, moving ahead a step and reaching out to show her acceptance of the apology.

"No, Lavinia, it isn't. I had no right to do that to you."

"Miss Catherine, y'all is just agitated about Mr. Creed, that's all. I understands. You didn't do it because I is black. I knows that."

"Even so—"

"Don't you pay no never mind, Miss Catherine," said Lavinia with a genuinely warm smile. "You wants to see Mr. Creed now. He's upstairs with the other gentleman, and he's all right."

Catherine looked wistfully at the stairs, then back at Lavinia. "I am sorry, Lavinia."

"Yes, ma'am, I knows. But it's all right. You go up them stairs now and see about Mr. Creed. He was cut by Colonel Hill in the jail house. I put a bandage on it, but I ain't so sure I did such a good job of it."

"Cut?"

"Yes, ma'am. In the arm. Here." She pointed to her own upper left arm. "Deep, too. I gave him some of Dr. January's pain medicine for his hurt."

"The laudanum?"

"Yes, ma'am."

"Come upstairs with me, Lavinia. I may need your help."

The two women hurried up the staircase.

Dr. January's office was almost dark. Catherine found the lamp and turned up the flame. She went to Bill Simons's bedroom door and started to open it but stopped when she heard the sound of a Colt's being cocked.

"Mr. Creed," she said softly, "it is I, Catherine Ramsdale."

"Who's that with you?" asked Creed, his words slightly slurred from the painkiller.

"It's me, Mr. Creed. Lavinia."

"Come in, ladies," said Creed from within, uncocking his Colt's as he did.

Catherine opened the door. The bedroom was dark. She carried the lamp inside.

Creed squinted at the sudden intrusion of light, which seemed more brilliant to him because of the effects of the opium-alcohol mixture he had been given by Lavinia. He had been sitting for several minutes, talking with Simons about the events of the day and evening, purposefully maintaining the darkness in order to keep his presence there as discreet as possible. A blanket was draped around his shoulders. When he stood up as a gentleman should when a lady enters a room, the cover fell away, exposing his naked chest. He wobbled a bit, having been made a bit unstable by the laudanum.

Catherine sucked in a deep breath at the sight of Creed's bare skin, then let it out, saying, "Mr. Creed, are you all right? Lavinia said you were hurt." Then she saw the bandage on his arm. It was clean, meaning no blood was leaking from the wound. She was also surprised to see that the skin on his arms and torso was almost as tan as that on his face and hands. She wouldn't take time to wonder why at this moment. She simply found it sensuously appealing and accepted it for that.

"I'm all right," said Creed.

"He's plenty tough, Miss Ramsdale," said Simons. "Little scratch like that ain't gonna slow him down much."

"I'd better look at it anyway," said Catherine. She moved close to Creed.

"No need, Miss Catherine," said Creed. "I've had worse wounds than this, and Miss Lavinia dressed it as good as any surgeon could."

"Yes, I can see that," said Catherine. "You did a good job, Lavinia."

"Thank you, Miss Catherine."

"Lavinia said Colonel Hill is the one that cut you," said Catherine. "Is that true?"

"Yes, it is," said Creed blandly.

Catherine's brow furrowed, not understanding. "Why?" she blurted.

"Miss Catherine, do you know what's happened tonight?"

"Yes, I do. Captain Spaulding told me that Colonel Hill was lynched and that you had escaped."

"Is that all he told you?"

"That was enough, wasn't it?"

"That isn't the whole story, Miss Ramsdale."

"It isn't?"

"No, ma'am."

"If you two don't mind," said Simons, "I've heard all this before, and I'd like to get some sleep now. Creed, you wake me if you need help or anything. I might still have a little buckshot in me, but I feel plenty good enough to shoot a gun if I have to."

"Let's hope you won't have to, Bill," said Creed.

"Good night, Mr. Simons," said Catherine.

Creed picked up his blanket and followed Catherine and Lavinia into the other room. He closed the door behind them.

"I's heard all this, too, Miss Catherine," said Lavinia. "If y'all won't be needing me for anything more, I'd like to turn in, too."

"Go right ahead, Lavinia," said Catherine. "I'll see you in the morning."

Lavinia left them.

Creed suddenly became aware of his appearance. A bit abashed he replaced his Colt's in its holster, then wrapped the blanket around his shoulders again.

"I've seen the bare chests of many men," said Catherine. "You need not be embarrassed on my account."

"Yes, ma'am," said Creed meekly.

"Now, you were going to tell me about everything that's transpired this evening."

They sat down, and Creed told her about everything that he had witnessed that day and night. Then Catherine took her turn, but she left out relating to him her second reason for going out that evening. Even so, Creed surmised it correctly and finally admitted to himself that Simons and Dr. January had been correct in their estimation of Catherine's feelings. She was quite smitten with him, and he felt quite flattered. In fact, he relished the thought that this provocative woman was attracted to him, and that brought forth a pang of guilt from his conscience. He quickly brushed it aside, thinking that looking was harmless, in spite of what the Good Book said about lusting in the heart being as sinful as doing the real thing. He would look all he wanted, but he would never touch. Or so he told himself then.

"So what are you going to do now?" she asked.

"I don't go looking for trouble, Miss Catherine. I think it would be best if I sort of laid low here for the night, then see what tomorrow brings."

"I think that's best, too. You can sleep in the room across from mine." She stood up and expected Creed to do the same, but he didn't.

"I don't think that's such a good idea, Miss Catherine. I think I'd better stay up here near Bill. There's no telling about lynch mobs. Any one of them might get a notion to come up here after Bill since they didn't get to put a rope around my neck. No, I think I'd better stay here."

Catherine studied him in the dim light and said, "I don't think that's the reason at all. I think you're afraid to sleep in a room so close to mine."

Creed was incredulous. Dr. January had said she could be straightforward, but he hadn't said she could be this blunt. Well, if she could be so frank, then he could, too.

"All right, I'll admit to that," he said.

"Do you find me so unattractive?"

Again, Creed was incredulous. "Unattractive? On the contrary, Miss Catherine. I don't think I could trust myself in the night."

She held out her hand for him to take and said, "That is a thought you should banish from your mind, Mr. Creed."

Without thinking, Creed reached out from beneath the blanket, took her hand, and stood up. Catherine's face was only inches from his own. All of his senses were alert to her, each one groping for her, consuming her. His heart palpitated. He felt a touch of vertigo. Their lips came together. Creed's were parted; hers weren't. Reacting, not really thinking about it, he flexed his lips to coax her to open hers. She did. Her mouth was silky, hot, wet. He was just about to let his tongue have its way when she broke the kiss.

"Come on now," she said huskily. "I'll take you to your room." She led him to the door to the upstairs hall.

The movement shook Creed's senses. He asked himself what he was doing. He had pledged his love to Texada, who was only fifty miles away in Hallettsville, and here he had kissed Catherine Ramsdale and was going with her to a bedroom. Ostensibly to sleep. Alone. At least, that's what he should be doing. But he knew that wasn't what Catherine had in mind, and it wasn't what he really wanted. He wanted Catherine. He wanted to make love to her all night long. Tonight. Tomorrow night. And for a lot more nights after that. She had stirred his desire that deeply. But he mustn't. Because of his love for Texada. He wouldn't, he told himself. He would beg off when they reached the room. Yes, that was it. He would tell Catherine about Texada and that would dampen her ardor as well. He would—

Creed was too late. They were already in the room, and Catherine was pressing her parted lips to his. He was caught up now in a euphoria that was induced partly by the laudanum and partly by his sexual desire for this woman; he was no longer in control of himself. He let the blanket drop and pulled her hard against him, and she pulled back, grinding her pelvis against him. They had the fire. Beads of salty sweat bubbled on their faces. Creed's mouth slid down her slender throat. She was so delicious. He'd never felt like this with any other woman. He'd never felt so . . . so . . . so woozy. Yes, he was definitely dizzy. His heart was pounding, doing its best to pump a steady torrent of blood to his hardened penis. He felt light-headed, weak, wobbly. He—

Creed had lost too much blood from the knife wound. When his sex organs needed an inordinate amount of the life liquid, all that was available had to come from his head. The drain was too much for him.

Creed fainted.

Catherine caught him, not realizing that he had passed out until his lips stopped their sensuous pursuit and his head lolled to one side. Damn! she swore silently when the reality of their situation set in. She lowered him to the bed, first in a sitting position, then on to his back. She lifted his feet and put them on the bed. She undressed him, then removed her dress and lay down beside him, hopeful that he might awaken in the night and continue their lovemaking.

22

Visions of Texada writhing in his arms danced through Creed's dreams. He could almost touch her. In fact, he was certain that he was touching her—or someone. He could smell her, too, and the scent was so inviting. He wanted her so much. His penis was erect and pulsating. He was in that half sleep where everything seemed so real. Texada purred. His eyes fluttered opened.

Catherine's head rested on his bare chest. She was also dreaming, but her dream was closer to true. She was holding Creed in her mind; she was holding him in reality, too.

Realizing Catherine was in bed with him startled Creed fully alert. He moved sideways, to his left, and was instantly reminded of the night before when a seering pain shot through his arm. "Damn!" he swore, reaching for the bandaged limb.

"What, Slate dearest?" muttered Catherine. She raised her head sleepily, blinking rapidly, trying to focus eyes that would have refused to see clearly even if she had been completely awake. It took her a few seconds to realize that she was no longer dreaming, that she was really in bed with Creed. Her first thought was embarrassment, but that passed as fast as it came. Then she, too, recalled the night before. She smiled and said, "Good morning, Slate dearest." She reached for him.

Creed shied away, winced with another pang in his arm, and swore again.

"I'm sorry," said Catherine. "Did I hurt you?"

"No, Miss Ramsdale."

"Miss Ramsdale?" she asked quizzically. She stared at Creed for a moment, then said, "You can call me Catherine now, Slate dearest. Especially after last night."

"After last night?" queried Creed. "I'm a bit fuzzy on that, Miss Ramsdale. How did I wind up in here? With my clothes off."

"You don't know?"

"No, ma'am, I surely don't."

Catherine was hurt, but she refused to show it. Instead, she attacked. "You mean to tell me that you led me in here and made passionate love to me and you don't recall any of it?"

Creed was shocked. And speechless.

"Well, I declare, *Mister* Creed! If you don't beat all! You deflower me and you don't recall any of it." She rolled away, turning her back to him. "I feel like some sort of riverfront strumpet that you men pay for favors," she pouted.

Creed rubbed his eyes, then ran his hand over the stubble on his face, all in an effort to shake his memory. For the life of him, all he could remember was kissing her in one room, then in this room. But that was it. Nothing more. Nothing lewd or lascivious. Just kissing. All right, passionate kissing, but he hadn't touched her. He hadn't deflowered her, as she put it. Had he? No, he told himself. He hadn't done that. Not consciously. Not that he was aware of, and if he wasn't aware of it, it didn't count. She had no right to hold it against him if he had, because he couldn't remember it.

"Miss Catherine, I don't recollect us . . . doing anything."

She rolled over again and faced him squarely. "You don't recollect any of it?"

"No, ma'am, I don't," he said firmly.

She buried her face in the pillow and forced herself to cry.

"Miss Catherine, you shouldn't carry on this way."

"And why not?" she snapped, raising her head again.

Creed saw the anger in her eyes and recalled Dr. January's warning that Catherine could be extremely vindictive. As that thought passed through his mind, he noticed something else in her eyes. Was it deceit? he asked himself. Maybe. If it was, did that mean nothing had happened between them besides their kisses? Maybe that was why he couldn't remember anything.

"Because nothing happened between us last night," said

Creed firmly. "Nothing except a few kisses."

"A few kisses? I slept with you. You deflowered me."

Creed glanced around the room. The only garment he could see was Catherine's dress.

"No, Miss Catherine, I didn't. For me to have deflowered you, I'd have to have been some sort of magician to get through all those ladies underthings while you were still wearing them."

Catherine realized that she was caught. She gasped, then turned away in shame.

Creed was empathetic. "Miss Catherine, I'm sorry," he said. "I'm not sure what to say here. On the one hand, I do recall kissing you. I liked it. I assure you of that. At the time, I wanted to go further than just kissing."

Catherine turned back to him and said, "You did?"

"Of course, I did. What sort of man wouldn't? You're a very desirable woman, Miss Catherine."

"Is that what you really think? Or are you only saying that because you think you've hurt my feelings?"

"No, ma'am, I mean it."

Catherine leaned toward him and said, "Then why don't we pick up where we left off last night?"

"Miss Catherine—"

"I know I'm being forward, Slate dearest, but I can't help myself. You make me feel . . . so . . . so . . ."

"Miss Catherine, you're a fine woman, and if I'd met you sooner, I'd certainly be entertaining thoughts of courting you seriously."

"You would?" asked Catherine hopefully.

"Yes, I would, but I can't because I'm already promised to another."

Catherine's eyes drooped. "Another?"

"Yes," said Creed. "Back home in Lavaca County."

"I'll bet she's real pretty, not plain like me."

"You're not plain, Miss Catherine," said Creed. He touched her cheek, then let his fingers drift down to her throat.

Catherine took his hand in hers, kissed the palm, then pressed it against her cheek.

Suddenly, he wanted to pull her close to him, but he resisted the urge. "No, you're not plain," he said. The heat was beginning to well up in his loins.

A knock on Catherine's bedroom door across the hall froze them. "Miss Catherine?" called Lavinia. "Is y'all up yet, Miss Catherine?" No reply. "Miss Catherine?" Another knock. "Miss Catherine?" Silence for another few seconds, then the rattle of the door latch. "Miss Catherine, is y'all in here?" No answer. The door was closed. Two footsteps, then a knock on Creed's door. "Miss Catherine, is y'all in there with Mr. Creed?"

Catherine started to answer, but Creed shook his head for her not to. "No, Lavinia," he said, "she's not in here."

"Well, she ain't in her room, Mr. Creed," said Lavinia, "and her bed ain't been slept in neither. Y'all sure she ain't in there with y'all, Mr. Creed?"

"If she was in here, Lavinia, don't you think I'd know it?"

"Yes, sir, I guess y'all would. Well, if she ain't in there, then where is she? It's breakfast time, and I needs to know what she wants me to fix for y'all."

"Anything would be all right with me, Lavinia," said Creed. "I'll be down as soon as I'm dressed."

"Yes, sir, y'all do that, and if y'all sees Miss Catherine, y'all tell her I's looking for her."

"I'll do that, Lavinia."

They waited until they were sure that Lavinia had gone back downstairs before speaking again.

"We'd better get dressed," said Creed.

"Yes, of course," said Catherine. She slid out of bed, picked up her dress, and covered herself with it instead of donning it. She looked at Creed as if she were waiting for him to get out of bed, too. When he didn't, she said, "It's all right. I undressed you last night."

"Maybe you did," said Creed, "but I wasn't awake then." He picked up her glasses from the nightstand and offered them to her. "Here. You'd better put these on."

She took the spectacles and put them on. Seeing Creed clearly for the first time that morning, she said, "I don't care if there is another girl in your life. You're in my life right now, and that's all that matters. Even if I only have you for a few more days, I intend to make the most of what little time we have together. I'm in love with you, Slate."

Creed sat up in bed but kept himself covered. He had a strong physical attraction for Catherine that he was trying his best to deny, but he was failing. He wanted her right then and there, and he might have taken her, too, if she hadn't turned and left the room.

23

Getting dressed was painful for Creed. But that was the least of his worries. His main concern was the Federal army, and it, in the person of Captain Linus Spaulding, was knocking on the front door of Dr. January's house before he left his room that morning.

Catherine was at the top of the stairs when she heard the knocking. "I'll answer it, Lavinia," she called out, then hurried downstairs. She saw Spaulding through the glass, and as much as she didn't want to face him first thing this morning, she knew it would avail her nothing to not answer. She opened the door and politely said, "Good morning, Captain."

Spaulding removed his hat and returned the greeting. "Good morning, Miss Ramsdale. I'm sorry to trouble you so early in the day, but it's about that man Creed. He's still missing, and I understand that he has a friend staying here under Dr. January's care. Is that true, ma'am?"

"Why, yes, it is, Captain," said Catherine. "Mr. Creed's friend, Mr. Simons, is a patient of Uncle's, and he's upstairs in the sickroom. But he's up there alone, I assure you."

"I'm sure he is, Miss Ramsdale, but I'd like to see him just the same, if you don't mind."

"Of course not, Captain. Won't you come in, and I'll show you to his room myself."

"Thank you, ma'am."

Spaulding entered the house and followed Catherine up the stairs. Creed heard them coming. He knew Catherine wouldn't betray him, but that didn't mean that Spaulding wouldn't take

it upon himself to open a few doors. If he did, Creed was prepared. He had his Colt's ready for action, but he hoped it would
be unnecessary to use the weapon.

"As you may or may not know," Catherine was saying as
she and Spaulding passed by Creed's door, "Mr. Simons was
wounded when those awful men down along Coleto Creek
attacked Mr. Creed and his friends last week."

"Yes, ma'am, I heard about the shooting," said Spaulding,
"but it's none of the army's concern."

"It isn't? And why not?"

"The way I understand it, Miss Ramsdale, Mr. Creed and
his friends are Rebs, or at least they were. And so were the
men who attacked them. The army could care less about Rebs
shooting each other."

"But you do care about a white man shooting a black man.
Is that it, Captain?"

Creed didn't hear Spaulding's response because the captain
and Catherine stepped into Dr. January's office at that moment,
but he could imagine Spaulding saying something to the effect
that it was the army's duty to protect the Freedmen from the
likes of Rebs like Colonel Hill and Slate Creed.

But all that wasn't important right now. Staying hidden
from Spaulding was. There was still no telling what Spaulding
might do. He might search the house, and he might not. Just
in case he did, Creed figured it would be in his best interests
to remove himself from the premises. He went to the window
and looked out at the backyard, hoping to see a way down
to the ground, but he saw none other than jumping, and that
wouldn't do because the leap could end with his breaking
a bone or two or more. But what about a way up? The roof
of the house was nearly flat, and a balustrade ran around
its outer edge. Could he open the window, then stand on its
sill and reach the balustrade? And upon doing that, could
he pull himself up, then close the window behind him? No,
of course not. His wounded arm wouldn't permit that. That
left him with two choices: either stay where he was or try
to sneak out through the house without being discovered.
If he left the room, he had to remove from the premises
any and all signs that he had been there, and that meant
making the bed. He was in the process of doing just that

when he heard Catherine and Spaulding coming back from Dr. January's office. He picked up his Colt's and knelt beside the bed, hoping again that Spaulding wouldn't open the door and discover him.

"I'll be posting men outside," Spaulding was saying, "just in case Creed should come here to see Mr. Simons."

"I don't think Mr. Creed would be so foolish as to come here, Captain Spaulding," said Catherine.

"Well, you never know about men like Creed, Miss Ramsdale."

"Men like Mr. Creed, Captain? How is that, sir?"

"Desperate men. Men trying to escape the law. You never know what foolish thing they might do, so you have to be prepared for everything if you expect to catch them."

"So I see," said Catherine, her voice fading as she and Spaulding started down the stairs.

Creed waited a half a minute, then cracked the bedroom door to listen. He was just in time to hear Catherine bid Spaulding adieu at the front door, which she closed behind him.

"What that Yankee want, Miss Catherine?" asked Lavinia.

"Mr. Creed, Lavinia."

"Y'all didn't tell him Mr. Creed is upstairs in the guest room, did y'all, Miss Catherine?"

"Don't be silly, Lavinia. Of course, I didn't."

"I didn't think so. Not after y'all slept the night together like y'all did."

Catherine gasped, then said, "Lavinia! What on earth made you say a thing like that?"

"I ain't stupid, Miss Catherine, and I ain't deaf neither. I heard y'all last night. Kissing and smooching and carrying on in the upstairs hall. And I only heard one door close, and that one was Mr. Creed's. And y'all don't sleep with your door open, Miss Catherine, so y'all must've been in with Mr. Creed. And if y'all wasn't sleeping together, then y'all is blind or stupid or something. Two healthy young folks like y'all. Y'all best be getting what y'all can when y'all can. There's no telling when y'all might get another chance. Leastways, that's how I sees it."

"Thank you very much, Lavinia," said Catherine, "but I'd appreciate it more if you would mind your own business."

"Yes, ma'am."

Yes, Lavinia, thought Creed, mind your own business.

"Now get Mr. Simons his breakfast," said Catherine.

"Yes, ma'am," said Lavinia before she hurried off to the kitchen.

Catherine then went upstairs, where Creed met her in the hall. "Did you hear?" she asked.

"Everything," said Creed.

"Everything?"

"Well, not everything," said Creed. "I didn't hear anything you and Spaulding said after you went into Dr. January's office."

"But you heard everything else?"

"Not after you went back downstairs," said Creed, lying.

Catherine was relieved but tried not to show it, and Creed pretended not to see it.

"Then you know that Captain Spaulding intends to post some men outside the house?"

"Yes, I heard him say that. That means I can't go outside and I have to stay away from the windows. I guess I'm trapped here until nightfall, but you aren't."

"I don't understand," said Catherine.

"I can't risk leaving here in the daylight, but you can come and go as you please. Last night you said something about having seen Dr. Goodwin and that he promised to help you get Dr. January and the others out of jail today."

"Yes, that's right," said Catherine.

"Well, I think you should go see him first thing this morning and start the ball rolling toward getting Dr. January and the others free before something happens to them like what Colonel Hill got."

"Yes, of course. I'd forgotten about Colonel Hill."

"So did I last night," said Creed. "It must have been the laudanum." Then he looked into Catherine's eyes and saw something that he liked. "Or maybe it was you that made me forget."

"Maybe," she said.

"Most likely it was you, Catherine. You do affect me that way, you know."

"I do?"

"Yes, you do," he said before he realized that their conversation was once again turning in the wrong direction. "But we don't have time to talk about us now. You have to go see Dr. Goodwin and get those other men out of jail."

"Yes, of course. Would you like me to have Lavinia bring you some breakfast?"

"That would be nice," said Creed. "I'm going to stay in Bill's room until you come back. Tell Lavinia that she can bring me something there."

"All right."

"And Catherine?"

"Yes, Slate?"

"Please be careful when you leave the house. There's no telling what you might see or hear out there. And be careful about who you talk to and what you say to them. After what happened last night, there's no telling what might happen now. So be careful."

Catherine threw her arms around his neck and kissed him. Not sure of what he should do, Creed returned the affection

Catherine broke the embrace and said, "I think you care more for me than you're willing to admit." Then she turned and left him thinking that she just might be right.

24

Dr. Goodwin was wearing his customary white costume when he greeted Catherine at his house that morning.

"No need to tell me what happened last night, Miss Ramsdale," said Goodwin. "Everybody within fifty miles of Victoria must know about the lynching by now. Ghastly business! Ghastly!"

"You could have prevented it if you'd only done what I asked last night," said Catherine quite righteously. During the walk to his home, she had prepared herself to be very indignant with Goodwin, and she was proud of herself for taking the first shot.

"I think not," he retorted. "While you and I were conversing last night, the foul deed was being done. If we had gone to see Colonel Rose then, we would still have been too late to save Colonel Hill from being murdered."

Catherine drooped and said, "Yes, I suppose you are correct in that, Dr. Goodwin. I went to see Colonel Rose myself, but I wasn't permitted to see him. Captain Spaulding came along and offered to help by going to the jail to make certain that Colonel Hill and Mr. Creed were safe. It was from him that I learned of Colonel Hill's fate."

"I was awakened at dawn with the news of it," said Goodwin. "I went over to the jail immediately and was in time to see the soldiers lowering Colonel Hill's body to the ground. He'd been killed with an axe, then hung."

"That much I know," said Catherine, her eyes filled with angry tears. "And I also know that those Negro soldiers did it.

They broke into the jail and killed Colonel Hill and then hung him outside. And Colonel Rose is responsible for his death. Those soldiers are under his command, and he let them do it. I even suspect him of ordering them to do it. At the very least, he's guilty of abetting them, because he ordered the white soldiers who were supposed to guard the jail to take Uncle and the other gentlemen across the river, leaving Colonel Hill and Mr. Creed unprotected by decent men and at the mercy of those Negro soldiers."

"Yes, you're quite right, Miss Ramsdale. And that brings up a curious point. What happened to this Mr. Creed? I understand he wasn't in the jail when the soldiers returned there last night. Captain Spaulding said the man must have fled the county by now."

Catherine turned away and said with all the innocence she could muster, "I wouldn't know about that."

"Well, he isn't our concern at this moment. We've got your uncle and Judge White to worry about first." Goodwin glanced out the window and saw his surrey being brought around to the front of the house. "If you're not worried about being seen riding in public with a known Yankee-lover, Miss Ramsdale, I'll drive us over to Colonel Rose's headquarters." He opened the door and offered his arm to her.

Catherine accepted the polite gesture and said, "I'd be honored, Dr. Goodwin."

At the Levi mansion, they were met at the front gate by Sergeant Hirsch. "Good morning, Miss Ramsdale, Dr. Goodwin," he said. "I suppose you've come to see Colonel Rose about the gentlemen in jail across the river."

"You are quite correct," said Goodwin.

"I was afraid of that," said Hirsch, his eyes lowered in frustration. Then looking up, he said, "Dr. Goodwin, the colonel isn't up to seeing anyone this morning."

"Poppycock!" snapped Goodwin. "I don't care how hungover he is, Sergeant. He'll see me and Miss Ramsdale immediately. Is that understood?"

Hirsch was well acquainted with Goodwin, having seen him at the mansion on several previous occasions and knowing exactly who he was. Besides being a Northerner by birth and a Unionist, the doctor was rumored to be related to some high-hat official in Washington, and for this reason, every man in camp stepped lightly when Goodwin was around.

"Yes, sir," said Hirsch, "but you'd better let me go in first, Dr. Goodwin, just to make sure the colonel is ready to receive a lady."

Goodwin's brow furrowed as he considered Hirsch's statement, but once he understood, he said, "Yes, of course."

They followed Hirsch into the house, and while he went upstairs to Rose's room, they waited in the foyer. In a minute, they heard shouting from above.

"What are you doing in my room at this hour, Sergeant?" yelled Rose. "I thought I told you never to disturb me before I'm up on my own."

A few seconds of quiet.

"What's that son of a bitch want at this hour?" demanded Rose.

Another few seconds of quiet.

"Miss who?"

More quiet.

"Goddamned son of a bitch! Where are my trousers? Get my trousers and boots. If I have to see the old son of a bitch and this Ramsdale woman, then at least let me put on my trousers and boots first. Have them wait in my office, and I'll be down as soon as I'm dressed. Now get out of here!"

Hirsch came downstairs and started to speak to Goodwin and Catherine, but the doctor halted his speech, saying, "Never mind, Sergeant. You just go back up there and tell Colonel Rose that the old son of a bitch and the Ramsdale woman will give him half a minute to get down here or we're coming up there."

Hirsch shook his head but said nothing. He knew it would do no good. He simply turned around and went back upstairs.

Several seconds later Rose appeared at the top of the stairs. His face, where Creed had struck him the day before, was black and blue and swollen so badly that his right eye was almost closed. He was wearing his riding boots and trousers but no tunic over the top half of his union suit.

Hirsch stood behind him.

As Rose began his descent, relying heavily on the banister and glaring at Goodwin the whole time, Catherine was aghast at the man's injury and felt a twinge of sorrow for him. But the feeling didn't last, because she reminded herself that this was the same man that she had heard screaming and swearing only minutes before.

Hirsch followed him down the stairs.

The colonel stopped quite purposely on the last step and said, "What in the hell are you doing here so early in the goddamned morning, Goodwin?"

"I would remind you, Colonel Rose," said Goodwin, "that there is a lady present."

Rose scanned the room, pretending to search for the "lady present" that Goodwin had mentioned, and when his view fell on Catherine, he glared hard at her and said, "All I see is this Rebel slut standing behind you, Doctor."

Goodwin moved menacingly toward Rose. The colonel stood his ground, but Hirsch stepped around him to place himself between the doctor and his colonel.

Catherine's quick temper intervened. "And all I see is a murdering Yankee bastard whose mother only knew his father in a biblical sense."

Rose wasn't so hungover that he didn't recognize the insult instantly. It was his turn to make a hostile movement. "You Rebel bitch!" he swore as he took the last step past Hirsch and headed toward Catherine. "I'll teach you to soil my mother's good name!" He raised his hand to strike her.

Goodwin was too surprised by Catherine's outburst to do anything but watch.

Hirsch followed his commander, thinking to stop him from doing Catherine any harm. He should have worried more about Rose's safety.

Catherine struck first, her right hand lashing out like the claw of a cornered cat, the palm and fingers catching Rose with a resounding slap on his left cheek. Dissatisfied with the blow, she repeated it before Hirsch could step between them.

"Out of my way, Sergeant!" screamed Rose.

Hirsch refused to budge, blocking the colonel's path to Catherine.

"Yes, Sergeant," said Catherine rather angrily, "out of his way so I can give the bastard more of what he deserves."

"What's this?" growled Rose.

"Hold on, Colonel," said Hirsch. "She's still a woman." He kept Rose in abeyance.

Goodwin was recovered now. He stepped forward, also placing himself between Catherine and Rose, and said, "Miss Ramsdale, remember yourself!"

The doctor's words disarmed Catherine, making her refocus her mind. She was a lady, but she certainly wasn't behaving like one. Of course, this Yankee son of a bitch deserved more than a few slaps on the face; he needed a good horsewhipping and maybe more. But a lady didn't administer such punishment, at least not a Southern lady.

"Yes, of course, Dr. Goodwin," said Catherine, straightening herself as if nothing had happened.

Rose was apoplectic. "You Rebel—!"

"Now, Colonel," warned Hirsch, putting his face directly in front of Rose's view of Catherine.

"Calm yourself, Rose," said Goodwin.

Rose turned his venom on Goodwin once again. "Calm myself? Who do you think you are coming in here and talking to me like this?"

"You know perfectly well who I am," said Goodwin. "Or do I have to remind you, Colonel Rose?"

Rose didn't need any reminding, but he didn't care either. Not at this moment, he didn't. "Do I have to remind you who is in charge here, Doctor?"

"You may be in charge now," said Goodwin, "but not for long. I promise you that, sir."

"Are you threatening me, Goodwin?"

"I warned you a month ago that if you didn't begin doing your duty properly I would be forced to take action. Well, sir, you've done nothing in that time to change my opinion of you. I am here to inform you that if you do not immediately release those men whom you hold captive across the river and do something to bring Colonel Hill's murderers to justice, I shall alert my foster brother posthaste as to your despicable conduct in these recent matters. Do I make myself clear, Colonel?"

"Go right ahead, Goodwin. Tell Sherman anything you want, and I'll go over his head to Grant."

"You do that, Colonel, and we'll just see which of us they

believe." Goodwin turned to Catherine and said, "Come along, Miss Ramsdale. We've done all we can do here."

"This woman isn't going anywhere accept to jail," said Rose.

"Jail?" queried Goodwin.

"Yes, jail," said Rose. "She's under arrest for striking a Union officer."

"If you arrest this young lady," said Goodwin, "I will personally lead a new rebellion, sir. Against you."

"You speak treason, Doctor," said Rose. "I warn you—"

"No, sir!" interjected Goodwin, shaking his finger at Rose. "You do not warn me! I was a loyal Unionist throughout the war, and there is no man in this county right at this very minute who is more loyal to his country than I am, sir. But I will not stand by and allow you to run roughshod over these good people who are my friends and neighbors. I promise you, Colonel Rose, that if you do not restrain yourself and your Negro soldiers from this moment forward, there will be hell to pay."

Rose fell dumb.

Goodwin offered his arm to Catherine. She took it, and they departed.

Hirsch was astounded by what he had just witnessed. A woman had slapped his colonel. An old man had shouted down the same officer. And to boot, the old man was General William Tecumseh Sherman's foster brother. What next? he wondered.

"Sergeant, fetch Captain Spaulding here at once," said Rose quite steadily and soberly.

25

Catherine had only reached the first step to the porch when Captain Spaulding and a squadron of troopers rode up to the front gate of her uncle's house. She turned to see them, then waited as Spaulding dismounted and came inside the yard. The thought that they had come to arrest her for slapping Colonel Rose crossed her mind.

"Good morning again, Miss Ramsdale," said Spaulding, tipping his hat as well. He was smiling. A good sign.

"Captain," she said curtly.

"I bring you good news this time, ma'am. Colonel Rose has ordered your uncle and the other gentlemen to be released from custody immediately."

"That is good news," said Catherine with genuine enthusiasm.

"I thought I'd come by and tell you myself before I ride across the river with the order."

"That was very nice of you, Captain. Thank you for being so thoughtful."

"I didn't want you to fret anymore, Miss Ramsdale."

Catherine smiled politely and said, "Thank you again, Captain. I'll be sure to tell Uncle how thoughtful you were in this matter."

"Yes, ma'am. Thank you, ma'am." Spaulding didn't know what to say next. He didn't wish to leave but felt he should. "Well, I guess I'll be going now." He was hoping to get some sort of invitation to stay or come calling later or something, anything that would indicate that she wanted to see him again.

But nothing. Disappointed, he tipped his hat and left.

Catherine didn't bother to watch the soldiers leave. Instead, she rushed inside and upstairs to tell Creed the news.

"Good," said Creed. "Now we can get out of here."

"Not all of us," said Bill Simons. "You can go, but I've got to stay a few more days, until Dr. January can get the rest of this buckshot out of me."

"Yes, of course," said Creed. "I'd forgotten, Bill. Sorry about that."

"Don't think nothing of it," said Simons. "You and the boys go on. I'll be just fine right here. As soon as I can, I'll be along home."

"No, I won't leave you behind, Bill. I feel responsible for you being here and—"

"You tell him to go on and get out of here, won't you, Miss Catherine?" interjected Simons.

Catherine was caught in a quandary. She knew Simons was right, but she didn't want Creed to leave. What to say? A compromise came to mind.

"Maybe your other friends should go on back to Lavaca County right away," she said, "and you could stay here, Slate. Just to be on the safe side."

Creed had halfway expected her to say something like that.

"She's right, Creed," said Simons. "I'd forgotten about the army being after you. You might be wise to hole up here with me for a while and let the boys go on home without us. That way the army will think you've gone off without them."

"I've thought of that myself," said Creed. "All right. When the boys get back here, I'll tell them to go on home and that we'll be along as soon as Dr. January says you're well enough to ride a horse again."

"Good," said Catherine. "Now you're being sensible."

"But I won't be able to stay in the room I slept in last night," said Creed. "You'll have to find some other place for me to hide until Bill's ready to leave."

"I know the perfect place," said Catherine happily. "Come on, I'll show you." She took his hand and started to pull him toward the door.

"You'd best do what the lady says, Creed," said Simons giddily.

"And you'd best mind your own business," said Creed over his shoulder as Catherine led him away.

She took him down the upstairs hall to a door just outside the doctor's office. She opened it to reveal a landing between two stairways: one that went up to the attic, and another that went down to the kitchen.

"Uncle had this built this way so the servants could come up here without disturbing any guests who might be visiting downstairs," said Catherine. "Leastways, that's what he said. I think he did it so he could sneak out of the house through the kitchen without my late aunt Virginia seeing him."

"Well, a man's home is his castle," said Creed.

"And should every castle have a queen?" queried Catherine.

"At least a princess."

Catherine liked the inference but didn't feel this was the proper time to exploit the sentiment. "The attic is up there," she said. "We can fix a pallet for you, and I'll bring your meals up to you."

Creed frowned and said, "I don't know that I really like the idea of hiding up there. There doesn't appear to be a second way out. Is there an attic window?"

"Yes."

"I still don't like it. I could be trapped there."

"What else would you do, Slate? Give yourself up to those Yankees? Or ride off to Lavaca County with your other friends?"

"I'm not sure," said Creed. "If Colonel Rose is willing to let your uncle and the others out of jail now, maybe he's willing to let me be as well. Captain Spaulding didn't say anything about me, did he?"

"Nothing this last time," said Catherine, "and you know what he said when he was here earlier."

"Yes, I do, but that doesn't mean things haven't changed now. Catherine, I'd rather not hide here if I don't have to. Could you—"

"Catherine? Are you up there?" It was Dr. January.

"It's Uncle," she said. Then she called out, "Yes, Uncle, I'm upstairs."

In a few seconds, January appeared at the other end of the

hall. He stopped abruptly, a look of disbelief on his face. "Creed, you're alive!" he said. "We heard that the niggers had chopped you up into little bitty pieces and threw you to the hogs."

"Not true," said Creed. "They killed Colonel Hill, and they would have done me in, too, but that sergeant who arrested Colonel Hill stopped them."

"Then you saw them lynch Colonel Hill?" queried January.

"Yes, sir. I saw it all."

"Tell me about it, son, then we'll go see Judge White and do what we can to bring those murdering niggers to justice!"

"Uncle, Slate can't leave the house," said Catherine.

January looked quizzically at Catherine, then asked, "Why not?"

"We're not sure about that, Dr. January," said Creed.

"But we think the army is still after Slate," said Catherine.

"Still after him? Didn't they release you like they released us?"

"No, sir. After Colonel Hill was killed last night, I left the jail and came here."

"You mean you just walked away from there?"

"That's about the size of it."

"I don't understand," said January. "Maybe we'd better sit down in my office, and you tell me everything that happened. Catherine, fetch me some coffee and some breakfast. Those damn Yankees didn't give us anything decent to eat or drink the whole time they had us under guard."

Catherine went off to do as she was told, while January and Creed went into the doctor's office. Creed retold the tale of Colonel Hill's murder and of how he came to be at January's house. He was certain to leave out the part about Catherine sleeping with him, although he had no reason to feel guilty about it.

"And you say Captain Spaulding was here this morning looking for you?" queried January.

"That's right," said Creed, "but he came back later to tell Catherine that you and the other men were to be set free. And speaking of the other men, where are my friends?"

"They had to walk back," said January. "Spaulding had the rest of us brought back in a wagon. Politics, you know. We

live here and your friends are just passing through. You know
how it is."

"Yes, I do," said Creed.

"But you say Spaulding didn't say anything about you on
his second visit?"

"That's right. Not a word."

Catherine appeared at the door carrying a wooden serving
tray that had a plate, knife, fork, three cups, and a tin pot
of steaming coffee on it; a napkin covered the plate, which
had bacon and biscuits smothered in gravy on it. She set
the tray down on the desk and began pouring the coffee.

"Slate and I were discussing Captain Spaulding's last visit
when you arrived home, Uncle," she said.

"Yes, sir, that's right," said Creed. "I was about to ask
Catherine to go into town and see if she couldn't find out
what the army's intentions were toward me."

"No need for that now," said January. "I'll go. I'm sure my
friends expect me to join them quite soon to discuss the current
situation in town. I'll find out then what the army has afoot."
He looked up at Catherine and said, "I understand that you
went to Goodwin and he's responsible for getting us released.
Is that true?"

"Yes, Uncle, it is," said Catherine. She uncovered his breakfast and placed the plate before him on the desk. "And there's
more. Did you know that Dr. Goodwin is that Yankee General
Sherman's foster brother?"

"Foster brother?" queried January. "Are you sure of this?"

"Colonel Rose is sure of it," said Catherine. "You should
have seen how he acted when Dr. Goodwin threatened to report
him to General Sherman."

"Well, I'll be," said January. "I always knew Goodwin was a
real Yankee, but I didn't know he was that much of a Yankee."

"I wouldn't judge Dr. Goodwin so harshly, Uncle," said
Catherine. "He was a perfect gentleman, and I think he's as
genuinely upset by all this business as you are."

"I wonder about that, Catherine. Goodwin is still a Yankee,
and that's that."

"But he did get you released," said Creed.

"We would have been released anyway," said January.

"But he got you released this morning," said Catherine.

"Why didn't he do it last night?" asked January. "Maybe if he'd done something then, Ben Hill would still be alive today."

"I don't think he could have helped last night," said Creed. "Those Negro soldiers meant to hang Colonel Hill, and that was all there was to that. No one was going to stop them from avenging that man Blair's murder."

"What murder?" queried January. "Hill shot that nigger in self-defense."

Creed was incredulous. "Self-defense? I was there, Dr. January. Colonel Hill had his gun out long before Blair picked up that pitcher. Hill meant to shoot Blair from the start."

January looked at Creed, then at his niece. "Catherine, I'd like to speak with Creed alone, please."

"Yes, Uncle," said Catherine. "I'll just take this cup of coffee into Mr. Simons, then I'll leave you two alone."

Catherine did as she said she would.

"Creed, you worry me," said January.

"You shouldn't worry about me, Dr. January. I can take care of myself."

"That isn't the kind of worry I meant. I'm concerned about your attitude toward the niggers, and I'm concerned about you and Catherine. But one thing at a time. First, Catherine. I warned you about her."

"Yes, sir, you did," said Creed warily.

"And are you still going to tell me that I have nothing to worry about concerning her?"

"Dr. January, Catherine is everything you said she was."

"Not good enough, Creed. Or should I call you Slate like Catherine does?"

"Creed will do, sir," he said stiffly.

January nodded, then tilted his head and squinted at Creed, trying to size him up. "All right, son. I'll get right to the point. You and she were here alone last night. What happened?"

"What happened?"

"Yes, what happened? Did you sleep with her?"

"If you're asking if I had a physical relation with Catherine," said Creed blandly, "then the answer is no."

"You'd say that even if you had slept with her," said January. "I believe you're that much of a gentleman."

"I thank you for that, sir."

"If you didn't sleep with her, then what did go on here last night?"

"I won't lie to you, sir. I don't recall everything."

"You don't recall everything? Were you drunk, man?"

"Yes, sir, I was, although not purposely. Lavinia gave me a good dose of laudanum for my pain before Catherine came home."

"Lavinia gave you laudanum for your pain? What pain?"

"The pain from my wound."

"The niggers wounded you?" queried January.

"No, sir. Colonel Hill slashed my arm when I tried to stop him from fighting off the lynchmen."

It was January's turn to be incredulous. "You did what?"

"I thought I could reason with them—"

January was astounded as he interrupted Creed. "Reason with niggers? Are you insane, man? They're niggers."

"They're human beings, Dr. January. People—just like you and me."

"Just like you, maybe. But they're nothing like me. No, sir. I have nothing in common with niggers."

Creed stared hard at January, then said, "No, sir, I guess you don't."

January didn't like the sound of that but decided to ignore the remark for the moment. "We've been over all that before, Creed, but it brings up the second point I was going to make and that's your attitude toward the niggers. Some of us discussed it while we were in jail across the river. Even two of your friends, those brothers, the Golihars. They even said they wondered about your feelings for niggers."

"What did my other friends say?" asked Creed.

"They said you were entitled to speak your mind and to feel any way you want to feel and it made no never mind to them. They'd still be your friends because of something you'd done for them up in Lavaca County."

"I see," said Creed.

"But that doesn't change things here, Creed. The way we figure it, you're either with us or against us."

"I told you before," said Creed. "I've got problems of my own with the army. Now I don't think those soldiers had any right to murder Colonel Hill, but he had no right to kill that fellow Blair."

"An eye for an eye?" queried January.

Creed chuckled and said, "You know, Doctor, that's just the way that Negro sergeant put it when he was talking those other men out of hanging me, too."

"And he convinced you he was right, didn't he?"

"No, sir, he didn't. They were a mob, not the law. They had no more right to kill Colonel Hill than Colonel Hill had to kill Blair."

"You said that already, Creed, and I tell you you're wrong. The difference was that Ben Hill was white and Blair was a nigger."

"Dr. January, we've gone over this ground before."

"Yes, we have, haven't we?"

Creed's frustration was beginning to show as he said, "Look, Dr. January, I appreciate what you've done for Bill in there, and I appreciate how your friends helped my friends. But I don't want to get any more involved in your problems with the Yankees than I already have. I want to get out of here . . . with my friends . . . as soon as we can . . . and in one piece. I want to go home where I belong and be left alone. That's all. Nothing more, but nothing less."

January took a deep breath, let it out, then said, "Yes, I guess you do want to go home. I'm sorry, Creed. I went off the deep end there. It's just those damn Yankees . . ." His voice trailed off.

"Yes, sir, I know," said Creed calmly. "I can't say that I'm particularly fond of them either."

"No, I guess you can't," said January with a weary smile. "All right, son. I'll go into town and nose around a bit and find out what they have in mind for you. I will, that is, as soon as I eat my breakfast and after I've looked in on your friend in the other room."

26

Dr. January walked into town, looking for the friends who had been incarcerated with him the night before. The first one he found was John McClanahan, the lawyer. They met on Main Street.

"See any of the others?" asked January.

"A couple," said McClanahan. "Andy Cunningham came by and said he was going over to the *Advocate*. Saw Jim Coffee and Bill Parker headed that way, too. Looks to me like Sam is planning something."

"Maybe we should go on over there," said January.

McClanahan nodded, and the pair strode off in the direction of the newspaper building. When they arrived, neither of them was surprised to see more than a dozen men gathered in the rear of the *Advocate*'s office. They were met at the counter by Judge White. He appeared to be a bit nervous as he greeted them.

"Glad to see you here, January," said White. "You, too, McClanahan." He looked over his shoulder at the group in back. "Quite a few boys here now. Maybe too many." He looked around the office until his view fell on reporter Victor Rose, sitting at his desk making notes on the events of the previous day and night, for a history of the town that he was planning to write. "Vic, pull the shades and put the Out to Lunch sign on the door and lock it. We're getting too many men in here. Just a precaution against the prying eyes of any Yankee-lovers who might be in the neighborhood."

Rose did as White ordered, while the judge, McClanahan, and January retired to the impromptu meeting in the back.

"I'm not going to put up with this any longer," Andy Cunningham was saying.

"Me neither," said Bill Parker.

"Now hold on, boys," said White. "Let's get ourselves organized here first and conduct this meeting like civilized men instead of a mob like that bunch of niggers that murdered Ben Hill last night."

"Sam's right," said McClanahan. "We can't go off half-cocked. We've got to organize and do this right."

"I once read something that John Hancock was supposed to have said on the eve of the American Revolution," said January. "He said, 'We can all hang separately or we can all hang together.' I don't think I have to explain what he meant by that to you boys."

"We're not talking revolution here, January," said White cautiously above the general din of agreement. "We tried that back in '61, and look where it got us."

"I'm not talking revolution either," said January.

"Then what are you talking about?" asked McClanahan.

"I'm talking about putting those niggers in their proper place," said January.

"Those darkies are Yankee soldiers," said White. "If we go against them, we're going against the whole Union army all over again, and you know what I said about that."

"I know most of those niggers who killed Ben Hill were soldiers," said January, "but they weren't all soldiers. Some of them came from Shantytown. It's them I'm talking about putting in their proper places."

"And just how do you propose to do that?" asked McClanahan.

"We ride down on them in the night and burn them out," said January. "Hell, we don't want them down there anyway, do we?"

"No!" was the general reply from the gathering.

"Then let's get rid of them!" said January.

"Yes, let's do it!" said Cunningham, and several others joined in with the same response.

"And just how do you figure we're going to do this?" asked Judge White when things became calmer.

"We get our guns and horses and meet somewhere," said January, "then we ride down there and burn them out."

"Who's going to lead us?" asked White.

"How about you, Judge?" said Parker.

"Not me," said White. "I'm too old to be toting any gun, especially on horseback."

"Then how about you, Doc?" said Cunningham.

"Sure, I'll do it," said January.

"That's all well and good," said White, "but how do you think you're going to assemble this fighting force without the Yankees wondering what's going on and then doing something about it?"

January's brow furrowed with perplexity. "I didn't think about that part yet," said the doctor.

"No, I guess you didn't," said White. "And I guess none of the rest of you did either from the looks of you."

"So what do we do, Judge?" asked Coffee.

"We stop and take a look at things here first," said White.

"How's that?" asked Parker.

"Look around us, boys," said White. "What do you see?" When no one replied, he went on, saying, "I mean Victoria, boys. What do you see around Victoria that isn't normally here?"

"Yankees," said January.

"Exactly," said White. "We've got Yankees here. White ones and black ones. And they've all got guns."

"We've got guns, too," said Cunningham.

"Yes, but there's only so many of us," said White. "We can fight these Yankee bastards, and we can kill every single one of them. But what good will that do? They'll only send more of them down here, and when they do, they'll come looking for blood. Our blood, boys. No, sir. We can't fight the Yankees, and we can't do anything about the darkies in Shantytown either as long as the Yankees are around to protect them."

"Then what do we do, Judge?" asked Coffee. "I don't know about you, but I'm getting real sick and tired of them coming into my store and acting like they're as good as me, and I can't do nothing to put them in their proper place because there's a nigger soldier standing outside just itching for me to do something wrong so he can come in and arrest me and work me over with the butt of his Springfield."

Others agreed.

"I know how you feel," said White. "I know how all of you feel. I don't like it myself, but it's how things are. Right now, that is. But things won't always be this way. Those Yankees won't be here forever."

"But how long do we have to put up with this?" asked Parker.

"As long as it takes," said White.

"So what can we do to make those Yankees leave here sooner?" asked McClanahan.

White pointed his finger at the lawyer, smiled, and said, "Now that's what we should be talking about here, boys. How we're going to rid ourselves of these damn Yankees."

"You can talk all you want about that," said Cunningham. "As for me, I'm still wanting to do something about those niggers down to Shantytown. Judge, you asked Dr. January how he was going to assemble a big fighting force to ride down on them black bucks, and he didn't have no answer. Well, I do."

Every man in the room focused on Cunningham, some, like Parker, Coffee, and January, with excitement and anticipation at the thought of action. Others, like White and McClanahan, men with cooler, wiser heads, worried that Cunningham might have a viable plan that the other fools in town would be willing to follow.

27

Jake Flewellyn, the Reeves brothers, and the Golihars were returned to the Victoria County jail house by the soldiers that had taken them across the Guadalupe River the evening before. Their belongings, what few there were, including the weapons they had been carrying, were returned to them, and Captain Spaulding advised them to find their horses and head north as soon as possible. They ignored him, of course, and walked to the first saloon they saw, which happened to be Scanlan's Gem, to have themselves a draft of lager before going on to Dr. January's to see Bill Simons and hopefully to get their horses.

"Say, aren't you boys from Lavaca County?" asked Scanlan as he set up their beers.

"That's right," said Flewellyn. "What of it?"

"Nothing much," said Scanlan as he set down the last mug, in front of Charlie Golihar. "It's just that there was a fellow in here this morning who was from Lavaca County."

"Is that so?" said Flewellyn.

"Said his name was Hendred or Hinderd or something like that," said Scanlan.

Flewellyn wiped the foam from his upper lip on his shirt-sleeve, glanced at Clark Reeves, then said, "It wasn't Kindred, was it?"

"Yes, that's it," said Scanlan. "Jim Kindred. Said he was on his way home from Mexico. Isn't that where you boys were coming from when you ran into that bunch down to Coleto Creek?"

"Yep," said Flewellyn.

"Then you boys know this Kindred fellow?" asked Scanlan.

"We know him," said Flewellyn.

"Friend of yours?"

"He's about as much of a friend of ours as a polecat is," said Clark Reeves.

"What else did he tell you?" asked Flewellyn.

"Nothing much," said Scanlan. "That he'd been down to Mexico fighting the French and that he'd had enough of that and was heading home now, back to Lavaca County."

"Fighting the French?" queried Crit Golihar. "Ain't that rich? Fighting the French." He chuckled.

So did Charlie Golihar.

"I take it he wasn't fighting the French down there," said Scanlan, looking at Crit now.

"Hell, no, he wasn't fighting no Frenchies," said Crit. "He was fighting with them against the Juáristas and us."

"You boys fought with Mexicans?"

"They're fighting for their freedom," said Clark Reeves.

"Same as we did for the Confederacy," said Kent Reeves.

"Besides," said Jake, "those Frenchies are a bad lot. Leastways, the ones we met were."

"They wasn't all French," said Clark.

"But most of them were," said Kent, "and those were bad."

Scanlan nodded and said, "I see, and you say this Kindred fellow fought with them."

"That's right," said Crit.

"Well, I wouldn't exactly say fought," said Flewellyn. "I'd say it was more like he ran with them. When we helped those Juáristas drive the French out of Matamoras, Kindred rode off with them. I can't say that he fired a single shot for their side, but I do know that he ran with them when they pulled out for Monterrey."

"And now he's come back here," said Crit. "You think maybe the Frenchies threw him out?"

"Most likely," said Flewellyn. "I know he'd be dead if the Juáristas had gotten their hands on him. Double-crossing little snake."

"Say," said Crit, "how long ago was it that he was here?"

"Left about an hour ago," said Scanlan.

"That ain't long," said Crit to Flewellyn. "We can get our horses and catch up to him before he gets back to Lavaca County."

Flewellyn was irritated by Crit's suggestion. Not that he didn't want to catch Kindred and string him up, but because Crit had said it in front of Scanlan.

"No, I think not," said Flewellyn, trying to be casual.

"Why not, Jake?" asked Clark.

"We got to find our horses first," said Flewellyn, "and then we have to look for Creed."

"Oh, yes," said Scanlan. "I'd forgotten about your other friend, who was in the jail with Colonel Hill. Word has it that he he was dragged out by the niggers and chopped up and thrown to the hogs."

"Were there any dead niggers found?" asked Crit.

"No, not that I know of," said Scanlan.

"Then Creed ain't dead," said Crit. "He would've killed a whole bunch of them bucks before they took him."

"With what?" queried Flewellyn. "His bare hands? He was in jail, Crit. He didn't have a gun or a knife."

"That's not what I heard," said Scanlan. "There was a knife in their cell."

"Well, if Creed had a knife," said Flewellyn, "then he took a few of them with him. If they got him, I mean."

"I don't think they did," said Scanlan.

The faces of the five Lavaca men posed the same question, but their tongues never moved to ask it.

"The soldiers are still looking for him," said Scanlan, answering their looks. "They wouldn't be looking for him if they thought he was dead. Especially since it was those nigger soldiers that killed Colonel Hill and everybody knows it."

"Yes, I see what you mean," said Flewellyn.

"Some other folks say your friend Creed escaped from the jail and left town," said Scanlan. "There's a few other rumors, too. Some say the soldiers still have him locked up, and others say he's hiding somewheres here in town."

"Which one do you subscribe to, Mr. Scanlan?" asked Crit.

"I'm not sure about any of them," said Scanlan, "but if I was a gambling man, I'd wager that your friend is back home in Lavaca County by now."

"That's what I think, too," said Crit, "and that's why I think we're wasting our time here, Jake. Let's get our horses and get the hell out of here while we can."

"Crit's right," said Charlie. "Let's get the hell out of here before those soldiers decide to lock us up again and those niggers do to us what they did to Colonel Hill."

Flewellyn didn't care for the way the Golihars were sounding: a little yellow to him. But this wasn't the place or the time to argue with them.

"Take it easy, boys," said Flewellyn. "Let's drink up and go over to Dr. January's and see if our horses are still there. If they ain't there, then we got us a problem that we'll have to take care of before we can go anywhere."

The five of them drank up and left the saloon. On the street, they saw Dr. January crossing at the intersection, hailed him, then met him on the corner.

"Have you boys been up to my office to see your friend yet?" asked January as he cautiously glanced around them to see who might be watching them.

"No, sir, we haven't," said Flewellyn.

"Then you'd better come with me and see him," said January.

"Have you heard anything about Creed?" asked Flewellyn.

"Only the rumors circulating about town," said January, "and that the army is looking for him. Dead or alive."

"Well, I hope he's still alive," said Clark.

"Me, too," said Kent.

January scanned the area again, then said, "I'm sure he's just fine, boys. Come on. We should go to my house immediately."

"Are our horses still there, Dr. January?" asked Crit.

"Yes, I have them in my barn out back. Now come along."

The six of them hurried off toward January's home but not without being seen. Captain Spaulding, at the head of a squadron of cavalry, came riding down the street from headquarters and saw the sextet leave the corner together. He thought this was suspicious and decided to follow them. He caught up with them before they reached the next corner.

"Dr. January, good afternoon, sir," said Spaulding from atop his horse.

January halted, as did the five men from Lavaca County. "Good afternoon, Captain," said January. "Something I can do for you?"

"Not so much you, sir," said Spaulding. "It's these men with you. They've been told to leave this town as soon as possible, and I see that they are still here."

"We're leaving, Captain," said Flewellyn. "Just as soon as we get our horses and see our pard up in Dr. January's hospital."

"Where are your horses?" asked Spaulding.

"They're in my barn," said January. "We're on our way there now just as Mr. Flewellyn has said."

"I see," said Spaulding. "Well, just to be sure you all do as Mr. Flewellyn says you plan to do, I think my men and I will accompany you there."

"Captain, I'm sure that won't be necessary," said January.

"I'm sure it will be," said Spaulding. "Shall we go now?"

"Whatever suits you, Captain," said Flewellyn. "Come on, boys. The sooner we get our horses, the sooner we can shed ourselves of these Yankees."

January heaved a sigh of resignation, then started off toward his house with Flewellyn and the others and with Spaulding and his men trailing behind them.

28

Creed heard the squadron of cavalry approaching on the normally quiet street. He went to the window in Bill Simons's room and saw Spaulding leading the unit toward the house. Then he saw January and the others and wondered what sort of trouble was afoot now.

"That Yankee captain and a troop of cavalry are coming up the street," said Creed, "and Dr. January and the boys are walking in front of them."

Simons rolled onto his good side and reached for his six-gun hanging on the back of the chair beside his bed.

Creed heard the movement, turned, and said, "No need for that now, Bill. There might be nothing to this at all. Spaulding won't do anything to you. It's me he's after, and I'm going up in the attic to hide." Creed made for the door. "You just sit tight right here. I'll be all right."

"Just the same," said Simons as he checked his pistol to make sure it was loaded properly, "I'll keep this where it's handier for now." Sure that the Colt's was in good firing condition, he slid it under the blanket beside him.

"Don't go shooting anyone unless you have to," said Creed. He waved at Simons, then left the room.

Catherine was in the hall when Creed came out of January's office. "Did you see those Yankees coming?" she asked.

"Yes, I did, and I'm going up to the attic until they're gone."

"Uncle is with them."

"Yes, I saw him and my friends." He took her by the arms,

pulled her close to him, and said, "Go downstairs now and act like nothing's wrong. I'll be all right up in the attic."

"Kiss me first," she said.

It was an order. Creed didn't like it, but he had no other choice. There was no time to argue. He kissed her, firmly, with affection.

"Now go do like I told you," said Creed, releasing her.

"Yes, Slate dearest," said Catherine, almost singing his name and the endearment.

Creed went up into the attic, and Catherine went downstairs to greet her uncle. She met him and Creed's five friends in the foyer. Coming up the porch steps behind them was Spaulding.

"Damn him!" muttered January. "Can't he leave us be?"

"I'll take care of Captain Spaulding, Uncle," said Catherine softly. "You take these gentlemen upstairs to see Mr. Simons."

"Where's he at?" whispered January.

"In the highest of places," said Catherine before stepping to the doorway to meet Spaulding. "Why, Captain Spaulding. Fancy seeing you again this day. How many visits is this now? Three? Why, I'm beginning to think you might have some ulterior motive for calling on us so many times in one day."

"Not at all, Miss Ramsdale," said Spaulding, tipping his hat. "It's just army business like before." He looked past her into the house.

"Army business?" She pulled the door closed behind her. "And here I thought you were coming to see me. What sort of army business could bring you back here again?"

"It's those men with your uncle," said Spaulding. "They're outsiders here, and Colonel Rose wants them out of Victoria as soon as possible. I saw them with your uncle and thought it would be best for him if he separated himself from them."

"I see," said Catherine. "Well, I don't think you have to worry about that, Captain. With their other friend having fled the county, I don't think they'll want to stay around here much longer."

"You mean that man Creed?"

"Yes, precisely. With him gone, why would these men stay here? Wasn't Mr. Creed their leader?"

"Yes, I suppose he was," said Spaulding, "but I'm not so sure he's left the county just yet. He could be hiding somewhere with some other Rebel, and God knows that there's plenty of them around this town."

"Yes, Captain, there is," said Catherine a little huffily. "Including me."

"I meant no offense, Miss Ramsdale."

"None taken, sir. I'm proud to be a Texan."

"Yes, ma'am, of course," said Spaulding nervously. "It's those other men. Colonel Rose fears they might stir up more trouble around here. He blames them for what happened yesterday. It's his opinion that they helped to incite Colonel Hill to kill Blair, and of course, the killing of Blair led to Colonel Hill's unfortunate demise last night."

"Please, Captain, I'd rather not discuss that horrible episode, if you don't mind."

"Of course not, Miss Ramsdale. Consider the matter closed."

Catherine stood there waiting. For what, she wasn't sure. Possibly for Spaulding to leave. Maybe for him to say something more.

Spaulding was just as tongue-tied as Catherine. He felt that he'd bungled most of his part of their conversation, and he feared that he would only make matters worse if he continued to speak with her.

"Was there anything else, Captain?" asked Catherine.

"Anything else?" queried Spaulding.

"Yes. Besides seeing Uncle home safely, that is."

Spaulding frowned, then said, "Why, yes, ma'am, there is. Those other men. I intend to see that they leave town immediately."

"I don't think they will be leaving immediately, Captain. I believe they intend to spend some time with their friend, Mr. Simons, who is upstairs in Uncle's hospital room."

"That's fine," said Spaulding. "We'll wait for them."

Frustrated, Catherine said, "As you wish, sir, but if you don't mind, I have duties to attend to. You may wait out here if you like."

"Yes, of course," said Spaulding, tipping his hat again.

Catherine went back into the house.

Spaulding stayed on the porch for a moment, then remembered that he was an officer in the Federal army who had a duty to do. He skipped down the steps and hurried to the gate. Outside the yard, he took the reins of his horse, looked at the animal, and was struck by a sudden thought: horses. Creed's friends said they had left their horses here at Dr. January's, and if they had, then he must have left his here also. Dr. January said their horses were in his barn. Just maybe Creed's was still there, and that would mean Creed was still in town. But if it wasn't there, then Creed was gone and good riddance.

A plan formulated in Spaulding's brain. He mounted up and gave the order to move out. The cavalry squadron rode to the next corner, turned back toward town, then halted.

"Sergeant, keep the men here," said Spaulding. He dismounted and handed the reins of his horse to Shannon. "I'm going to do a little snooping around Dr. January's barn."

An alley for carriages divided the block into east and west halves. Spaulding walked down the lane to the rear of January's lot, where his barn and corral were located. Two horses milled around in the corral; neither of them was Creed's gray Appaloosa. Spaulding opened the back door of the barn, went inside, and immediately saw Nimbus in a pen with five others.

So Creed was still around, thought Spaulding. Although he couldn't see the house, he looked in its direction and thought further that Creed was probably hiding in January's house.

Spaulding's mind was awhirl.

Good! Now I can catch the son of a bitch and—

No wait! Miss Ramsdale is in the house, too, and she's probably hiding Creed at her uncle's orders. If I arrest Creed, I'll have to arrest her, too. I can't do that. That would ruin everything. No, I've got to capture Creed some other way. Or do I have to capture him? Maybe he could be dealt with another way. Yes, of course.

A smile spread over Spaulding's face as the solution to his problem came to him. He left the barn and ran back to his horse. Mounting up, he said, "We must hurry, Sergeant. I have to see Colonel Rose at once."

29

"Miss Catherine! Miss Catherine!"

Damn! thought Catherine, annoyed that Lavinia was calling her. She didn't want to be bothered, because she was listening at the door to her uncle's office, trying to overhear the conversation within.

Dr. January had led the Lavaca men upstairs to his office, then had called Creed down from the attic to join them once Captain Spaulding and his cavalry had left the front of the house. After they had greeted each other, Creed began telling his friends about the events of the previous eve and that morning.

"Miss Catherine!" Lavinia was at the bottom of the stairs now. "Miss Catherine!"

Damn! She would have to go or risk being discovered by her uncle, and that would never do. She turned and scurried down the hall to meet Lavinia.

"Oh, there y'all is, Miss Catherine," said Lavinia.

"What is it, Lavinia?" asked Catherine, quite exasperated.

"Miss Catherine, that Captain Spaulding was snooping around the barn out back," said Lavinia.

"Captain Spaulding out back?" queried Catherine. "Are you sure about that, Lavinia?"

"Yes'm. I saw him with my own eyes from the kitchen window. He poked around the corral, then went to the back of the barn and had himself a look inside."

And saw Slate's horse, thought Catherine. "Then what did he do, Lavinia?"

"He just left. Went back where he come from, I guess."

"Are you sure?"

"Yes'm."

"Thank you, Lavinia. Now go back downstairs and keep watch for the soldiers to return."

"Is there gonna be shooting, Miss Catherine?"

"I don't know, Lavinia. I hope not. Now go on."

As Lavinia traipsed down the stairs, Catherine hurried back to her uncle's office and knocked on the door twice before entering.

"What is it, Catherine?" asked January, irritated by the interruption.

"That Yankee captain was snooping around out back," she said. "Lavinia saw him nosing around the corral and the barn."

"The barn?" queried January.

"Yes, sir."

The men looked at each other with the same question on their minds: Why?

"Do you think he knows your horse, Creed?" asked January.

"I don't know," said Creed. "I can't recall meeting up with him while I was riding Nimbus, but that's not to say he didn't see Nimbus somewhere in town and ask around about who he belonged to."

"Yes, that stallion is about the only Appaloosa around here," said January. "He'd be hard to miss."

"Lavinia said he went back where he'd come from," said Catherine, "and I'd guess that would be—"

"Thank you, Catherine," said January, cutting her short. "This is men's business, girl. You run along now and keep an eye out for those Yankees."

Flustered, Catherine said, "But, Uncle—"

"Now go on, girl," said January sternly.

She left the room.

"So what do you think?" asked January. "Do you think Spaulding suspects anything?"

"Of course he does," said Creed. "Him poking around the barn says he thinks I'm here, and if he knows my horse, he knows I'm here."

"So what do you plan to do?" asked January.

"Well, if we stay here," said Creed, "the Yankees are bound to catch on sooner or later, and when they do, there's sure to be trouble. The problem is I can't exactly go riding out of here in broad daylight."

"But that don't mean we can't," said Crit Golihar.

"That's right, Crit," said Creed. "You boys should ride out of here as soon as you can and as fast as you can. I thought the Yankees we had up in Lavaca County were a bad lot, but they're pussycats compared to this bunch down here. Markham might be a sly son of a bitch as far as I'm concerned, but he's been decent as far as everybody else goes."

"Kindred was in town, Creed," said Flewellyn.

"Kindred?"

"That's right," said Flewellyn. "This morning. Barkeep at the saloon said he stopped in there, then rode out right away."

"Was he sure it was Kindred?" asked Creed.

Flewellyn nodded.

"Who's this Kindred you're talking about?" asked January.

"The son of a bitch who led the rustlers who killed my brother," said Creed.

"And who double-crossed us down in Mexico," said Crit.

"That's right," said Charlie.

"I take it you've got an axe to grind with this fellow," said January.

"More like a rope to swing around his neck," said Creed. "Him and a couple of others back home."

"We thought we'd head out after him," said Crit, "and catch up with him before he gets back home. Of course, that was before we knew you were safe up here."

"Not a bad idea, Crit," said Creed. "Like I said, you boys should get out of Victoria right away."

"But what about you?" asked Flewellyn. "Suppose those Yankees come back here looking for you. How are you going to hold them off by yourself?"

"Don't worry about me," said Creed. "I don't think they'll find me here. Dr. January will see to that."

"That's right," said January. "He's plenty safe here."

"What about Bill?" asked Flewellyn. "How's he going to get home?"

"Don't worry about us," said Creed. "We'll be all right here.

You boys get on out of here and catch up to Kindred if you can. Jake, if you catch Kindred, don't kill him. Just take him to Somer's Thicket and hold him there until I can come back and hang him myself. I know I said I was going to let it go as far as he was concerned, but that was in Mexico before he turned traitor on us. Now we're back in Texas, and I intend to hang the son of a bitch as soon as I can get my hands on him."

"Don't worry, Creed," said Flewellyn. "We'll catch him and hold him for you. You just make sure these Yankees here don't get hold of you."

"I'll be all right," said Creed. "Now you boys go on."

"Yes, you should go," said January. "Creed will be safe here until tonight, and he can slip out of town then."

"I don't think that's such a good idea," said Creed.

"Don't worry about it, Creed," said January. "Trust me. You'll be able to get away tonight."

Creed wasn't so sure he liked the idea of leaving town just yet, and he suspected that something evil was in the air. Until he knew for certain what that might be, he would play along with January.

"All right, if you say so, Doc," said Creed.

"Is there anything you want me to tell Miss Texada?" asked Flewellyn.

"Yes, there is," said Creed, "but I'd better put it in a letter. You might feel a little funny saying my words to her."

"I know what you mean," said Flewellyn.

January let Creed use his desk, pen, and paper. He wrote the missive as quickly as he could, while Flewellyn and the others said farewell to Simons.

Creed gave the letter to Flewellyn and said, "You boys be careful now."

"Don't worry about us," said Flewellyn. "You just get out of here as fast as you can."

"You'd best be on your way," said January.

"You heard the man, boys," said Creed. "Now git!"

They left, and Creed watched them ride off, wishing he was going with them.

30

Captain Spaulding was quite excited when he entered Colonel Rose's office. His enthusiasm waned instantly once he saw his commander's condition. As best as Spaulding could tell, with Rose's face as swollen as it was, the colonel's eyes were glassy, indicating an inebriated state.

"What is it, Spaulding?" asked Rose, slurring his words slightly.

Good, thought Spaulding, he's not too drunk yet. "Colonel, it's the escaped prisoner, Slate Creed. I think I've located him."

"You *think* you've located him?"

"Yes, sir."

"You don't know for certain, Spaulding?"

Spaulding stammered, "Well, no, sir, not for certain, but I'm fairly sure he's——"

"I don't want to hear fairly sure!" snapped Rose. "I want to hear certainties, Captain. Have you located him or not?"

Damn! thought Spaulding. He's hardly drunk at all. "Well, sir, I've located Creed's horse."

"And you arrested the animal, didn't you?" said Rose snidely.

The son of a bitch is making fun of me, thought the captain. Damn him! "No, sir, I didn't arrest the horse," said Spaulding calmly.

"Well, good for you, Captain. At least you did one thing right."

"Yes, sir."

The colonel poured himself a glass of brandy, then said; "So where did you find Creed's horse?"

"In Dr. January's barn."

Rose perked up. "In January's barn?"

"Yes, sir."

Rose smiled deviously and said, "You don't say? Well, this is a curious turn of events." He eyed his brandy. "Yes, indeed. A very curious turn of events." Then, looking up at Spaulding, he said, "But you don't know whether Creed is in the house. Is that it, Captain?"

"Yes, sir. I went into the house this morning and went up to see Creed's friend who's in January's hospital room, but there was no sign of Creed. Miss Ramsdale—"

Rose lurched forward at the mention of Catherine's surname and interrupted Spaulding. "Ramsdale? January's niece?"

"Why, yes, sir."

"That four-eyed bitch! She's just like the rest of them. She needs putting in her place the same as that goddamned uncle of hers."

Spaulding didn't like this sort of talk, especially from a drunk like Rose. However, he knew better than to protest too much. "Sir, Miss Ramsdale is a lady."

"A lady my ass!" raged Rose. "That bitch slapped me this morning and cast aspersions on my mother's good name. A lady wouldn't use such language, Captain." Then it struck him. He squinted hard at Spaulding. "You aren't taken with this woman, are you, Captain?"

Feeling bold, Spaulding said, "As a matter of fact, sir, I have entertained thoughts of courting the lady."

"Well, you can just forget that, Spaulding. You'd be better off diddling with a waterfront whore down on Bridge Street."

"I'm sorry, sir, but I wholly disagree."

Rose concentrated his view on Spaulding's face and said, "Yes, I suppose you would. But never mind her. What about this Creed? You don't think he's in the house, do you?"

"No, sir."

"And you base that belief on the Ramsdale woman's say-so. Is that right?"

"Yes, sir, and the fact that I looked in the house myself."

"That's not worth more than a pile of horse shit, Spaulding. You couldn't find your ass if it wasn't trailing behind you all the time."

"There's no need to be abusive, Colonel."

"You make me sick, Spaulding. All you New Yorkers make me sick. But that's not what's important here. It's that god-damned Rebel who hit me yesterday. Creed. I want him found. If he's in January's house, then drag him out and get him back in my jail, where he belongs."

"I'd like nothing better than that, Colonel, but I don't think it would be wise for our men to go barging into Dr. January's house looking for Creed."

"And why not?"

"Dr. January isn't there alone. Creed's friends are with him. There's liable to be some bloodshed, sir."

"So what? They're only Rebels, Spaulding, and if some of our boys get hurt, so what? They didn't enlist to be pampered. They're supposed to be soldiers."

"Colonel, if we force our way into Dr. January's house," said Spaulding, "some innocent people might get hurt."

"Yes, of course, Miss Ramsdale. That would be who you're referring to as being innocent, wouldn't it, Captain?"

"Not just Miss Ramsdale, sir. Dr. January has a Negro house servant living there. If anything should happen to her, there could be real trouble. I mean since she's a Negro and all."

Rose screwed up his face as he considered the implications of Spaulding's statement. Realizing the captain was right, he said, "All right, Spaulding, what would you have us do instead?"

Spaulding had had a plan when he entered the room, but now he wasn't so sure about it, considering how Rose felt about Miss Ramsdale and Dr. January. He twitched nervously and said, "Well, sir, I think we should place men about the neighborhood and keep an eye on the house. Sooner or later, Creed will come back for his horse."

"Or he'll come out of the house," said Rose.

"I don't think he's in the house, sir."

"Yes, yes, we've been over that ground already, Captain." He paused and studied Spaulding for a moment before saying, "All right, Spaulding, we'll do it your way for now. Post your men in January's neighborhood, and we'll see what we'll see."

Spaulding smiled and said, "Yes, sir." He saluted and left the room.

"Yes," said Rose, pouring himself another glass of brandy, "we'll see what we'll see." Then he laughed evilly.

31

Even in the twilight, the men Spaulding had posted in Dr. January's neighborhood to watch for Creed were quite visible from the windows of January's house. January was perturbed by their presence; Catherine was delighted; and Creed had mixed feelings.

January had hoped to see Creed out of his house that night, because he knew that as long as Creed remained in Victoria Andy Cunningham's plan to teach the Freedmen of Shantytown a lesson in good manners would have to be delayed.

Catherine was happy to have Creed staying in her uncle's house for one more night at least. It would afford her another opportunity to claim him as her own, and hopefully, he would begin to love her as she loved him.

As for Creed, he told himself that he was glad to be able to stay with Bill Simons another night because he felt Simons's life might be in jeopardy, considering the state of affairs in Victoria. That was on the one hand. On the other, he wanted to get home to Texada as soon as he could, because he knew he couldn't trust himself with Catherine. Beyond that, he didn't care. Not now, he didn't anyway. Christmas was only a few weeks away, and he did want to be home for the holiday this year.

But first things first. For now, he was stuck in Victoria, and he was the centerpiece of events.

No one was more aware of this fact than Dr. January. Creed had been there when Ben Hill murdered Blair. Creed had been there when Sam White confronted Colonel Rose about Hill's

safety in the county jail house. Creed had been there when Hill
was lynched. Creed had been the only man who had witnessed
all three episodes, and this would have been a plus for January
and the others of his ilk except that Creed wasn't an integral
part of their anti-Negro clique.

On the other side, Colonel Rose wanted Creed gone for two
reasons: Creed had struck him and Creed was the only eye-
witness to all that had happened that fateful day and night.
This fact worried Rose because of the distinct possibility that
if Dr. Goodwin carried out his threat to report him to General
Sherman, the colonel would be brought up on charges. The
exact charges would be up to Sherman or some other ranking
officer, but they would be charges all the same, and Rose knew
he wouldn't be able to withstand any investigation that might
include Creed as a witness against him.

As for Captain Spaulding, he was beginning to see Creed as
a stumbling block in his path to Catherine's heart. He wasn't
exactly sure about how Creed fit into Catherine's life, but he
knew he didn't like Creed for being so close to her.

Dr. Goodwin was the single most disturbed man in Victoria
that night. He had seen the mutilated body of a neighbor, Ben
Hill, hanging from the balcony rail of the county jail house.
He had seen the drunken misuse of power by Colonel Rose.
He had seen that day terror in the faces of the good people of
his town as they feared that they might be the next victims of
the mob that had murdered Ben Hill, and it had brought tears
to his eyes. He had seen hate and anger in his own soul, and
although these emotions were usually quite foreign to him, they
dealt a mighty blow to his heart. He knew that he alone had the
power to act, the power to initiate change; and that afternoon,
he had set the wheels of change into motion.

No one else knew about Goodwin's move. He confided in
no one, and he felt all the more alone.

Creed stationed himself in January's attic, guns ready in
case Spaulding and his men should decide that waiting wasn't
enough. While he kept a watchful eye on the street below, he
recounted the last few days and wondered how he had let himself get into this fix. More than that he wondered how he would
get out of it, especially now that Spaulding was obviously aware
of his presence in January's house, and this led him to think of

Texada, waiting for him back in Hallettsville. He passed into a pleasant reverie that manifested itself in him as a hunger for her touch, for the sound of her voice, for the warmth and the feel of her body against him.

The moment dissolved to black with the creak of the attic door and the soft padding of Catherine's feet coming up the stairs. Creed smelled food. She was bringing him his supper.

Creed sat on a chest next to the window, which was covered with an old blanket to keep the light from shining through. He held the plate in one hand and the fork in the other.

"I'm glad you're having to stay another night," said Catherine, "although I wish you didn't have to stay up here in this dusty attic."

"It's not so bad," said Creed between bites. "At least it's warm and dry."

"Yes, I suppose you have slept in worse places. In the war, I mean."

Creed nodded and chewed.

Catherine casually scanned the room and said, "It seems awfully lonely up here. I mean, it seems that you might prefer some company this evening instead of being up here all alone."

Creed knew what she was getting at. The thought of lying with her was enticing, but his conscience conjured up Texada's image to dispel the thought.

"Catherine, your uncle said something about he was certain that I could get away from here tonight. He said it like he was positive it would happen because something else was in the works. Have you got any idea what he did today in town?"

"Only thing I know is he met with some of the other men to figure out what they should do now."

"Do you know what they decided?" asked Creed.

"No, I don't. Uncle doesn't confide those things in me."

"I sure wish I knew what they might be up to. Something tells me that whatever it is will only lead to more trouble." He washed down the last bits of food with a drink of cider, then said, "Your uncle isn't telling me anything either, Catherine, but I'd sure like to know what they're up to. Do you think you could find out for me?"

"How would I do that?"

"I don't know," said Creed. "Just keep your ears open, I guess, and maybe ask a question or two without raising his suspicions that I put you up to it. I really need to know, Catherine. Two men are already dead because matters are out of control here in Victoria, and I don't want to be the third, and I don't want anyone else to die on my account."

"Yes, of course, I'll do it, Slate," she said. "I'll go down right now and see what I can find out for you, but I'll be back later. I promise."

Catherine took the dishes and went down to the kitchen by way of the hidden staircase.

"Miss Catherine, Dr. January has got that Mr. Cunningham in the drawing room," said Lavinia.

"Mr. Cunningham? Andrew Cunningham?"

"Yes'm."

"How long has he been here?" asked Catherine.

"Only a minute or so. They just now went in there."

Catherine hurried through the dining room to the parlor, where she saw that the drawing room door was closed. She stepped lightly up to it and put her ear close to the crack.

"We'll have to hold off for now," January was saying. "Creed is still here."

"Still here?" said Cunningham. "What difference does that make? He's not part of my plan."

"That's not the point, Andy. He's here and so are all those soldiers you must have seen on your way over here."

"So what?"

"So they're too close to things," said January.

"But I've already sent a rider out," said Cunningham.

"Then send another to stop him or there will be hell to pay, I tell you."

Odd, thought Catherine, but that was the same expression that Dr. Goodwin had used with Colonel Rose.

"But we won't be involved," said Cunningham.

"We can't take that risk, Andy. Now go. And get another rider to stop them immediately. Go yourself, if you have to, but stop them tonight."

Catherine heard the movement of feet and decided it would be best for her not to be seen lurking outside the drawing room door. She passed out of the parlor just as January and

Cunningham emerged from the drawing room. She stopped, turned around, and came back as if she was just then entering the room.

"Good evening, Mr. Cunningham," she said lightly. "Lavinia said you were here."

"Good evening, Miss Ramsdale," said Cunningham, giving her a stiff half bow.

"Shame on you, Uncle," said Catherine, "for keeping our guest all to yourself."

"We had business to discuss," said January, smiling nervously. "You wouldn't have been interested."

"Well, maybe not," said Catherine, "but it's always nice to see Mr. Cunningham."

"Thank you, Miss Ramsdale," said Cunningham. "It's always a pleasure to see you, too."

"We're through with our discussion," said January, "and Andy has to be going."

"Nonsense," said Catherine. "You mustn't hurry off, Mr. Cunningham. Please sit down, and I'll have Lavinia bring us some refreshment."

"Thank you, but no," said Cunningham. "I really must be off, Miss Ramsdale."

Catherine heaved a forced sigh, then said, "Well, if you must, then you must. But it certainly was nice to see you again, Mr. Cunningham."

"Yes, ma'am." He bowed again, donned his plug hat, and headed for the door.

"I'll see you out," said January, following his guest. At the door, January peeked over his shoulder to make certain Catherine was out of earshot, then softly said, "Don't waste any time, Andy. Stop those men tonight."

"I'll do my best," said Cunningham. And with that, he was gone.

32

Dr. January was exhausted from the excitement of the past few days. He retired early that night.

As soon as she heard her uncle's first snore, Catherine tiptoed up the attic stairs to see Creed.

"You were right," she said. "Uncle and some other men are up to something."

"Did you find out what?" asked Creed.

"No, not exactly. Andrew Cunningham was in the drawing room with Uncle when I went downstairs earlier."

"Cunningham? The man who was arrested with us the other day?"

"Yes, that's the one."

Creed nodded and said, "Go on."

"Well, I listened at the door, and I heard Uncle tell him that he'd have to send a rider to stop the first rider he'd sent."

"That who sent? Your uncle?"

"No, Mr. Cunningham. He sent a rider somewhere—"

"Did they say where?" asked Creed, interrupting.

"No, just somewhere. He said he'd better stop him or there would be hell to pay."

Creed stood up and paced the room. "I knew they were up to something. The fools! Don't they know the war is over and we lost?"

"Uncle said they couldn't do anything until you were gone. He seemed to be worried about all the soldiers around here."

"So am I," said Creed. "I can't figure why they haven't come

184

to search the house. If Spaulding saw my horse, he must know that I'm in here."

"What makes you think that?" asked Catherine.

"If he wasn't sure that I'm in here, he would have at least come to the house and asked about my horse."

"Yes, I see," said Catherine. "He must know you're here."

"Yes, but why hasn't he come in here searching for me?"

"It might be because of me," said Catherine.

"You?"

"Yes, me." She paused intentionally, hoping to arouse a little jealousy in Creed. "Captain Spaulding has asked to call on me."

Quite calmly, Creed said, "And he might not wish to spoil his chances of courting you by doing something overt like searching the house. Yes, that must be it." He stopped pacing. "Well, maybe I'm meant to remain here for a while. Your uncle and his friends won't act as long as the soldiers are around here, and the soldiers aren't going to leave until I do. A stalemate, but at least it'll keep the peace around here for the time being."

Catherine moved closer to him and said, "Does this mean you'll be staying longer than you'd planned?"

"It means I'm not leaving here until those soldiers leave," said Creed.

"I'm glad," said Catherine. "I hope they never leave."

Creed looked at her sideways and said evenly, "Catherine, I can't stay here forever."

"I know, but you're here now." She moved closer to him. "And I love you, Slate, and that's all that matters to me."

The air was heavy with her scent. It attacked his senses, exciting them to a feverish pitch. He reached out and held her arms, thinking he could reason with her about their relationship; but the touch only served to weaken him all the more.

"Catherine, I—"

Her hand went to his lips, interrupting him. "No, don't tell me what I don't want to hear," she said. She lowered her hand and whispered, "Just kiss me, Slate."

His passion was now in full control of his good sense. He pulled her to him and kissed her.

Catherine responded by throwing her arms around his neck and pressing her hardening breasts against him.

Creed's loins were aflame. He clasped her waist and ground himself against her. His lips parted, and his tongue darted forward, coaxing her mouth to open, then searching out her tongue. His knees wobbled. He pulled her down on the pallet with him.

"Oh, yes, Slate!" she whispered breathlessly as their lips separated and his mouth sought her throat.

His hand felt for her breasts, found one, and caressed it with gentle fingers. "Catherine, I want you," he whispered in her ear.

"Yes, my love, and I want you."

They kissed again, deeper, longer. Their hands explored their bodies, discovering new joy with each touch.

"We shouldn't . . . do this," said Catherine.

"No, we shouldn't," said Creed.

Neither of them really believed the other.

"I want you, Slate. I love you."

"Yes, but I shouldn't do this," he said hoarsely, not hearing himself say anything. "There's another . . . back home."

"Yes, I know," said Catherine. "I don't care. I'm here with you . . . now, and I want you to love me. Love me now, Slate! Love me!"

Creed heard her, took a deep breath, and started to comply with her wish.

"Yes, Slate, love me. I know I can't have your heart. I don't care. Just give me your seed. I want your child."

Catherine couldn't have poured a colder bucket of water on Creed at that very moment. He jerked to attention, propped himself up on one elbow, and looked down at her, not knowing exactly what to say.

"Don't stop," she said, still in the throes of passion, her eyes closed. When he didn't resume their lovemaking, she opened her eyes and saw the concern in his face. "What's wrong, Slate dearest?"

"Do you know what you just said?" asked Creed.

"Yes, I do. I said that I want your child. What's wrong with that?"

Creed shook his head and said, "You don't want my child, Catherine. Not out of wedlock. Don't you know what that would mean?"

"Yes, but I don't care. I told you, if I can't have your heart, then I'll take what I can get. I love you, Slate. I want your child . . . to love . . . because it will be our child. Yours and mine."

"And it will be your hold on me," said Creed. "Isn't that it, Catherine? You think I'll love you if you have my child."

"No, Slate, I don't think that at all," she said sincerely.

"Maybe you don't know it, but that's what's in your head, Catherine. A child is how a woman holds on to any decent man."

"No, Slate dearest, I swear that isn't what I'm thinking. I love you, but I know you love another. Like I said, if I can't have your heart, then let me have your child."

Creed said nothing. He was too intent upon studying her face as he looked for the truth.

"Oh, please, Slate," she said desperately. "I love you. I know I can't have you. I know that. So please let me have your child."

"No, Catherine," he said slowly. He saw tears welling up in her eyes. "It isn't because I wouldn't be proud to be the father of our child. It's just that I know what it would do to your life. To the baby's life, too. It wouldn't be right for either one of you. As for me, I won't be around, Catherine."

"It's that girl back in Hallettsville, isn't it?"

"No, it's not. A minute ago I was all set to take you, and I would have enjoyed every second of it, Catherine. Not just for the act itself, but because I was doing it with you. Because I do have feelings for you, Catherine. I can't deny that. I don't know that they're the same feelings I have for Texada, but—"

"Texada? Is that her name?"

"Yes, it is," said Creed softly, almost with reverence. "We can't do this, Catherine. It wouldn't be right. Not for you. Not for me. Not for any child we might have. Not for . . ." He let his voice trail off.

"Not for Texada?" prompted Catherine.

"No, and not for Texada either. Catherine, I've known her most of my life, and I love her like no other woman that I've ever known."

"I see," said Catherine.

Creed rolled away from her. "Catherine, I do want you to understand. It isn't you. It's me. Even if I hadn't given Texada my heart, I couldn't give it to you. Not because I wouldn't want to, but because I'm not . . . in a position to make a commitment like that. Not now."

"But you gave your heart to Texada? I don't understand."

"I fell in love with Texada before my troubles began," said Creed.

"Your troubles?"

"Yes, troubles. Catherine, Creed isn't my real name. But that isn't important. I was accused and convicted of a crime I didn't commit, and I've taken this name until the day I can clear my real name. Until then, I'm Slate Creed. A man without a home. A man who can't make the sort of commitment you're asking me to make, Catherine."

"I don't care about all that," said Catherine. "I just want your child." She reached for him.

Creed stood up and said, "No, Catherine, I can't do it."

Pleading shaded her eyes, but only for a moment. It was replaced by hurt, then anger.

Creed bent down to help her to her feet.

"No, thank you, sir!" she snapped. "I'm quite capable of standing on my own." She stood up, straightened her clothes, then said, "I'll be going now." And she left.

Damn! thought Creed. The things I get myself into!

33

Creed was surprised that Lavinia brought him his breakfast the next morning. He wasn't surprised to see Spaulding's men still at their posts.

Dr. January came up to the attic after breakfast and informed Creed that he planned to operate on Bill Simons that morning. "If all goes well," said January, "he should be up and ready to leave here tomorrow."

"Tomorrow?" queried Creed. "That soon?"

"Yes. The pellets that are left in his side aren't as deep as the ones I pulled out of his leg. Since I won't have to probe so far, he won't bleed as much and should come through it all pretty well. Mr. Simons is a fast healer."

"Well, I know he'll be glad to be up and out of here."

"And you won't?" queried January.

"Of course, I'll be glad, too," said Creed hesitantly.

January perused Creed's face, then said, "What went on up here last night?"

Creed was too embarrassed to reply.

"Did Catherine come up here?"

He couldn't lie, and it was too late to evade the question. "Yes, sir, she did," said Creed.

January was disturbed but not angry. He was too old and too wise in the ways of life not to understand. "And you deflowered her, didn't you?"

"No, sir, I didn't," said Creed firmly.

January had expected the words but not the way they were delivered. "You didn't?"

189

"No, sir, I didn't."

The doctor studied Creed for a second, then said, "I find it hard to believe that a healthy young man such as yourself didn't take advantage of a vulnerable girl like Catherine. Are you, uh, funny or something, son?"

"It isn't that I didn't want to . . . lay with her, sir," said Creed. "It's just . . . well, I have a girl back in Hallettsville, that's all."

"And you're being faithful to her, is that it?"

Well, that's part of it, thought Creed, but he said, "Yes, sir, that's it."

"All right, I believe you. I'm not sure that I don't think you're crazy, but I believe you left Catherine alone. I respect you for it, too. I guess." He turned to leave, then over his shoulder, he said, "You might want to see your friend before I go to digging into his side. Don't worry about being seen by those bluebellies out there. I've got the shades pulled over all the windows in my office."

Creed went downstairs with January and visited with Simons while the doctor and Catherine prepared for the minor surgery. Once they were ready he went back up to the attic to wait. He had only been up there for a few minutes when he looked outside and saw Spaulding riding up the street at the front of a whole company of cavalry.

Damn! thought Creed. Spaulding must have tired of waiting and is coming in after me now.

He continued to watch, and much to his surprise, Spaulding was the only man to dismount when the soldiers halted in front of the house.

Now what? wondered Creed.

He heard Spaulding ring the doorbell, then heard Lavinia answer it. He wished he could hear what they were saying, but whatever it was didn't take long because Spaulding was soon back on his horse and leading his men away. That was a relief to see.

Creed went down the hidden stairs to the kitchen. He cracked the door and saw Lavinia talking with another Negro woman.

"Who was that?" asked Cleo.

"That Yankee captain," said Lavinia. "Come by to tell Miss

Catherine he's going away for a few days."

"Going where?" asked Cleo.

"He say he's going over to Clinton on some sort of army business and I's to tell Miss Catherine that he won't be calling for a while."

"Clinton? What's going on over there?"

"Captain Spaulding didn't say. Just say he's going over there."

"Well, makes no never mind to me. Fact is, all them white soldiers can leave and I wouldn't care none."

"How's about them colored soldier boys?" asked Lavinia. "Y'all wouldn't want them to leave now, would y'all?"

"Course not," said Cleo. "Ain't enough men around here without them boys. Course, I wants them to stay. What about you, Lavinia? You wants them to go?"

"Not me, girl. They's all so dashing in them blue uniforms. I wants them all to stay."

The two women giggled and continued chattering about the soldiers and how good this one looked or that one.

Creed had heard the only important part of their conversation, so he went back upstairs to the doctor's office to wait for January to finish operating on Simons.

When the surgeon and his assistant emerged from the sickroom, Catherine ignored Creed's presence and went straight downstairs.

"I thought I believed you before about her," said January, "but now I am one hundred percent positive that you had no relations with Catherine last night. That was a scorned woman that just walked out of here. Yes, sir, a scorned woman. I warned you about her, Creed. She can be quite vindictive, you know."

"You've said that before," said Creed, "but I still have trouble thinking she could be that way."

"Well, take my word for it. Catherine is not a woman to be trifled with. You've evidently crossed her, and I don't think she's taking it too lightly. Be aware, my young sir. She intends to punish you."

"I don't think she has that in mind at all," said Creed, "but I'll be on my guard just the same."

"Wise man. Now, about Mr. Simons. I believe I got every single pellet out of his side, and his leg is healing nicely. If no infection shows up by this time tomorrow, the two of you can ride out of here tomorrow night. Providing, of course, that the Yankees let you pass peaceably."

"Speaking of Yankees," said Creed, "Spaulding was here while you were operating on Bill."

"I thought I heard the doorbell, but how do you know it was him?"

"I overheard Lavinia telling another girl about it. He came by to tell Catherine that he was going over to Clinton on some army business and wouldn't be calling on her for a few days."

"Clinton? What's going on over there?"

"Lavinia didn't say."

"Hm! I think I'd better get into town and find out what's going on around here. You stay up in the attic, Creed. This could be a ruse of some sort to get you out of here."

"Yes, I thought of that already. Don't worry about me. I'm not going anywhere until I can take Bill with me and those Yankees that are still posted in this neighborhood are gone."

"Whatever," said January. "Just stay up there until I get back." He took his coat and hat down from the hat tree and left.

Creed started to go back to the attic but met Catherine in the hall. She ignored him, walking on to the office door.

"He's gone," said Creed.

"Who's gone?" asked Catherine.

"Your uncle. He went into town."

"Thank you for telling me," she said coldly. Then she turned and walked past him again.

Creed reached out and grabbed her arm. "Catherine, you shouldn't be hurt by last night."

She wrenched herself free and said, "I wouldn't worry too much about me, Mr. Creed."

"Oh, so that's how it is. Mr. Creed again. All right, Catherine. Have it your way. I still have very strong feelings for you, but you go ahead and act like this if you want. I know I did you no wrong last night."

"Are you finished, Mr. Creed?"

"For now."

Without another word, Catherine turned and went downstairs.

Creed shook his head in bewilderment. His grandfather had always told him that women were hard to figure. Well, he wasn't wrong.

34

When she reached the foyer, Catherine went to the closet for a wrap and hat, donned them, then left the house afoot. She marched directly to the Levi mansion, where she was met by Sergeant Hirsch at the gate.

"Not again, Miss Ramsdale," said Hirsch heavily.

"Yes, again," said Catherine as she stormed into the yard. "I wish to see Colonel Rose immediately, Sergeant."

Hirsch followed her up the walk, then scurried past her to open the door for her. They went inside, and Hirsch said, "I'll see if he's receiving anyone, Miss Ramsdale." He moved off toward Rose's office, not realizing that Catherine was right behind him every step of the way. He knocked on the door, then waited for an answer.

Catherine didn't. She turned the knob and walked right in.

Rose was seated behind his desk. The usual glass of brandy was within easy reach. It was nearly empty.

"What's the meaning of this?" snapped Rose, rising automatically because a woman had entered the room. Then he recognized Catherine, sat down, and said, "Not you again."

"Yes, Colonel, it is I," said Catherine.

"Haven't you abused me enough, Miss Ramsdale?"

"I didn't come here to abuse you, Colonel Rose," said Catherine, seating herself in the chair opposite him.

"Then what demands are you going to make of me now?"

"I've come here to help you, Colonel."

"Help me?" queried Rose. He laughed and said, "You? A

Rebel? Help me? I can hardly wait to find out how, Miss Ramsdale."

"Yes, Colonel," said Catherine. "I can understand your disbelief, but I assure you, sir, that I mean to help you."

"How?"

"The man you're searching for? Slate Creed? He's hiding in my uncle's house."

"We've already surmised that, Miss Ramsdale," said Rose haughtily as if he'd made that deduction instead of Spaulding. "His horse is in your uncle's barn."

"Then why haven't you come for him?" asked Catherine.

"Because we think we'd have to lay siege to Dr. January's house in order to get him out," said Rose, "and if that didn't work, we'd have to storm the place, which wouldn't do because you or Dr. January might be hurt in the process and there could be considerable property damage. Since we don't have funds to pay for such things, storming the house is out of the question. Creed will come out sooner or later, and then we'll grab him."

"I would like him out sooner," said Catherine.

"You would like him out?"

"Yes, I want Creed out of our house."

"That's all well and good, Miss Ramsdale, but I need to know about your uncle. How does he feel about Creed? Obviously, he's there with your uncle's approval."

"Yes, he is, but Uncle would also feel much better if Creed were gone."

"I see," said Rose. "So what do you propose I should do about Creed, Miss Ramsdale?"

"Remove your soldiers from our neighborhood, and he will leave this very night. He will take the Hallettsville Road, and you can capture him there."

Rose studied her for a moment, then said, "Why are you taking this attitude, Miss Ramsdale?"

"What do you mean, sir?" she asked defensively.

"Only yesterday you were in this house being quite belligerent with me, and now you come barging in here and willingly give up one of the men you sought to protect yesterday. Why?"

"Slate Creed means nothing to me," said Catherine. Her

words rang hollow. "He's interfering with our household, and he's endangering all of us as well. I wish for him to be gone from us. There's been nothing but trouble in Victoria since he and his friends arrived here last week."

"But his friends have left, Miss Ramsdale."

"Yes, thank goodness."

"Then what you're telling me is that you're doing this for the good of the community. Is that it, Miss Ramsdale?"

"More or less, Colonel."

"I see," said Rose. "All right, Miss Ramsdale, I'll remove the men I've posted in your neighborhood, and I'll have a squadron of cavalry waiting for Creed on the Hallettsville Road tonight. You just go home now and act as if you had never been here."

"Very well, Colonel. Good day, sir." She stood, turned, and left the room and the house.

As soon as she was gone, Hirsch asked, "Colonel, how are you going to send a squadron of cavalry out to the Hallettsville Road tonight when Captain Spaulding has all of them on the march to Clinton?"

"You let me worry about that, Sergeant," said Rose, not looking Hirsch in the eye. "In the meantime, have those men removed from Dr. January's neighborhood, and send a message down to the fairgrounds to Colonel Barry. I want him and his officers to join me across the river for a march to Clinton in support of Captain Spaulding."

"Just Colonel Barry and his officers, sir?" queried Hirsch.

"That's right," said Rose as he picked up a pen and paper and began to write the order for Barry.

"But, sir, that won't leave any troops here except Colonel Barry's Michigan regiment."

"Yes, I know," said Rose without looking up.

"But, sir, those are the colored troops."

Rose glared at Hirsch and said, "Sergeant, I gave you an order, and I don't expect you to question it. Now carry out that order or I'll have you placed under arrest for insubordination."

"Yes, sir," said Hirsch reluctantly. He saluted, spun on a heel, and left the room.

As he walked away, Hirsch tried to add up the facts as he knew them in order to make some sort of sense out them.

Rose was pulling all of the white soldiers out of Victoria and was leaving the Negro units but without their white officers. He had promised Miss Ramsdale to have a cavalry squadron on the Hallettsville Road that night in order to catch Creed, but all the cavalry had gone to Clinton with Captain Spaulding.

Why was he doing this? Hirsch wondered. It didn't make sense. Unless, of course . . .

35

Word about the movement of the white soldiers from Victoria spread around town like a prairie fire in a high wind. To say it caused excitement among Victorians was an understatement. As soon as the leaders of the community heard, a town meeting was called at the courthouse.

"Rose has left us at the mercy of the niggers!" shouted Dr. January, coming straight to the point of the conference.

Andy Cunningham stood up and said, "We don't need those goddamned Yankees to protect us!" He brandished a Colt's over his head. "I've got five balls in here, and that means five dead niggers!"

Silas Newcombe, who had served under January in Company A of the 13th Texas Cavalry, stood up and announced, "I've got two barrels of buckshot for any nigger that comes near my place!"

"Wait a minute!" shouted Dr. Goodwin. "We can't start shooting people just because they aren't white."

"Sit down, Goodwin!" said January.

"Yeah, sit down, you Yankee-lover!" added Cunningham.

"Judge White, are you conducting this meeting?" asked Goodwin. "Or are we going to be a mob like that bunch that murdered poor Ben Hill?"

The judge banged his gavel to get everybody's attention. "Dr. Goodwin is right," said White. "We are supposed to be civilized white men, so let's conduct ourselves accordingly, gentlemen." When no one objected, he said, "Go ahead, Dr. Goodwin, and have your say. And from this point on, don't anybody else speak up until you're recognized by the chair, and that means me. Now go ahead, Dr. Goodwin."

"Gentlemen, the argument about the Union versus the Confederacy has seen its day," said Goodwin. "I would prefer to let it rest in peace and concentrate on the present situation, which is our mutual condition here in our fair city of Victoria. I chose to become a Texan and reside in this town fifteen years ago, and when I took up residence here, I also took on the responsibility of being a good friend and a good neighbor to all about me. Every man should accept this responsibility, in my opinion. When I came here, I tried to set aside my opinions on national politics and concentrate my efforts on our local situation, whatever that may be."

"Get on with it, Goodwin," said January.

White banged his gavel again, then pointed it at January and said, "Dr. January, if you persist with these interruptions, I will have you removed from this meeting." It was a hollow threat, but it was still enough of a chastising to quiet January. "Go on, Dr. Goodwin."

"As I was about to say," said Goodwin, "I feel my duty lies within this city of ours, to each and every one of my friends and neighbors. I have felt from the beginning of the Federal occupation of Victoria that the cause of our troubles here isn't the Negroes. Nay, it is Colonel Isaac Rose that troubles us so much. The man has set himself above the law, as witnessed by the episode of two days ago when he defied Judge White's orders to release the prisoners and to provide adequate protection for Ben Hill. Before that, he misused his powers as provost marshal and closed down Moses Schwartz's store, then took Schwartz's stock for his personal use without compensating him. From my travels to the most distant points of our county, I have learned that the commanding officers in neighboring counties are not anywhere as high-handed as our Colonel Rose. This evil man, I believe, gave his Negro soldiers free rein when he ordered all his white soldiers who were guarding the jail to take all their prisoners except Ben Hill and that other man, Mr. Creed, across the river, thereby removing the only opposition to the Negroes. And now he deserts his post, taking all the white soldiers with him, leaving us at the mercy of his Negro soldiers and the Freedmen of Shantytown. It is my opinion, gentlemen, that we need to rid ourselves of this man as soon as possible, and to that end, I have taken steps.

"Yesterday, after demanding that Colonel Rose release our friends and neighbors that he had incarcerated the day before and upon seeing this demand met, I took the train to Indianola and sent a telegram to my foster brother, General William Tecumseh Sherman, of whom I am certain you are all acquainted, and I apprised him of our circumstance here in Victoria and asked him to relieve us of this evil man at once."

This last started the entire room to buzzing. Judge White banged his gavel to restore order.

"I remained in Indianola until I received my foster brother's reply," said Goodwin, continuing. He reached inside his coat, removed a piece of paper, then held it up for all to see. "Here is his reply, gentlemen." He lowered the telegram and began reading: "'I had no idea of conditions in your town. My apologies. I am ordering Colonel Markham in Hallettsville to be sent to relieve Colonel Rose immediately until a permanent replacement for him can be posted in Victoria.'" Goodwin folded the message and replaced it in his pocket. "There's more, but it's of a personal nature."

Again, the room resounded with murmuring, and Judge White had to silence the throng with his gavel.

"There you have it, gentlemen," said Goodwin. "As soon as Colonel Markham arrives from Hallettsville, our problems should be over." He sat down.

"How do we know this Colonel Markham will be any better than Rose?" demanded Cunningham.

"That's not the problem yet, Andy," said January. "Before we can worry about what sort of Yankee this Markham is, we've got other catfish to fry."

"What do you mean, January?" asked White.

"I mean, what do we do until this Colonel Markham arrives from Hallettsville?" said January. "Until he gets here, we are still at the mercy of the niggers, gentlemen."

The elder statesman of Victoria stood and asked to be recognized. White rapped his wooden hammer on the bench and said, "The chair recognizes the Honorable John Linn."

John Linn was among the first Anglo settlers of Victoria County, arriving in 1830 from New Orleans. He had served the town as its last alcalde under Mexican rule and as its first mayor under the Republic. He had served on the city council on several occasions and had always been a civic leader. He was a hero of the Revolution and Victoria's delegate to the Republic's constitutional convention. Although now a sexagenarian, he was still a man of great stature, and when he spoke, all about him listened with dignified respect.

"Gentlemen, I have heard of the plan to enlist the rabble at Coleto Creek in an adventure against the unfortunate people who reside in Shantytown, and frankly, I am appalled that such a dastardly plot could have been devised by any member of this community." He was looking squarely at Andy Cunningham, who averted his eyes. "Now I hear talk among my friends and neighbors of arming themselves and commencing open warfare against the Negro soldiers. How foolish can we be, gentlemen? From what I have seen and heard, those black men would show us about as much mercy as Santa Anna showed Travis and Bowie at the Alamo. And should we win, then what? We would have the rest of Yankeedom—white and black—come riding down upon us, all quite ready to put Victoria to the sword.

"That is on the one hand, gentlemen. On the other, we must protect ourselves from the rabble element among the Negroes of Shantytown and within the ranks of the Federal army. There is no doubt in my mind that they would do us harm if they thought for one second that they would not suffer any retribution for it. Therefore, I say we should arm ourselves, but for defensive purposes only. And when we do so, we should notify some authority somewhere, such as this Colonel Markham in Hallettsville, of our situation and how we plan to deal with it, meaning that we will not stand idly by while our homes and property are being destroyed.

"I recommend that we send a messenger immediately to this Colonel Markham and ask him to hasten to our relief, while at the same time we patrol our streets against the rabble element."

"Here! Here!" shouted January and a chorus of others as Linn sat down.

White banged his gavel to restore order, then said, "First things first. We need a volunteer to ride to Hallettsville immediately. Who's it going to be?"

Several men jumped up and offered their services. White chose Andy Cunningham.

"You go on now, Andy," said White. "Just remember that we're all counting on you."

Cunningham said, "Don't worry about me, Judge. I'll be back tomorrow with or without that Yankee colonel." And with that, he left the courthouse and was soon on his way to Hallettsville.

"Now let's get organized around here," said White.

January stood up and said, "You forgot one thing with Andy, Judge."

"What's that?" asked White.

"He's the only man in town who's dealt with that bunch down to Coleto Creek," said January. "Now that Andy's gone, who's going to ride down there and stop those boys from raiding Shantytown tonight?"

36

Before leaving Victoria with the white soldiers, Colonel Rose met with Sergeant Jones at the 3rd Michigan's camp on the fairgrounds. He told Jones in front of several other soldiers that he was taking the Pennsylvania regiment to Clinton in support of Captain Spaulding, who had taken the 18th New York Cavalry there to quiet some disturbance. The colonel said that he expected Jones to keep his men under control the whole time he was absent.

As an apparent afterthought, Rose said, "By the way, we received a report that the Rebel Creed is hiding in the neighborhood of Dr. January's house on Liberty Street. He might even be in January's house. You might see if there's any truth in that, Sergeant."

"Yes, sir," said Jones.

"Now, Sergeant, a word in private." Rose took Jones aside and said, "That Ramsdale woman, Dr. January's niece, she came by headquarters and told me Creed is hiding in January's house. The bitch struck me yesterday when she came to headquarters with Dr. Goodwin. It wouldn't upset me any if she should meet with an accident of some sort while you and your boys are trying to capture Creed. She's a Rebel just like her uncle and all the others around here, Jones, and they need to be taught another lesson. Do you understand, Jones?"

"Yes, sir," said Jones grimly.

"Oh, and one more thing," said Rose. "If you boys should want to have a little . . . fun with the Ramsdale woman before she has her accident, well, that's all right, too." He laughed out

loud. "Hell, I wouldn't mind having a little of that fun myself."
He laughed again. "Nope, I wouldn't mind at all." He turned
serious again. "It wouldn't bother me at all if Creed, January,
and the Ramsdale woman all met with accidents. Do you know
what I mean, Jones?"

"Yes, sir, I believes I does."

"Good! Now you boys do your duty, you hear, Jones?"

"Yes, sir," said Jones. He saluted his commander, then
watched the white soldiers and officers depart. As soon as
they were gone, Jones was surrounded by his fellow soldiers,
all of them with the same question on their lips: When were
they going after Creed?

Marcus Jones was no fool, and he wasn't stupid. He knew
that the 3rd Michigan was all that stood between Shantytown
and Diamond Hill, between black and white, between life and
death. Rumors had been rampant throughout the camp that the
white folks of Victoria were up to something. Exactly what, no
one was sure; that was the nature of rumors. Nonetheless, he
knew that Victoria was akin to a big kettle filled to the brim
and set over a growing fire. It would be just a matter of time
before it boiled over and burned somebody.

Instead of answering the soldiers' question, Jones told them
to leave him be until he could figure out how to go about catching Creed. He sat by himself and gave the situation plenty of
thought. In his mind, Creed wasn't like the others; he'd treated
Jones with respect, the same respect that one white man usually
reserved for another white man. No, better than that. Creed
had given him the respect one man should give another no
matter what his color might be, and Jones felt a friendship for
Creed for it.

Even so, Jones knew he had to do something about Creed.
Colonel Rose wanted Creed captured, and although he didn't
say so outright, Rose had intimated that it would be fine with
him if Creed met with the same end as Colonel Hill. Making
this harder for Jones was the fact that his friends also wanted
Creed dead. They saw him as a sliver in their big toe; they
wouldn't be happy until he was removed permanently. Some
of them had suggested to Jones that they march into town and
storm Dr. January's house. This wouldn't do, because as soon
as a large force went into town, the white folks would be up

in arms to oppose them, and at their head would be January; bloodshed, lots of it, would be the result, and what would that accomplish?

If he could have had it his way without anyone complaining or second-guessing him, Jones would have kept his men in camp until the white soldiers and officers returned. That would have been the easiest way to avoid trouble. But he wasn't going to get his way; that much he knew for sure. Therefore, he had to do something, especially after it was reported that the white folks were holding a meeting in the courthouse and that one of them had left there and rode out of town, heading north, lickety-split, on the Hallettsville Road.

"I wants ten volunteers," said Jones after he called the men together again.

"Ten?"

"Only ten?"

"That's right," said Jones. "Only ten."

"How come, Marcus?"

"We's going into town and see if Colonel Rose is right about Creed being in Dr. January's house."

"But only ten men going?"

"That's right. Only ten."

"How come, Marcus?"

"Because that's all it's gonna take," said Jones. "Lookey here, y'all. If too many of us go into town, the white folks is gonna be ready to fight, and we can't be having that. If all I takes with me is a squad, then they ain't gonna be nervous and start nothing. We just go up to Dr. January's house and see if Creed is there or not."

"And what if he is?"

"Then we arrests him like the colonel say," said Jones. "Now who's going with me?"

More than enough men volunteered. He picked his squad of ten and marched them into town. He made only one mistake. He failed to leave anyone in charge with specific orders about what the others should do. All he said was for everyone to sit tight until he came back.

The town meeting broke up at about this same time, and the men who had been in attendance scattered to their homes and businesses. Some went to arm themselves and prepare to do their part in protecting the streets of Victoria that night, while others—particularly those of the so-called upper gentry, the planters—gathered their families and a few possessions and made hasty retreats to their ranches and plantations or to other towns, where they thought they would be safer.

Jones noted much of this activity as he led his men to Dr. January's house, and it worried him. These were people preparing for war, he thought. He was very concerned about the way the women appeared to be frightened at the sight of his squad and how the men seemed to hurry a little faster when they saw him and his soldiers coming. The closer they came to January's house, the more he thought they were marching into a hurricane.

37

Through the attic window, Creed saw January turn the corner and hurry toward the house, while farther down the street he spotted Jones and his ten picked men marching in formation, shouldering their Springfields with bayonets in place. He wondered if they were coming for him or January, both or neither. No matter. He had both of his revolvers ready for action. There was no way he would permit them to take him or January.

Creed stood at the top of the stairs and waited for January to enter the house. He heard the door open and close, then January called out.

"Catherine, the niggers are coming down the street! Get my shotgun! Creed? Are you up there, Creed?"

"Right here, Doctor," said Creed calmly.

"The niggers are coming down the street," said January. He stood at the bottom of the stairs. "I suspect they're coming for you. You going to let them take you?"

"How do you know they aren't coming for you, Doctor?" asked Creed.

Catherine appeared beside her uncle and said, "They're coming for you, Mr. Creed."

"How do you know?" asked January.

"So that's where you went," said Creed. "To see Rose."

"That's right," said Catherine, "I did."

"You did what?" asked January.

"She went to Rose and told him I was here," said Creed.

"You didn't, did you, Catherine?" asked January.

"Yes, Uncle, it's true. I told Colonel Rose he was here."

207

January threw up his arms in exasperation and said, "That does it. They're coming for both of us, Creed."

The sound of footsteps, heavy and thudding, could be heard on the front porch.

"My God, they're here!" said January. "Catherine, where's my shotgun?"

"You won't need it," said Creed as he came down the steps.

Lavinia came into the foyer. There was a knock at the door. She went to answer it.

"Wait, Lavinia," said January. "Creed, you stay up there for now."

Creed halted three-quarters of the way down.

"I'll answer the door," said Catherine. "Uncle, your guns are in the closet beneath the stairs."

There was another knock. Catherine went to answer it. She opened the door a few inches and peered out.

"Afternoon, ma'am," said Jones. When Catherine didn't reply, he said, "Is Dr. January at home, ma'am?"

January stepped up behind Catherine and pulled the door wide open. He held his Colt's at his side. "What is it, boy?" he asked with all the venom he could muster.

"Sir, I am Sergeant Marcus Jones of the 3rd Michigan Infantry. Am I addressing Dr. James January?"

"That's me, boy."

"Colonel Rose sends his compliments, sir," said Jones.

"To hell with Rose, boy. What is it you want here?"

"Dr. January, Colonel Rose said I should come by and ask you if a certain Mr. Creed is hiding in your house."

"Captain Spaulding has been by here several times in the past few days," said January, "and he's asked us the same thing and the answer is always the same. Creed isn't here."

Jones looked at Catherine, his eyes accusing her.

January raised his revolver at Jones and said, "Lower your eyes, boy, when you're looking at a white lady."

Jones looked January straight in the eye and said, "It's my understanding, Dr. January, that your niece, Miss Ramsdale, visited Colonel Rose this morning and told him that Mr. Creed is hiding here."

January cocked his pistol and said, "Did you hear what I said, boy?"

Creed didn't want another killing on his account. He leaped down the last few steps, guns in hand, came up behind January and Catherine, and said, "Put it down, Doctor." To emphasize his point, he pulled back on the hammers of both of his revolvers.

January heard the clicks, flinched, blanched, then did as he was told. "What the hell are you doing, Creed?" he asked over his shoulder.

"Just trying to stop you from starting a new war, Doctor," said Creed.

Jones looked past January and Catherine to Creed and said, "Mr. Creed, I'd like to speak to you, sir." He glanced over his shoulder at his squad of men waiting at the front gate, still in formation, still at attention, with their eyes aimed down the street instead of at him and the house. "In private, sir."

"You ain't coming into my house, boy," said January.

"Stand aside, Doctor," said Creed, "and let that man come inside." When January didn't move or say anything, Creed said, "Dr. January, you know I won't shoot you unless it's the only way to save another life, so I appeal to your good sense of morality, sir. I think Sergeant Jones wants to avoid trouble here as much as I do. And you do. Isn't that right, Sergeant?"

"Yes, sir, it is," said Jones eagerly.

"I don't give a damn," said January. "He's a nigger, and I won't permit him inside my house."

Lavinia stepped forward and said angrily, "I's a nigger, too, Dr. January. Y'all wants me to leave?"

January was totally unprepared for this. "You're, uh, different, Lavinia," he said.

"No, I ain't," she said. "I was your slave before the war, and I only stayed on because I ain't got nowhere else to go to and no one there for me if I does leave here."

"But, Lavinia," said Catherine, "you can't go. You're part of this household."

"That's right, Lavinia," said January. "Why, you're almost, uh, like a . . ."

"Almost like a member of the family?" offered Creed. "Is that what you intended to say, Dr. January?"

"Well, no, not quite."

"Then what?" asked Creed. "Like a good horse, maybe? Or how about a piece of furniture? Maybe a good dog?"

"No!" said Catherine, looking at Lavinia with compassion and genuine feeling. "No, like a member of our family. Lavinia, we practically grew up together, and although I never thought of it before, we've been friends all these years. At least that. Friends. Maybe even like sisters."

"Catherine!" snapped January. "What are you saying?"

"I know exactly what I'm saying, Uncle."

"Listen, folks," said Creed, "I don't mean to interfere with a family debate here, but—"

"Why not?" asked January. "You're the one that started it."

"It seems to me, Dr. January," said Creed, "that we're in a tight situation here that can only be resolved by letting Sergeant Jones come into the house."

"Uncle, you should allow Sergeant Jones to come inside," said Catherine.

January looked at her with total disbelief. He stammered, "My own niece. I can't believe it. This . . . this *Negro* is the one who led that mob that lynched Ben Hill, and you say I should let him into my house? I'd sooner be dead."

Jones took a step closer and said in a perfectly conspiratorial tone, "Dr. January, I don't want to take Mr. Creed prisoner. I don't want no trouble with anyone, sir."

"Then why are you here?" asked January.

"Because Colonel Rose told the whole camp Mr. Creed was here," said Jones, "and if I didn't do something about it, every man in the regiment would have marched up here and burned your house down around you, Dr. January, and then they'd set fire to the rest of the town until someone stopped them. I know those men, sir. They would have done it."

"So you came instead," said January.

"Yes, sir."

"To prevent bloodshed?"

"Yes, sir, that's right," said Jones. "At least that's what I hope I'm doing here."

"What else is on your mind, Sergeant?" asked Creed.

"It's all the rumors, sir," said Jones. "The men in camp and all the folks in Shantytown is plenty worried, sir, that there's going to be trouble tonight."

"We're worried about the same thing," said January.

"Well, sir, I don't want no trouble with the white folks," said Jones. "I've had my fill of killing. I want to stop the trouble before it starts. If you folks are planning on doing something to the folks in Shantytown, I hope I can do something or say something that will make you stop it. I got the feeling Mr. Creed wants the same thing."

"You're right about that," said Creed. "I've had my fill of killing, too. I don't want to do it, but I will if I'm forced into it. What about it, Doctor? Is there a plan afoot to harm those people in Shantytown?"

January looked at the floor and said nothing.

"Uncle, Slate knows about your meeting with Andy Cunningham," said Catherine. "I told him."

"That's right," said Creed.

"We tried to stop it," said January softly, "by sending Andy to Hallettsville to fetch Colonel Markham down here as soon as possible to replace Rose."

"What's this?" asked Creed.

January quickly explained everything that had transpired at the town meeting, including the part about Cunningham's plan and ending his remarks with, "Because we were uncertain whether Parker could find that bunch from Coleto Creek in time to stop them from raiding Shantytown, we decided we'd better get to our homes and arm ourselves against the, uh, Negroes."

"Sergeant," said Creed, "I think you'd better take your men back to your camp and prepare to defend Shantytown against those men from Coleto Creek."

"Then what, Mr. Creed?" asked Jones. "What do I do after we stop those men? How do I tell my men that the white folks here in town had nothing to do with it and that we shouldn't come into town looking to kill every one of them we can find? How do I stop them from doing that, Mr. Creed?"

Creed couldn't answer him.

38

When he rode out of town to look for the Coleto Creek gang, Bill Parker had no idea who they were individually. He figured he'd find a bunch of ragged men who looked mean and ornery and that would be them, and once he found them he'd tell them that their services were no longer needed and that they could go back to doing what they did before, which was robbing just about anyone who came near them. It was a simple enough task. Or it was until Parker started thinking that he might wind up as a victim of their felonious pursuit if he met up with them. Then he remembered from his school books how that Greek messenger was killed way back when. Maybe the job wasn't so simple after all. Parker decided against finding the gang and rode back to town late that afternoon.

Victoria was all astir when Parker returned with the bad news that he hadn't been able to locate the creek bottom bandits and give them the message that they shouldn't raid Shantytown that night. "I didn't see any sign of them," said Parker. "I must have rode up and down the Coleto for a couple of miles on either side of the road, and I couldn't find hide nor hair of them. They must have left already and come around to town by a different route."

Among his listeners were Creed, Dr. January, Judge White, and John McClanahan.

"Are you sure about this, Bill?" asked the judge.

"Yes, sir, I am."

"Seems mighty strange that they'd pick some sort of circuitous route to come to town," said McClanahan.

"Well, that's what they must have done," said Parker.

"There's only one place below here where they could cross the river," said January, "and that's at Kemper's Bluff. I can't imagine those boys using White's Ferry to cross the river when there's a perfectly good bridge right here at Victoria."

"Yes, but the army guards the bridge day and night," said McClanahan. "I'd think they'd be a bit reluctant to try and cross the bridge."

"The army isn't guarding it now," said Creed.

"But they don't know that," said January.

"Then they must have crossed at Kemper's Bluff," said White, "and that means they'd be coming up the Indianola Road and that leads right through Shantytown."

"How far away is Kemper's Bluff?" asked Creed.

"Twelve miles or so," said January.

"How far is it from where the Refugio Road crosses Coleto Creek to Kemper's Bluff?" asked Creed.

"About the same distance," said January. "Why?"

"Well, it's about seven miles to Coleto Creek from here," said Creed. "I can't see those men riding twelve miles to Kemper's Bluff, then twelve miles back here when all they have to do is ride seven miles to get here. Especially when they're planning to ride through Shantytown and get out of here as fast as they can. They can't do that on spent horses. I think they're still coming by way of the bridge."

"So what if they are?" asked Parker. "I'm not riding down there to stop them. I got a family to look after, and that's what I'm going to do right now." He mounted up again and rode away.

"Someone should go down to the bridge and stop them," said Judge White.

"Let them come," said January. "Jones and the other niggers will be waiting for them."

"You still don't get it, do you, Dr. January?" said Creed. "Jones knows as well as I do that as soon as those soldiers get stirred up with a fight, they're likely to come this way looking for more blood."

"We can handle them," said January. "There's a lot of men here who wore the gray."

"But they're not an army," said Creed, "and the 3rd Michigan is."

"Creed's right," said McClanahan. "We're not prepared to
take on the army, January."

"But they're just niggers," said January.

"No, sir, they're not," said Creed angrily. "They're soldiers,
and if Jones is a sample of what kind of soldiers they are, then
I'd say I wouldn't want to go into battle against them unless
I had a force of equal size and armament."

"You're just yellow, Creed," said January.

The warrior in Creed showed in his face. "Dr. January, I have
a great deal of respect for you as a physician," said Creed, "and
I also respect your age. Those are the only two reasons I'm
holding back right now from knocking you down and stomping
you in the ground, sir."

January put his hand on the butt of the revolver sticking out
of his trousers.

"That'll be enough out of both of you," said White. "Let's
try and remember what we're doing here. I'm surprised at you,
January, carrying on this way."

January looked a bit sheepishly at White and said, "Aw, it's
just that I can't abide a nigger-lover."

"Well, you'd better get used to the idea," said Creed, "because they're free now and soon they'll have all the rights of
white men. You can bet on that."

"Not if I have anything to say about it," said January.

"Will you two stop?" said White.

"I'll tell you what, Judge," said Creed. "I've had my fill
of this town, and I'd like nothing better than to shed it for
all time. But I can't ride out of here knowing that fools like
January are willing to risk starting the war all over again when
a little common sense can keep everybody out of harm's way.
So I'm going to ride down to that bridge myself and wait for
those bandits to come my way. If any one of you has the balls
to join me, you're more than welcome. But even if you don't,
I'm going."

"You go right ahead," said January. "Just try and stop them
by yourself and see what you get for it."

Creed glared at January one last time, then mounted Nimbus
and rode off toward the bridge.

39

Jones called his men into formation as soon as he returned to camp. Someone asked him where Creed was, and when he explained, many of them grumbled and wanted to go into town and get him. Jones ordered them to stay in formation, and they reluctantly obeyed him.

"We gots us a real problem here, men," said Jones as he addressed the troops. "Some of the white folks in town don't like how our people is living down to Shantytown. They wants them out of there and back on the plantations picking cotton like always before."

"That ain't right, Marcus."

"I knows it, and y'all knows it," said Jones, "but the white folks ain't got used to the idea that we's free now, that we ain't breaking our backs for them no more lessen they pays us a good wage, just like they pays white folks who works for them."

"Amen, brother!"

"But that ain't the whole problem here," said Jones. "Like I was saying, some of the white folks wants to git rid of Shantytown, so they's gone and hired them some bandits down to Coleto Creek to come and raid Shantytown tonight."

"We ain't gonna let it happen, is we, Marcus?"

"No, we isn't," said Jones. "We's going to march down to Shantytown and protect those folks. Now everybody fall in, and let's get going down there now."

Jones formed up the troops and started them marching toward Shantytown. The sun was nearly down when they arrived.

"What's going on here, Marcus?" asked Gilmore. "What y'all doing here with all them soldiers?"

"We's here to protect y'all," said Jones.

"You mean it's true that the white folks is coming to burn us out?"

"Not the white folks in town," said Jones. "Some bandits from down to Coleto Creek."

"Same thing," said Gilmore. "They's white, ain't they?"

"Far as I knows, they is," said Jones.

"Then it's the same thing," said Gilmore. "What y'all gonna do here?"

"I'm posting guards all around," said Jones. "We'll be waiting for them when they comes."

"Why don't y'all go into town and stop them there?" asked Gilmore. "Git them before they gits us."

"We can't be starting no fight with the townfolks," said Jones. "We's the army. It wouldn't be right."

"But they's peckerwoods, Marcus," said Gilmore.

"Not all of them," said Jones. "Some of them is decent folks, and it's my duty to protect them as well as y'all."

"Y'all protecting white trash?" queried Pembroke. "I ain't believing that. Not after what we done to that peckerwood Hill."

"I told you then, Cassius," said Jones. "That was one of them for one of us. An eye for an eye, like the Good Book say. We don't go around killing white folks just 'cause they is white. We start doing that, and that makes us as bad as they is."

"Still don't seem right," said Pembroke. "Y'all shouldn't be worrying none about the white folks. They can takes care of themselves."

"Never mind that, Cassius," said Gilmore. "Come on. Let's us go say hello to Rafe."

The two of them found Rafe Moon at his post on the road that led to the Guadalupe River Bridge.

"What y'all doing here?" asked Moon when the pair of Freedmen joined him.

"Come to see how y'all is doing, Rafe," said Gilmore. "Just being friendly is all."

"Thought y'all might be cold and thirsty," said Pembroke. He produced a small jug of whiskey from beneath his coat.

With a broad smile, he said, "Like Pompey said, we's just being friendly is all." He pulled the cork from the jug.

"Well, y'all shouldn't be here," said Moon as he watched Pembroke take the first drink. "There's bandits coming tonight, and there's gonna be shooting. Y'all might get hurt or something."

"We ain't worried none," said Gilmore. "From the way Marcus is telling it, no one gonna get hurt tonight excepting those bandits." He took the whiskey from Pembroke.

"That's right, Rafe," said Pembroke. "Marcus say y'all is gonna take them by surprise when they comes riding in. Gonna shoot down every one of them peckerwoods."

"We gonna do our best," said Moon.

"What if they don't come, Rafe?" asked Gilmore. He offered the jug to Moon. "Then what? Y'all just gonna pack up and go back to your camp or something?"

"Don't know," said Moon, taking the liquor from Gilmore. "Maybe. I guess." He chugged down a few burning gulps. It felt good inside him.

"And them peckerwoods is gonna be let off free, ain't they?" said Pembroke. He took the jug from Moon and drank again.

"Don't seem right to me," said Gilmore. "They's white folks planning to do us bad, and they's gonna get off free just 'cause they is white. Don't seem right to me."

"Me neither," said Pembroke, passing the whiskey to Gilmore.

"What y'all talking about?" asked Moon

"We's talking about not gitting any sleep tonight 'cause we's feared them peckerwoods is coming to burn us out," said Gilmore. "Now that ain't right that we should be feared like that. Ain't it so, Cassius?" He took a hard pull on the whiskey, then wiped his mouth on his sleeve.

"Sure is, Pompey," said Pembroke. "White folks is always gitting the best, and we's never gitting what's ours by right. Only way we's gonna git what's ours is to take it."

"That's right," said Gilmore. "We gots to take it when we can, Rafe." He passed the jug to Moon.

"Now what y'all talking about?" asked Moon. He drank again and felt even better.

"This land," said Gilmore. "This is our land. We earned

it. Y'all earned it, too. We earned it by breaking our backs under the lash, and y'all earned it by fighting in the army. It's ours, and now them peckerwoods is trying to take it back from us."

"Yeah, and Marcus is letting them do it, too," said Pembroke. "He say he's protecting the white folks as well as us black folks. That ain't right. He's black like us, and he should be protecting us and to hell with the white folks."

"He shouldn't just be protecting us from the white folks," said Gilmore. "He should be leading the soldiers against the white folks in town and take back what's ours."

"Yeah, that's right," said Pembroke. "Don't y'all agree, Rafe?"

"Don't know," said Moon, feeling quite loose now.

"Course, y'all do," said Gilmore. "Trouble is, Marcus ain't gonna do it. He thinks too much like a white man. He ain't got the guts to stand up to them like y'all do, Rafe. Hell, he'd never swung that axe at Hill, and remember how he stopped y'all from finishing off that other peckerwood?"

"Yeah, that wasn't right," said Moon, slurring his words.

"Marcus needs help in this, don't y'all think, Cassius?" said Gilmore.

"That's right," said Pembroke. "Marcus needs our help. We gots to git him started toward emancipating this town for us colored folks."

"How we gonna do that, Pompey?" asked Moon.

"Brother, I is glad y'all asked that question," said Gilmore with a big grin, " 'cause I has got the answer."

40

The sun was almost down when Creed positioned himself on the Victoria side of the bridge and waited. He had loaded all six chambers in both revolvers, and if that wasn't enough, he had a Henry rifle ready for action as well.

As darkness settled around him, Creed realized that he wouldn't be able to see anyone coming across the bridge until they were nearly on him. This wouldn't do. He needed light. He looked about him, wondering where he could get a lantern or two. His view fell on the riverfront saloons a few hundred feet away at the foot of Bridge Street. Quickly making up his mind, he ran to the nearest one.

A solitary patron and a woman barkeeper looked at Creed as he entered the saloon. He didn't take time to notice who or what they were. Without asking, he took the first two lanterns he saw.

"Hey, what do you think you're doing?" demanded the woman. She moved toward the door as if to intercept Creed.

Creed saw her as a hard case that had been aged beyond her years by whiskey. He stopped, looked her in the eye, smiled, and said with all the friendly persuasion he could muster, "Darling, I'm in need of these right now, but I promise I'll bring them back as soon as I'm done with them."

Disarmed by his sweet attitude, she said, "What y'all need them for?"

"I got business at the bridge, darling," said Creed, "and I need to see who's coming across it in the dark."

She glanced down at the guns on his waist, nodded, and said, "You aiming to kill someone?"

"Not if I can help it," said Creed.

She touched his cheek, smiled, and said, "Well, when you finish your business at the bridge, come on back here and have a drink with me."

Creed smiled back and said, "I'll do just that, darling. Now if you'll excuse me, I don't want to miss those boys at the bridge."

The woman stood at the door of her saloon and watched him walk back to the bridge. Her patron came up behind her, put his arm around her waist, and said, "Come on back inside, Sudie, and let's have us some fun."

"The fun's gonna be out here," she said, still watching Creed. "That boy ain't gonna take no for an answer, and when he don't, somebody's gonna die for it."

Creed placed the two lanterns on opposite sides of the bridge, setting them atop the railings midway across the structure, making it appear that they belonged there all the time. Then he returned to the Victoria side and waited—but not for long.

Less than an hour passed before Creed heard a group of riders coming down the road across the river. He wondered if he should mount Nimbus to block their way or face them afoot. He looked at the stallion, and flashes of past battles went through his head. The Appaloosa had conducted himself admirably in every fight, had suffered wounds of a minor nature, but had always obeyed his master's every command. Creed saw no reason to endanger the animal now. He stepped into the middle of the road, a Colt's in each hand, and walked to the end of the bridge.

The beating of the approaching horses' hooves on the hard dirt road drew closer to Creed. They were coming on at a trot. He estimated them to be about ten to fifteen men in number. More than he had hoped.

He moved a few paces onto the bridge, then halted, waited.

The horsemen came on. Creed could see their vague shadows in the faint light of the half moon. They reached the bridge, and the dull thudding of their horses' hooves became a resounding rumble.

Creed raised the Colt's in his left hand over his head and fired a warning shot.

The riders came to a halt near the middle of the bridge. They were easy to see now. They looked much like the scraggly bunch that had jumped Creed and his friends the week before down on Coleto Creek.

"Turn back!" shouted Creed. "You are not wanted here; nor are you welcome in Victoria tonight."

"Who the hell are you?" asked one man.

"I've been sent here by the citizens of Victoria to tell you to turn around and go back where you came from," said Creed. "They do not want you here."

"We was hired to do a job, mister," said the same man, "and we aim to do it."

"The man who hired you, Andrew Cunningham, has gone north to Hallettsville to bring back a Yankee colonel and his men to take control of the town," said Creed.

"So what do we care about that?" said the man. "He hired us to ride through Shantytown and raise hell with the niggers."

"And I'm telling you that your services are no longer wanted," said Creed. "Now turn back or I will shoot the first man to move any closer to me."

"You hear that, boys?" said the man. "He's going to shoot us. All by hisself."

"Hey," said another man, "ain't you one of them that bush-whacked us last week?"

"Don't you mean that you bushwhacked my friends and me?" said Creed.

"Yeah, that's him," the second man said to the others. "He's the one that killed Jed and Davey."

"Let's get the son of a bitch!" swore another.

The leader reached for his gun but never broke leather.

Creed raised the Colt's in his right hand, took quick aim, and fired. The leader toppled backward from his horse, forcing the animal to rear up. The other mounts danced skittishly about, one even throwing its rider over the side of the bridge into the river below. The man screamed his fright before splashing into the water. Those men who could control their horses drew their guns and tried to take aim at Creed. Their leader fell silently

to the bridge, landing with a thump that was drowned out by
the scared horses.

Calmly, Creed drew a bead on another man who was trying
to aim at him. He squeezed off a second round, and the target
let out a scream as the ball pierced the man's chest. He, too,
fell dead.

One man decided to ride down Creed. He hunkered down,
spurred his horse, and came on at a run, firing in Creed's direction.

Just as he had in dozens of engagements during the war,
Creed denied fear, took perfect aim, and shot his attacker from
the saddle.

"He got Nate!" shouted one man.

"I'm getting the hell out of here!" shouted another.

The other riders decided to follow his example.

Creed considered firing once more and taking one more life,
but he didn't. Why? he asked himself. Because this wasn't
Virginia or Tennessee, and they weren't Yankees. This was
Texas, and those men were Texans, the same as he was. For
a moment, he hated himself for having killed them; then he
rationalized that they had intended to kill him and would have
killed him if he hadn't shot them first. Damn! he swore silently.
What an insane world this had become!

41

The whole town had heard Creed shooting at the bridge, and it set everybody's nerves to grinding because no one was sure what was happening around them.

Judge White had organized many of the men into groups to patrol the town against the rumored threat of the Freedmen from Shantytown and the Negro soldiers of the 3rd Michigan. Should any large body of black faces be seen coming toward the business district, the town fire bell would be rung and all good white men were to turn out in defense of their property, their families, and their own lives. Those who were on patrol were to hasten to the plaza for their orders.

Pembroke, Gilmore, and Moon didn't know what was happening around them either as they stealthily made their way into town by cover of darkness and the back alleys. They, too, had heard Creed's shots, and they had become frightened men They had no idea from where the shots had come and could only speculate.

"What's going on, Pompey?" asked Moon after the trio of skulkers had found a spying place beside Scanlan's Gem Saloon. "Who doing that shooting?"

Gilmore was wide-eyed with fear as he said, "Don't know, Rafe. Sounds like it's coming from back to Shantytown." He and Pembroke had no weapons and were very much afraid of guns. The echoing gunshots only heightened their phobia.

"Y'all reckon them peckerwoods from Coleto Creek is attacking Shantytown?" asked Pembroke nervously.

"Must be," said Gilmore.

"I best git back to my post," said Moon.

"This is your post," said Gilmore. "With us. Y'all is protecting us from the white folks."

"But I's only one man," said Moon.

"Lookey there!" said Pembroke, pointing to a patrol of Victorians coming down the street. "They's coming for us!"

Leading the group was Silas Newcombe. With him were Jim Coffee, Jack Moody, George Williams, Harry Thurmond, Sam Gaylord, and Bill Mitchell. Each man was armed with a rifle or a shotgun, and four of them carried torches, making them easy targets in the dark.

"Shoot them, Rafe!" said Gilmore. "Y'all has got to protect us. Shoot them before they comes to git us."

Without thinking about it, Moon leveled his Springfield at the patrol and sighted in on the first man's chest. He squeezed the rifle's trigger.

Newcombe never heard the shot that killed him. The ball crashed through his sternum just above his heart, destroying the artery that supplied the pump with blood. He fell backward into his fellows, two of whom caught him while the others knelt down quickly, as if they expected to hear another shot.

"It came from over there!" said Jim Coffee, pointing to the alley beside the Gem.

The Victorians fired in the direction that Coffee had indicated. Most of their shots struck wood, but not all.

"Ai-ee-ee!" screamed Moon as a ball tore into his knee. He dropped his rifle and grabbed the wounded joint with both hands.

"Rafe, is y'all hurt?" asked Pembroke.

"I's hit! I's hit! I been shot!"

"Come on, Cassius," said Gilmore. "Let's get the hell out of here." He broke into a run toward the rear.

"Come on, Rafe!" said Pembroke.

"I can't run," cried Moon. "Y'all go on and git."

"Come on," said Pembroke. "I'll help y'all." He tried to take Moon's arm, but the soldier would have none of it.

"They're niggers!" shouted Coffee. "Let's get them, boys!"

"Git, I say!" said Moon.

Pembroke heard Coffee, and he heard Moon. The sound of the patrol coming toward him bore heavier on him. He ran for his life in the same direction that Gilmore had gone.

Coffee led all but Moody and Thurmond to the alley. Mitchell drew his revolver, cocked the hammer, and aimed at Moon's head.

"No, don't!" shouted Coffee, knocking Mitchell's arm aside. "Can't you see he's one of them nigger soldiers?"

"But he just killed Silas," said Mitchell.

"Yeah, let's shoot the bastard," said Williams.

"No, Jim's right," said Gaylord. "We can't shoot him. If we do, all those other nigger soldiers will come in here looking for a real fight and we don't want that."

"Let's take him to the jail," said Coffee, "and see what Judge White has got to say about it."

"I say we hang the bastard," said Mitchell.

"We'll let the judge decide," said Coffee. "Git up, boy."

"I can't," said Moon, his voice quavering. "I's shot in the knee."

"Don't that figure," said Mitchell. "Lazy nigger can't even walk to his own execution."

"Well, let's get hold of him," said Coffee, "and carry him over to the courthouse."

They picked Moon up by his arms but didn't carry him. They dragged him all the way.

Everybody in town had heard the shooting in front of the Gem Saloon, and someone had the forethought to ring the fire bell in the square, calling out every able man. Close to a hundred men were in the plaza by the time Coffee and Mitchell dragged Moon up to the courthouse and Moody and Thurmond carried Newcombe's body there.

"This nigger shot and killed Silas Newcombe," said Coffee to the crowd. "There was at least one other nigger with him, but he got away."

"Let's hang him!" cried someone deep in the mob.

"Yeah, let's hang him!" shouted others.

"Someone get a rope!"

"Let's do him like they done Ben Hill!"

"Yeah, like Ben Hill!"

Tears rolled down Moon's cheeks. He was a dead man, and he knew it.

42

Certain that the bandits from Coleto Creek wouldn't return, Creed retrieved the two lanterns he had borrowed from Sudie, the saloonkeeper. He was taking them back to her when he heard Moon's Springfield discharge its lethal missile. He immediately recognized the sound as that of an army rifle, and his first thought was that there was trouble in Shantytown, that he had killed three men for nothing. He decided he was wrong when he noted how the folks around him were looking toward town. This ghoulish gathering of riverfront flotsam had come out to see the results of his fight at the bridge, but now their attention was drawn elsewhere. Unsure of what to do but very much afraid of the night, most of them scurried back to the holes from which they had crawled.

Now what? wondered Creed. He spurred Nimbus, rode up to Sudie, who was standing in front of her saloon, handed her the lanterns, and tipped his hat in gratitude for their loan. He was about to thank her for them, but the echoes of the patrol's shots at Rafe Moon interrupted him. He looked toward town, then back at Sudie.

"Thanks for the loan, ma'am," he said.

"What about that drink?" she asked.

"I'll try to come back," he said, knowing he never would. He tipped his hat, then rode off at a gallop for the plaza. As he raced up the hill on Bridge Street, he heard the fire bell ringing and thought that Jones had been unable to control his troops.

Damn! he thought. What a mess!

He reached the plaza just as someone threw a rope over the balcony railing of the jail house. He saw Judge White, John McClanahan, and Dr. January pushing their way through the crowd from one direction, while Dr. Goodwin was trying to get to the county building from another. Then he spotted Moon on the porch. Quickly, Creed figured out what was going on: a lynching. And he knew it had to be stopped.

"Hold on there!" shouted White over the din of the mob. He worked his way up the jail-house steps and motioned for the crowd to settle down to silence. "What do you think you're doing there?"

"We're hanging us a nigger," said Mitchell.

"No, we're not," said Coffee. "Not yet anyway."

"Hanging him?" queried White. "What for?"

"He murdered Silas Newcombe," said Moody, pointing through the open jail-house doors to Newcombe's body lying inside.

"Is this true, Jim?" asked the judge.

"He shot him all right," said Coffee.

"Did you see him do it?" asked White.

"Yes, sir, I did," said Coffee.

"So did I," said Moody and each of the other men in Newcombe's patrol.

White looked at the mob, saw their thirst for blood, and realized he had no other choice but to give in to them. Even so, he felt the need to lend legality to the moment. He said, "All right, boys, you've heard the testimony of these witnesses. What say you?"

To a man, they roared the same word: a mighty "Guilty."

White turned to Moon and said, "Have you got anything to say, boy?"

Poor Rafe was too frightened to say anything. He just let his head hang low and the tears flow.

"Then the sentence is hanging," said White.

"String him up!" shouted Mitchell.

And this started another chorus of such calls for blood.

Creed knew he would never be heard above the mob, so he fired a shot into the air to silence the throng.

"You can't hang that man!" he shouted at the Victorians

from atop Nimbus. He nudged his horse and moved closer to the jail.

"Why not?" demanded January from the jail-house steps. "We gave him a trial. With a judge and a jury. How much more justice do we have to give a nigger?"

"We hang him!" shouted Moody and several others.

Creed fired another shot to silence the crowd. "You can't try him in your court," said Creed. "He's in the army. It's up to the army to try him."

"He killed Silas Newcombe," said Judge White. "Silas wasn't in the army. He was one of ours."

"I know that," said Creed, "but don't you see what will happen if you hang that man?"

"He ain't no man," said Mitchell. "He's just a nigger."

"He's a man," said Creed angrily. "A soldier in the Federal army, and guilty or not, you have no right to hang him. You've got to wait for the army."

"To hell with the army!" said January. "Let's hang him!"

"For God's sake, January!" yelled Creed. "Use your good sense! You hang him, and Jones will lead his men into this town and burn it to the ground."

"Just let them try it!" said January. "We're hanging this nigger, and you can't stop us."

Creed raised his Colt's at January and said, "I can sure as hell try."

Before he could fire, a man in the mob grabbed him from behind and pulled him out of the saddle. Nimbus reared up. Another man grabbed the horse's bridle. Others aided the first man in subduing Creed. Someone shouted to hang him alongside Moon, and he was carried up to the jail-house steps.

Judge White called for the crowd to settle down again, and it did.

"Now we're not going to hang this man," said White.

"He's a nigger-lover!" shouted someone. "Let's hang him!"

"Put him down," said White. Once Creed was on his feet, White said to him, "Mr. Creed, we heard the shooting from down at the bridge. Was that you?"

"Yes, it was," said Creed.

"And did you stop the bandits from Coleto Creek?" asked White.

"Yes, sir, I did."

White nodded officiously and said, "Well, we're grateful for that, Mr. Creed, and we thank you. But we're still going to hang this boy."

"But, Judge—"

White held up a hand to silence Creed and said, "We've given him more trial than we would give a lot of men who were caught murdering a decent man like Silas Newcombe. It makes no difference that he's in the Federal army. He's a convicted murderer, and he's been sentenced to hang. And now we're going to hang him. Go ahead, boys."

Moody slipped a rope around Moon's head and fitted it around his neck. "Lift him up on the rail," said Moody.

Mitchell and Thurmond started to do just that, but a distant rumble stayed their hands.

"What the hell is that?" asked January.

"Shake your memory, Doctor," said Creed. "That's the sound of an army marching at double time."

"The soldiers are coming!" shouted a man at the rear of the crowd. "They're coming up Common Street!"

"They're coming up Main Street, too!" yelled another man.

"Take cover, boys!" yelled January. "We got us a fight on our hands!"

Before the crowd could begin to look for hiding places, the judge stepped forward and shouted, "Hold on, men! There's no need to run! We are the law here! Not those soldiers! Just hold your ground! They won't fight!"

"You're as crazy as January, Judge," said Creed. "Those men will kill every one of you and me, too, if they're provoked."

"That's just it, Mr. Creed," said White. "I don't aim to provoke them."

All held their ground as White had ordered, and they waited as Jones brought his men into the square and deployed them in two ranks on Main Street between Common and Commercial. He ordered them to fix bayonets, and as soon as they had, he gave the command to move forward across the plaza.

The Victorians backed away, moving toward the courthouse, becoming a more compact group as they did.

Jones halted his men at the edge of the street, only a few

feet from the crowd of Victorians. He ordered the front rank
to kneel, then he stepped forward to parley. The crowd parted
as he slowly crossed the street alone, carrying a Springfield
in front of him. He stopped a few paces from the courthouse
steps.

"Mr. Creed, are you all right, sir?" asked Jones.

"I'm fine, thank you, Sergeant," said Creed.

Jones's gaze fell on Moon, and he asked, "Why is one of
my men up there with you gentlemen?"

"He's killed one of our citizens," said Judge White, "and
we aim to hang him for it."

"You are Judge White, aren't you, sir?" asked Jones.

"I am he."

"This man is a soldier in the Federal army, sir," said Jones.
"It's up to the army to decide whether he's killed anyone."

"Not in this town, it isn't," said White. "We've given him
a fair trial, and I've passed sentence on him. I believe that is
my right as an officer of the court."

"I already said, Judge, that your court can't try a soldier.
He's the army's responsibility."

"Sergeant, we've already tried him, and we intend to hang
him." White turned aside and said, "Carry out the sentence,
boys."

Moody and Thurmond lifted Moon onto the railing.

"Don't let them hang me, Marcus!" cried Moon.

"Stand away from that man!" shouted Jones. He shifted his
rifle as if he intended to take aim at the first man to lift a hand
against Moon.

"Hang him!" said January.

"You hang that man," said Jones, "and my men will open
fire on you." He raised his rifle high over his head as a signal
to another soldier who gave the command for the two ranks
of infantry to take aim.

"You won't do it, nigger," said January. "They'll shoot you,
too."

"I'll take that chance," said Jones.

"Sergeant, this man is a convicted murderer," said White,
"and we will hang him."

"No, sir, you will not," said Jones emphatically. "Now stand
away from him."

No one moved for several seconds. Finally, the judge gave the order.

"Do like he says, boys," said White. "Move away from the prisoner."

"I say hang him," said January, "and damn the consequences!" He started toward Moon, but Creed broke free of his captors and stopped him.

"No!" shouted White. "I won't have the blood of all these people on my hands. Stand away from him."

Moody and Thurmond moved back.

Jones turned around and yelled back to the troops, "Stand down, men!" Then he lowered his rifle.

Both ranks did as ordered.

Jones turned and looked at Moon and said, "Rafe, I told y'all before not to go near Gilmore and Pembroke. Now look at the mess y'all is in. Y'all kill that man like they say, Rafe?"

Moon looked at Jones with the saddest of eyes and said, "Yessuh, I did."

Tears began to stream down Jones's cheeks as he said, "Why, Rafe? Why?"

"I don't know, Marcus," whined Moon. "I don't know. It was Pembroke and Gilmore made me do it, Marcus. It was their idea."

"But y'all still pulled the trigger, Rafe," said Jones.

"Yessuh, I did."

"Oh, Rafe," said Jones ever so softly, his tears falling copiously. And without warning, he leveled his Springfield at Moon's heart and fired.

The impact of the bullet jolted Moon from the railing. The rope stretched tight, preventing his feet from reaching the porch floor. But it made no difference. He was dead before his neck snapped.

No sooner had he fired the shot than Jones spun around and yelled back at his men, "Hold your ground! It's all right! I's all right!"

The men in the front rank leaped to attention. The men in the back line moved ahead to get a better look.

"Hold your ground, y'all!" shouted Jones. He heard their murmurs, heard them speak their disbelief that he had shot Moon. He moved toward them, motioning with his arms for

them to stay back. "I told y'all before," he said, his voice full
of anguish. "One of ours for one of theirs. An eye for an eye
and a tooth for a tooth. Like it say in the Good Book. It
works both ways, brothers."

43

With one bullet, Sergeant Marcus Jones defused the powder keg that was about to explode in Victoria. The soldiers had no one to blame and seek revenge on, and the Victorians had their justice.

After some initial complaint from the troops, which he quickly put down, Jones ordered his men to return to their camp, and they sullenly obeyed. Before he departed, Jones promised that he would take care of Pembroke and Gilmore for their part in Newcombe's murder.

Judge White ordered the people of Victoria to go about their business, which was still to protect themselves until Colonel Markham arrived from Hallettsville. All of them obeyed, although some wanted to punish all of the Negroes for Newcombe's murder. As Dr. January had argued, "We shoot ten Mexicans for every Texan they kill. Why shouldn't we do the same with niggers?" Several agreed with him, but wiser heads, such as White and Dr. Goodwin, swayed the populace to peace.

As for Creed, he returned to Dr. January's house to pick up his belongings, telling Catherine that he would spend the night at the Globe House, one of Victoria's hotels. He looked in on Bill Simons, briefly told him what had happened that evening, then said he would come by for him in the morning and they would ride out for home.

When morning came, Creed rose early, ate in the hotel dining room, then rode over to January's to fetch Simons. When he arrived, he was surprised to see the horses of Jake Flewellyn

233

and the Reeves brothers tied up in front. He met them on the porch as they came out of the house with Simons, who wasn't moving too fast.

"What the hell are you doing back here?" asked Creed a bit testily. "I thought I told you boys to go home."

"We did," said Jake. "Just like you said. And we delivered your letter to Miss Texada, too. She read it, then sent us back here to give you her answer." Jake reached inside his coat, pulled out a folded piece of paper, and offered it to Creed.

"Her answer?" queried Creed. He took the letter, opened it, and read:

My dearest darling Clete,

I hope this letter finds you well and hardy. I am fine, but Granny is not well. She grows weaker every day. I pray she lives to see Christmas and the New Year. She asks about you all the time, and I do not know what to tell her all the time except that you are well and that you are about the business of clearing your good name. This makes her happy, and every time I tell her she says she has a great surprise for you once you have cleared your name. I do not know what she means by that, but I fear it is only the chattering of an old woman.

I have read your letter, and I miss you, too. And I love you, too. I wish you could come to me right this minute and hold me in your arms, but I know this cannot be until you have cleared your name.

Jake has told me that they tried to catch Jim Kindred before he could get back to Hallettsville but that they failed to catch him. He rode into town this morning and went straight to Markham and told him that he knows that you are in Victoria. Markham has been ordered to take some of his men to Victoria to relieve the Yankee colonel there. He is preparing to leave this very minute, and I expect him to do so within the hour. That is why I am asking Jake to take this letter to you immediately—to warn you about Markham.

I want to see you so much, Clete darling, and I want you to hold me in your arms and love me the way you do. But I know this cannot be yet because of the danger you are in with Markham and the army. As much as I loathe writing this next part, I must tell you to stay away from here and from me until you can come home without worry of being punished for the crime you did not commit. The army has placed a bounty on you, and the Detchen brothers have been bragging that they intend to collect it if you ever come back here because the army does not care whether you are captured dead or alive. If anything should happen to you on my account, my darling, I would never be able to live with myself or in this world without you.

So as much as I love you and miss you, I must ask you not to come home again until you are a free man. I will be all right, and I promise you I will remain faithful to you until that wonderful, glorious, beautiful day comes. Until then, my darling, I am

Your ever loving,
Texada

Creed folded the letter again, put it in his coat pocket, and looked at his four friends through misty eyes. "Well, boys, I suppose we better be riding out of here before Markham shows up," he said.

"Where to, Creed?" asked Flewellyn.

"That's a good question, Jake," said Creed. "A very good question."

GILES TIPPETTE

Author of the bestselling WILSON YOUNG
SERIES, BAD NEWS, and CROSS FIRE
is back with his most exciting
Western adventure yet!

JAILBREAK

Time is running out for Justa Williams, owner of the Half-
Moon Ranch in West Texas. His brother Norris is being
held in a Mexican jail, and neither bribes nor threats can
free him.

Now with the help of a dozen kill-crazy Mexican *banditos*,
Justa aims to blast Norris out. But the worst is yet to come:
a hundred-mile chase across the Mexican desert with fifty
federales in hot pursuit.

The odds of reaching the Texas border are a million to nothing . . . and if the Williams brothers don't watch their backs,
the road to freedom could turn into the road to hell!

JAILBREAK
by
Giles Tippette

On sale now, wherever Jove Books are sold!

*Here is the first chapter
of this
new Western
adventure.*

At supper Norris, my middle brother, said, "I think we got some trouble on that five thousand acres down on the border near Laredo."

He said it serious, which is the way Norris generally says everything. I quit wrestling with the steak Buttercup, our cook, had turned into rawhide and said, "What are you talking about? How could we have trouble on land lying idle?"

He said, "I got word from town this afternoon that a telegram had come in from a friend of ours down there. He says we got some kind of squatters taking up residence on the place."

My youngest brother, Ben, put his fork down and said, incredulously, "*That* five thousand acres? Hell, it ain't nothing but rocks and cactus and sand. Why in hell would anyone want to squat on that worthless piece of nothing?"

Norris just shook his head. "I don't know. But that's what the telegram said. Came from Jack Cole. And if anyone ought to know what's going on down there it would be him."

I thought about it and it didn't make a bit of sense. I was Justa Williams, and my family, my two brothers and myself and our father, Howard, occupied a considerable ranch called the Half-Moon down along the Gulf of Mexico in Matagorda County, Texas. It was some of the best grazing land in the state and we had one of the best herds of purebred and cross-bred cattle in that part of the country. In short we were pretty well-to-do.

But that didn't make us any the less ready to be stolen from, if indeed that was the case. The five thousand acres Norris had been talking about had come to us through a trade our father had made some years before. We'd never made any use of the land, mainly because, as Ben had said, it was pretty worthless and because it was a good two hundred miles from our ranch headquarters. On a few occasions we'd bought cattle in Mexico and then used the acreage to hold small groups on while we made up a herd. But other than that, it lay mainly forgotten.

I frowned. "Norris, this doesn't make a damn bit of sense. Right after supper send a man into Blessing with a return wire for Jack asking him if he's certain. What the hell kind of squatting could anybody be doing on that land?"

Ben said, "Maybe they're raisin' watermelons." He laughed.

I said, "They could raise melons, but there damn sure wouldn't be no water in them."

Norris said, "Well, it bears looking into." He got up, throwing his napkin on the table. "I'll go write out that telegram."

I watched him go, dressed, as always, in his town clothes. Norris was the businessman in the family. He'd been sent down to the University at Austin and had got considerable learning about the ins and outs of banking and land deals and all the other parts of our business that didn't directly involve the ranch. At the age of twenty-nine I'd been the boss of the operation a good deal longer than I cared to think about. It had been thrust upon me by our father when I wasn't much more than twenty. He'd said he wanted me to take over while he was still strong enough to help me out of my mistakes and I reckoned that was partly true. But it had just seemed that after our mother had died the life had sort of gone out of him. He'd been one of the earliest settlers, taking up the land not long after Texas had become a republic in 1845. I figured all the years of fighting Indians and then Yankees and scalawags and carpetbaggers and cattle thieves had taken their toll on him. Then a few years back he'd been nicked in the lungs by a bullet that should never have been allowed to head his way and it had thrown an extra strain on his heart. He was pushing seventy and he still had plenty of head on his shoulders, but mostly all he did now was sit around in his rocking chair and stare out over the cattle and land business he'd built. Not to say that I didn't go to him for advice when the occasion demanded. I did, and mostly I took it.

Buttercup came in just then and sat down at the end of the table with a cup of coffee. He was near as old as Dad and almost completely worthless. But he'd been one of the first hands that Dad had hired and he'd been kept on even after he couldn't sit a horse anymore. The problem was he'd elected himself cook, and that was the sorriest day our family had ever seen. There were two Mexican women hired to cook for the twelve riders we kept full-time, but Buttercup insisted on cooking for the family.

Mainly, I think, because he thought he was one of the family. A notion we could never completely dissuade him from.

So he sat there, about two days of stubble on his face, looking as scrawny as a pecked-out rooster, sweat running down his face, his apron a mess. He said, wiping his forearm across his forehead, "Boy, it shore be hot in there. You boys shore better be glad you ain't got no business takes you in that kitchen."

Ben said, in a loud mutter, "I wish you didn't either."

Ben, at twenty-five, was easily the best man with a horse or a gun that I had ever seen. His only drawback was that he was hotheaded and he tended to act first and think later. That ain't a real good combination for someone that could go on the prod as fast as Ben. When I had argued with Dad about taking over as Boss, suggesting instead that Norris, with his education, was a much better choice, Dad had simply said, "Yes, in some ways. But he can't handle Ben. You can. You can handle Norris, too. But none of them can handle you."

Well, that hadn't been exactly true. If Dad had wished it I would have taken orders from Norris even though he was two years younger than me. But the logic in Dad's line of thinking had been that the Half-Moon and our cattle business was the lodestone of all our business and only I could run that. He had been right. In the past I'd imported purebred Whiteface and Hereford cattle from up North, bred them to our native Longhorns and produced cattle that would bring twice as much at market as the horse-killing, all-bone, all-wild Longhorns. My neighbors had laughed at me at first, claiming those square little purebreds would never make it in our Texas heat. But they'd been wrong and, one by one, they'd followed the example of the Half-Moon.

Buttercup was setting up to take off on another one of his long-winded harangues about how it had been in the "old days" so I quickly got up, excusing myself, and went into the big office we used for sitting around in as well as a place of business. Norris was at the desk composing his telegram so I poured myself out a whiskey and sat down. I didn't want to hear about any trouble over some worthless five thousand acres of border-land. In fact I didn't want to hear about any troubles of any kind. I was just two weeks short of getting married, married to a lady I'd been courting off and on for five years, and I was mighty anxious that nothing come up to interfere with our plans. Her name was Nora Parker and her daddy owned and run the general mercantile in our nearest town, Blessing. I'd almost lost her once before to a Kansas City drummer. She'd finally gotten tired of waiting on me, waiting until the ranch didn't occupy all my time, and almost run off with a smooth-talking Kansas City drummer that called on her daddy in the harness trade. But she'd come to her senses in time and got off the train in Texarkana and returned home.

But even then it had been a close thing. I, along with my men and brothers and help from some of our neighbors, had been involved with stopping a huge herd of illegal cattle being driven up from Mexico from crossing our range and infecting our cattle with tick fever which could have wiped us all out. I tell you it had been a bloody business. We'd lost four good men and had to kill at least a half dozen on the other side. Fact of the business was I'd come about as close as I ever had to getting killed myself, and that was going some for the sort of rough-and-tumble life I'd led.

Nora had almost quit me over it, saying she just couldn't take the uncertainty. But in the end, she'd stuck by me. That had been the year before, 1896, and I'd convinced her that civilized law was coming to the country, but until it did, we that had been there before might have to take things into our own hands from time to time.

She'd seen that and had understood. I loved her and she loved me and that was enough to overcome any of the troubles we were still likely to encounter from day to day.

So I was giving Norris a pretty sour look as he finished his telegram and sent for a hired hand to ride it into Blessing, seven miles away. I said, "Norris, let's don't make a big fuss about this. That land ain't even crossed my mind in at least a couple of years. Likely we got a few Mexican families squatting down there and trying to scratch out a few acres of corn."

Norris gave me his businessman's look. He said, "It's our land, Justa. And if we allow anyone to squat on it for long enough or put up a fence they can lay claim. That's the law. My job is to see that we protect what we have, not give it away."

I sipped at my whiskey and studied Norris. In his town clothes he didn't look very impressive. He'd inherited more from our mother than from Dad so he was not as wide-shouldered and slim-hipped as Ben and me. But I knew him to be a good, strong, dependable man in any kind of fight. Of course he wasn't that good with a gun, but then Ben and I weren't all that good with books like he was. But I said, just to jolly him a bit, "Norris, I do believe you are running to suet. I may have to put you out with Ben working the horse herd and work a little of that fat off you."

Naturally it got his goat. Norris had always envied Ben and me a little. I was just over six foot and weighed right around a hundred and ninety. I had inherited my daddy's big hands and big shoulders. Ben was almost a copy of me except he was about a size smaller. Norris said, "I weigh the same as I have for the last five years. If it's any of your business."

I said, as if I was being serious, "Must be them sack suits you wear. What they do, pad them around the middle?"

He said, "Why don't you just go to hell."

After he'd stomped out of the room I got the bottle of whiskey and an extra glass and went down to Dad's room. It had been one of his bad days and he'd taken to bed right after lunch. Strictly speaking he wasn't supposed to have no whiskey, but I watered him down a shot every now and then and it didn't seem to do him no harm.

He was sitting up when I came in the room. I took a moment to fix him a little drink, using some water out of his pitcher, then handed him the glass and sat down in the easy chair by the bed. I told him what Norris had reported and asked what he thought.

He took a sip of his drink and shook his head. "Beats all I

ever heard," he said. "I took that land in trade for a bad debt
some fifteen, twenty years ago. I reckon I'd of been money
ahead if I'd of hung on to the bad debt. That land won't even
raise weeds, well as I remember, and Noah was in on the last
rain that fell on the place."

We had considerable amounts of land spotted around the
state as a result of this kind of trade or that. It was Norris's
business to keep up with their management. I was just bringing
this to Dad's attention more out of boredom and impatience for
my wedding day to arrive than anything else.

I said, "Well, it's a mystery to me. How you feeling?"

He half smiled. "Old." Then he looked into his glass. "And
I never liked watered whiskey. Pour me a dollop of the straight
stuff in here."

I said, "Now, Howard. You know—"

He cut me off. "If I wanted somebody to argue with I'd
send for Buttercup. Now do like I told you."

I did, but I felt guilty about it. He took the slug of whiskey
down in one pull. Then he leaned his head back on the pillow
and said, "Aaaaah. I don't give a damn what that horse doctor
says, ain't nothing makes a man feel as good inside as a shot
of the best."

I felt sorry for him laying there. He'd always led just the
kind of life he wanted—going where he wanted, doing what
he wanted, having what he set out to get. And now he was
reduced to being a semi-invalid. But one thing that showed
the strength that was still in him was that you *never* heard
him complain. He said, "How's the cattle?"

I said, "They're doing all right, but I tell you we could do
with a little of Noah's flood right now. All this heat and no
rain is curing the grass off way ahead of time. If it doesn't
let up we'll be feeding hay by late September, early October.
And that will play hell on our supply. Could be we won't have
enough to last through the winter. Norris thinks we ought to sell
off five hundred head or so, but the market is doing poorly right
now. I'd rather chance the weather than take a sure beating by
selling off."

He sort of shrugged and closed his eyes. The whiskey was
relaxing him. He said, "You're the boss."

"Yeah," I said. "Damn my luck."

I wandered out of the back of the house. Even though it was nearing seven o'clock of the evening it was still good and hot. Off in the distance, about a half a mile away, I could see the outline of the house I was building for Nora and myself. It was going to be a close thing to get it finished by our wedding day. Not having any riders to spare for the project, I'd imported a building contractor from Galveston, sixty miles away. He'd arrived with a half a dozen Mexican laborers and a few skilled masons and they'd set up a little tent city around the place. The contractor had gone back to Galveston to fetch more materials, leaving his Mexicans behind. I walked along idly, hoping he wouldn't forget that the job wasn't done. He had some of my money, but not near what he'd get when he finished the job.

Just then Ray Hays came hurrying across the back lot toward me. Ray was kind of a special case for me. The only problem with that was that he knew it and wasn't a bit above taking advantage of the situation. Once, a few years past, he'd saved my life by going against an evil man that he was working for at the time, an evil man who meant to have my life. In gratitude I'd given Ray a good job at the Half-Moon, letting him work directly under Ben, who was responsible for the horse herd. He was a good, steady man and a good man with a gun. He was also fair company. When he wasn't talking.

He came churning up to me, mopping his brow. He said, "Lordy, boss, it is—"

I said, "Hays, if you say it's hot I'm going to knock you down."

He gave me a look that was a mixture of astonishment and hurt. He said, "Why, whatever for?"

I said, "*Everybody* knows it's hot. Does every son of a bitch you run into have to make mention of the fact?"

His brow furrowed. "Well, I never thought of it that way. I 'spect you are right. Goin' down to look at yore house?"

I shook my head. "No. It makes me nervous to see how far they've got to go. I can't see any way it'll be ready on time."

He said, "Miss Nora ain't gonna like that."

I gave him a look. "I guess you felt forced to say that."

He looked down. "Well, maybe she won't mind."

I said, grimly, "The hell she won't. She'll think I did it a-purpose."

"Aw, she wouldn't."

"Naturally you know so much about it, Hays. Why don't you tell me a few other things about her."

"I was jest tryin' to lift yore spirits, boss."

I said, "You keep trying to lift my spirits and I'll put you on the haying crew."

He looked horrified. No real cowhand wanted any work he couldn't do from the back of his horse. Haying was a hot, hard, sweaty job done either afoot or from a wagon seat. We generally brought in contract Mexican labor to handle ours. But I'd been known in the past to discipline a cowhand by giving him a few days on the hay gang. Hays said, "Boss, now I never meant nothin'. I swear. You know me, my mouth gets to runnin' sometimes. I swear I'm gonna watch it."

I smiled. Hays always made me smile. He was so easily buffaloed. He had it soft at the Half-Moon and he knew it and didn't want to take any chances on losing a good thing.

I lit up a cigarillo and watched dusk settle in over the coastal plains. It wasn't but three miles to Matagorda Bay and it was quiet enough I felt like I could almost hear the waves breaking on the shore. Somewhere in the distance a mama cow bawled for her calf. The spring crop were near about weaned by now, but there were still a few mamas that wouldn't cut the apron strings. I stood there reflecting on how peaceful things had been of late. It suited me just fine. All I wanted was to get my house finished, marry Nora and never handle another gun so long as I lived.

The peace and quiet were short-lived. Within twenty-four hours we'd had a return telegram from Jack Cole. It said:

YOUR LAND OCCUPIED BY TEN TO TWELVE MEN STOP
CAN'T BE SURE WHAT THEY'RE DOING BECAUSE THEY
RUN STRANGERS OFF STOP APPEAR TO HAVE A GOOD
MANY CATTLE GATHERED STOP APPEAR TO BE FENCING
STOP ALL I KNOW STOP

I read the telegram twice and then I said, "Why this is crazy as hell! That land wouldn't support fifty head of cattle."

We were all gathered in the big office. Even Dad was there, sitting in his rocking chair. I looked up at him. "What do you make of this, Howard?"

He shook his big, old head of white hair. "Beats the hell out of me, Justa. I can't figure it."

Ben said, "Well, I don't see where it has to be figured. I'll take five men and go down there and run them off. I don't care what they're doing. They ain't got no business on our land."

I said, "Take it easy, Ben. Aside from the fact you don't need to be getting into any more fights this year, I can't spare you or five men. The way this grass is drying up we've got to keep drifting those cattle."

Norris said, "No, Ben is right. We can't have such affairs going on with our property. But we'll handle it within the law. I'll simply take the train down there, hire a good lawyer and have the matter settled by the sheriff. Shouldn't take but a few days."

Well, there wasn't much I could say to that. We couldn't very well let people take advantage of us, but I still hated to be without Norris's services even for a few days. On matters other than the ranch he was the expert, and it didn't seem like there was a day went by that some financial question didn't come up that only he could answer. I said, "Are you sure you can spare yourself for a few days?"

He thought for a moment and then nodded. "I don't see why not. I've just moved most of our available cash into short-term municipal bonds in Galveston. The market is looking all right and everything appears fine at the bank. I can't think of anything that might come up."

I said, "All right. But you just keep this in mind. You are not a gun hand. You are not a fighter. I do not want you going anywhere near those people, whoever they are. You do it legal and let the sheriff handle the eviction. Is that understood?"

He kind of swelled up, resenting the implication that he couldn't handle himself. The biggest trouble I'd had through the years when trouble had come up had been keeping Norris out of it. Why he couldn't just be content to be a wagon load of brains was more than I could understand. He said, "Didn't you just hear me say I intended to go through a lawyer and the sheriff? Didn't I just say that?"

I said, "I wanted to be sure you heard yourself."

He said, "Nothing wrong with my hearing. Nor my approach to this matter. You seem to constantly be taken with the idea that I'm always looking for a fight. I think you've got the wrong brother. I use logic."

"Yeah?" I said. "You remember when that guy kicked you in the balls when they were holding guns on us? And then we chased them twenty miles and finally caught them?"

He looked away. "That has nothing to do with this."

"Yeah?" I said, enjoying myself. "And here's this guy, shot all to hell. And what was it you insisted on doing?"

Ben laughed, but Norris wouldn't say anything.

I said, "Didn't you insist on us standing him up so you could kick him in the balls? Didn't you?"

He sort of growled, "Oh, go to hell."

I said, "I just want to know where the logic was in that."

He said, "Right is right. I was simply paying him back in kind. It was the only thing his kind could understand."

I said, "That's my point. You just don't go down there and go to paying back a bunch of rough hombres in kind. Or any other currency for that matter."

That made him look over at Dad. He said, "Dad, will you make him quit treating me like I was ten years old? He does it on purpose."

But he'd appealed to the wrong man. Dad just threw his hands in the air and said, "Don't come to me with your troubles. I'm just a boarder around here. You get your orders from Justa. You know that."

Of course he didn't like that. Norris had always been a strong hand for the right and wrong of a matter. In fact, he may have been one of the most stubborn men I'd ever met. But he didn't say anything, just gave me a look and muttered something about hoping a mess came up at the bank while he was gone and then see how much boss I was.

But he didn't mean nothing by it. Like most families, we fought amongst ourselves and, like most families, God help the outsider who tried to interfere with one of us.

An epic novel of frontier survival...

"Johnny Quarles brings a fresh approach to the classic western."—Elmer Kelton

———— JOHNNY QUARLES ————
———— BRACK ————

Brack Haynes knew what he wanted: a homestead of his own, a wife, and family—and peace from the haunting memories of war and bounty hunting. So he and a half-breed rancher led his cattle to the edge of Indian territoy—a hostile stretch of wilderness that no white man had ever dared to claim. Everyone called Brack Haynes a crazy dreamer...and he couldn't deny it.

__BRACK 0-425-12299-9/$3.95

VARRO

Varro Ramsey's been a hired hand for the law longer than most sheriffs have been able to aim a pistol. But this time Varro wants more than cash—he wants revenge. The twisted Hall brothers left him to die in the desert, and robbed him of the woman he loves. Now there aren't enough hideouts in Texas to keep the Halls safe from Varro...

__VARRO 0-425-12850-4/$3.95